**"The diadem belongs to the RMoahl,"
said the spidery being.**

"The diadem belongs to the wearer," answered Aleytys. "It is not a simple piece of jewelry. You imprisoned three souls in your treasure vault. How do you account to them for four hundred years of solitary confinement?"

The RMoahl clicked his nipper claws impatiently. "What does it matter? We will never let slip away what is ours."

Aleytys shrugged angrily. "The three are vehemently opposed to returning to that vault. We fought you before and won. I'll always have help. Remember Lamarchos? I can't always control the summoning.

"Push me too far and men will die, no matter what I want."

MAEVE

Jo Clayton

DAW BOOKS, INC.
DONALD A. WOLLHEIM, PUBLISHER
New York

FIRST PRINTING, JUNE 1979

3 4 5 6 7 8 9

DAWsf
BOOKS
DAW TRADEMARK REGISTERED
U.S. PAT. OFF. MARCA REGISTRADA.
HECHO EN U.S.A.

PRINTED IN U.S.A.

Book I:

THE FOREST

Chapter I

Gwynnor crouched beside his lover, Amersit. A churning distaste stirred his insides as he watched the strangers come down the side of the ship and approach the drieu, Dylaw. More of them coming to put their damn feet on Maeve's breast.

"One's a woman," Amersit whispered, his eyes glowing violet, like spring asters on the Maes. He sniffed, then wiggled excitedly. "She smells . . . ha . . . good!"

Face folding in a grimace of repugnance, Gwynnor stared at the smugglers. "They wouldn't come if Dylaw stopped dealing with them."

Mischief sparkling in his eyes, Amersit patted his shoulder. "Yeh, little one, and we wouldn't have any guns."

Gwynnor rubbed his cheek against the hand resting on his shoulder. "Do we need them so much?" He straightened his back, turning troubled eyes on his trail lover. "Do those guns really make any difference when we face the energy weapons of the starmen?"

Amersit stroked the soft gray curls coiling close about Gwynnor's head. "You take things so seriously, little one. Relax. You know we haven't got enough support from the people yet. Let the starmen hit the villages a bit more and we'll have them all storming the city. In the meantime, we make them pay a little anyway for their raids. The day's coming through. We'll lock them tight in that damn city and burn it down around their ears."

"Someday. Always someday." Gwynnor refused to let Amersit cheer him out of his depression.

"Hey." Amersit stared at the group sitting on the deep black tradecloth. "The woman speaks cathl maes. Dylaw looks like she hit him over the head with a rotten squash."

I don't like it." Gwynnor moved away, glowering angrily at the red-haired woman. The sun shone off the glowing mass of

7

her hair, surrounding her head with a golden halo. He pinched his nostrils to shut out her disturbing odor. "It means she had to come from the city. What if the city sent her, knowing we're here?"

Amersit slapped his hand on his thigh. "Ah, mannh, Gwynnor, you're right. I didn't think of that. We'd better tell Dylaw." He started to get to his feet, then hesitated. "If we interrupt the bargaining, he'll peel skin with a dull knife." He rubbed a hand over his gray fuzz, a rueful grin turning the ends of his long mouth.

"I'll do it." Gwynnor jumped up and walked with small, quick steps over to the bargainers. The woman finished translating the drieu's last speech to the starman and looked up at him, her blue-green eyes bright with interest. Gwynnor sank his teeth into his tongue as he knelt before Dylaw, body in question-submission.

The drieu frowned, his pointed ears twitching fretfully. Gwynnor knew he'd have a lot of explaining to do later. Trying to speak softly enough to keep his words from her, he said, "The woman speaks the cathl maes. It might be important to discover where she learned it."

He saw Dylaw's face go rigid as he digested the implications of the question. Gwynnor swallowed this further indication of his leader's stupidity. He struggled to suppress his growing sense of futility. Then Dylaw's hand moved through the ritual acknowledgment and dismissal.

Gwynnor rose and walked slowly away. He glanced briefly over his shoulder, his dark-green eyes involuntarily seeking hers . . . blue-green like the sea on a bright day . . . strange round pupils like small targets . . . so different, so different . . . He wrenched his eyes free and settled beside Amersit, thigh against thigh, drawing a little comfort from the contact.

The drieu, Dylaw, picked up one of the sample weapons. Turning it over in his hands he ran the tips of his fingers over the checked grip, then along the blue-black of the metal parts. As he put the weapon down he said, as casually as if mere curiosity prompted the question, "How do you come to speak the cathl maes?"

Aleytys spread out her hands, the fingers long and golden in the rusty light of the orange sun. "Not in the city. This is the first time I've put foot on this world." She rubbed a forefinger beside her nose. "Do you know another language?"

"I know some words of another tongue." Dylaw spoke slowly, thoughtfully. "Why?"

"I have the gift of tongues, drieu Dylaw." The corners of her mouth twitched at his look of blank disbelief. "I can prove it. That language you know—would anyone in the city know it also?"

"Why should they learn what they don't need to learn?" His mouth drew down in an unpleasant sneer. "Few of them bother to learn enough cathl maes to give a man a proper good morning."

She nodded. "That being so, give me a few words in that language."

After a moment of thoughtful silence, Dylaw lifted his head and stared at her. "Watiximiscisco. Ghinahwalathsa lugh qickiniky."

She covered her eyes with the heels of her hands, wincing as the translator's activity made her head ache fiercely but briefly. When she looked up, she was smiling. "I speak in anger. I carry the fire of my anger to the south."

He nodded. "Laghi tighyet lamtsynixtighyet."

"The best laugh is the very last laugh."

"Lukelixnewef hicqlicu."

"A hunter is a man of pride."

Dylaw sat in silence, eyes turned toward the cold blue sky where the sun was a bronzed orange disc creeping toward the zenith. Then his shallow, pale gray eyes, with their narrow slit pupils, ran over her body and fixed on her face. "Remarkable," he said dryly.

"It's what I do for the Captain."

"Are there more among the starfolk who can do this?"

"I don't know." She spread out her hands and shrugged. "I've never met any."

The drieu, Dylaw, picked up the gun again, dismissing the talent as unimportant since he saw no way to profit from it. "If we bought weapons in Caer Seramdun, we'd pay only fifty oboloi. The maranhedd in one phial alone should buy five hundred."

When Aleytys translated this for Arel his dark, sardonic face expressed surprise and contempt. He spoke briefly and forcefully, then jumped to his feet and stood waiting for her to give his answer to the drieu.

"The Captain says if that is so, then he will take his merchandise elsewhere." She started to rise.

"Yst-yst, woman. No need for such haste." He tapped fingers on his thighs and waited for her to settle herself. "Why not see if we can reach some kind of agreement rather than leave here having wasted our time?" He pulled a bag made of leather from inside his gray homespun tunic. With deliberate slowness he worked the knot loose on the drawstring, then thrust his stubby fingers inside and pulled out a small glass phial. "One trom of maranhedd."

The Captain leaned forward and spoke briefly.

Aleytys nodded. To Dylaw she said, "Fifty guns. Five hundred darts."

"Four hundred guns and four thousand darts."

Arel snorted when Aleytys translated for him. He snapped out an answer, a look of scorn on his dark face.

Aleytys said calmly, "You dream, ergynnan na Maes. One hundred guns. Five hundred darts."

Gwynnor turned his back on the disturbing sight of his leader bargaining as greedily as any huckster in the market square. "I don't like this," he muttered.

"You said that before." Amersit grinned widely, his mobile mouth stretching in the quick flashing smile that usually delighted Gwynnor. "I wonder what the Synwedda would think of that red witch."

"Tchah!"

"I doubt she'd say that." He broke into a chuckle. "I daresay you've not had a woman yet, little love. Trust me. That's one fine woman, starbred or not." He sniffed then pantomimed an exaggerated ecstasy.

"I won't listen to you." Gwynnor jumped up and ran to the kaffon and stood next to his own mount, combing unsteady fingers through the kaffa's thick fur, finding a measure of calm in the animal warmth of the placid, dozing animal. He ignored the sound of voices continuing behind him.

The drieu, Dylaw, grunted. "Agreed. For three trom of maranhedd, five hundred weapons and ten thousand darts." He blinked round eyes, his slitted pupils little more than a narrow black line crossing the silver-gray mirrors of his irises. His long hooked nose twitched its mobile tip as he dropped the leather sack into Aleytys' hand. "I presume the man from the stars will test this as usual, not trusting our word."

Aleytys glanced at the Captain, then nodded. "We aren't included in your people, ergynnan na Maes. No doubt your word is good to your own. You'll trust us to keep our part of the bargain?"

Dylaw's mouth gash clamped shut; the gray fuzz patches over his round eyes slid together as he frowned in irritation. "I trust your greed for maranhedd, gwerei. To cheat me now would mean empty hands next year."

"True." As Aleytys handed the bag to the Captain, she switched languages. "He knows you'll want to test it before handing over the guns."

"Yeah." He dumped the three phials out of the bag and began peeling off the wax. Then pulled the rolled leather stoppers out and poured a few grains of the drug from each phial into the palm of his free hand. "Looks like dream dust all right." He stirred the amethystine crystals with a forefinger, then poured them back. Head twisted back over his shoulder, he called, "Vannick."

The long, pale man came from the shadow of the ship's tail, leaving Joran there. The little killer's eyes prowled the canyon, measuring the small band of natives, alert for any sign of trouble.

Arel handed the bag to his second. "Test."

"Right." Vannik scrambled up the ladder and disappeared into the ship.

The drieu, Dylaw, crossed his arms over his meager chest, dropped his head and stared at the ground in front of his crossed legs. He let his leathery eyelids sink until the silver-gray was veiled, leaving only narrow slits. He appeared to settle into a light doze.

Aleytys sighed and pushed the hair out of her face. The fitful breeze meandering down the canyon alternately lifted and let fall gouts of coarse grit; now and then it played at her hair, sending loose, tickling ends waving around her face. She touched Arel's arm. "You've got some energy weapons stored there." She nodded at the ship. "You'd get a lot more for them." She reached out and touched his knee. "Why?" Pinching the flesh lightly, she grinned at him. "Though I think you've screwed these poor ignorant creatures out of their back teeth. I can feel the cat inside you licking the cream off its whiskers. But they'd really put out for energy weapons. They want them."

"They'll have to want. If I gave them energy guns, I'd have a Company search-and-destroy mission on my tail. No thanks."

"Oh." She looked around the canyon. Dry barren walls. Small spring, its water carefully hoarded in a cistern built from rough stone blocks joined with yellow-brown mortar. A few scraggly weeds, gray with dust, clinging to the cracks of the rock. A small gray lizard ran a jagged race across the wall, disappearing into one of the larger cracks.

"This is a damn inhospitable place."

One eyebrow went up increasing the sardonic amusement in his face. "You expected me to land in some farmer's field?"

"I suppose that wouldn't be too safe. It's hard on me though, unless one of them would guide me down from here."

"He might."

"For a price, maybe." Aleytys rubbed her nose.

"That one'd sell his grandmother for more guns."

"They hate us."

"Why do you think they want the guns, love?" The crow-tracks at the corners of his eyes deepened momentarily. "They don't hunt the kind of game you'd want to eat."

"Doesn't it bother you? By selling them these guns you help them kill people."

He shrugged. "Company men. If I had my way, I'd dump them all into a drone and junk it on the nearest sun." For an instant, hatred leaped from him across her sensitive nerves, along with hurt, loneliness, and loss. Something bad out of his past, she surmised, knowing she'd never find out what it was now that she was leaving him.

"I'll buy the guns from you, Arel."

"Don't waste your money, Lee. You'll need it to bribe your way onto a ship."

She grinned. "I wasn't about to give you all the jewels."

"Keep them. I'll supply the guns."

She shook her head. "No, Arel. I know how close to the line you run. I'll pay for the guns."

"You don't like owing people, do you."

"It's hard for me to take things. I . . . I've learned to put a premium on my independence, Arel." She brushed her head with quick, nervous hands. "I'm going to pay my way from now on."

"Dammit, Lee. You've earned . . ."

"Then pay me off with money. I expect I'll need it for living expenses when I make it to Star Street."

"What about advice? Willing to take that?"

"Why not."

"Don't let anyone know about the jewels. When you get to the city, use everything you've got to find a man you can trust before you let anyone see them."

"Man?"

"Wei-Chu-Hsien Company believes in male supremacy, Lee. Most likely the only women you'll find in the city will be streetwalkers or menials like cooks and cleaners."

"Phah!" She sniffed. "Their loss."

He shrugged, then grinned. "When you start working on those grubs, let me do the bargaining. Even with that on-off empathy of yours, you drive a lousy bargain. You give away too much."

"Well, I don't intend to set off trudging on foot across that mess." She waved her hand at the cliffs rising above the ship.

"I still think you should sign on with us." He scowled at her. "You seemed to like it."

"I did." She stroked her fingers over his arm. "And the three of you, too." Then she shook her head and sighed again. "I have a baby somewhere. I've got to find him, Arel. He needs me more than you do. And . . . and there's a lot more you don't know about me. It's not pretty."

"I know your nightmares." He reached out and slid his fingers down her cheek. "We'll all miss you, Lee. Even Joran."

At that moment Vannik leaned out of the lock. "Captain."

Arel looked around, one eyebrow sailing up into the tangle of black slanting across his forehead.

"Right stuff."

"Then let down the sling." Arel turned back to Aleytys. "I wouldn't trust that bunch far as I could throw one of those four-footed hairballs they ride." Frowning at the patient, hunched figure of the drieu, he curled fingers around her hand until the pressure hurt. "Probably slit your throat the minute we leave."

She gently freed her hand. "No. I can protect myself. You should know that by now."

He was silent a minute, then swung around. "Vannik, break out another half dozen guns and a thousand more darts."

Vannik's shaggy eyebrows rose and he ran a bony hand through the white thatch on his head. Then he moved back up the ladder, his awkward-looking body agile as a monkey.

"Wake your fuzzy little fanatic." The Captain moved his long body around to face the native.

The lighter gravity of this world fooled Aleytys again as she attempted to follow his example. Her heavy-world muscles overreacting, she caught herself at the edge of an undignified sprawl.

"Drieu Dylaw."

"Yes, woman?"

"The weapons are ready. The Captain is anxious to leave before the city spies find him. I suppose you'd like to get out, too." As the drieu started to stand, she said quickly, "However, there's another thing. My service to the Captain concludes here and we part company."

"Why tell me?"

"Name a price for supplying a kaffa and a guide to take me to the sea."

A sudden fierce anger exploded from the stiffening figure of the drieu. Then he was on his feet, turning to leave, unable to be in her presence any longer without destroying his honor by breaking trade truce.

In the shadow of the wall, young Gwynnor's eyes stayed fixed on her with a growing fascination despite the fear which was turning his body cold.

The kaffa stirred nervously.

The gray lizard poked his head out of the crack, scuttled in a tight circle, eyes jerking from side to side. A moment later he plunged back into his hiding place.

The wind sang down the canyon with an eery mourning note, a dirge portending fateful events.

"A price, drieu Dylaw. More guns, more darts to fill them." Her voice sang in his ears, whispering temptation.

A small dust devil broke over the drieu's feet, showering desiccated leaves and other debris on his legs, breaking his mood. He shuddered and turned to face her, hating her all the more because he knew he couldn't refuse.

"I will not take you." His voice was harsh and abrupt.

"I don't expect that. You have your people to care for."

"But I'll ask those." He swung a hand at the squatting figures. "If one will do it, then we can bargain. If not . . ."

Aleytys looked over scowling faces alike in their ingrained xenophobia. Then she focused on one face, a young face twisted in the most malignant scowl of all. She reached out. Touched the turmoil boiling in him. Snatched the probe back.

Reeled under the impact of his confusion. The drieu stared at her, then turned his back on her.

"If one among you would take this—this person to the sea, our cause would benefit greatly. They have offered additional guns and darts to pay for this service." Aleytys could see the long muscles of his neck tighten, then loosen. "Is any willing?"

Gwynnor ran the tip of his tongue over his lips as he fought the pull of the starwitch. He . . . he must . . . he must . . . no! He almost shouted the words, but clamped his lips over the impulse to speak, swallowing the soaring words, afraid to answer, afraid to acknowledge her influence in any way. But the pull strengthened. She reached out touching him tickling gently along his nerves whispering comecomecome . . . until, his feet scraping heavily over the sand-littered stone, he stepped forward. "I . . ." His voice cracked. He cleared his throat and spat, grudging briefly the expenditure of his body's moisture here in this desert. "I'll do it." He forced himself to meet Dylaw's incredulous eyes, drawing back his narrow shoulders in a mockery of stiff pride while his anger beat futilely at invisible seals. "Let the weapons be my gift to the cause." The words were proud also, but he felt hollow inside, knowing that the woman had laid a spell on his soul.

"So be it. Come, Musician, sit beside me till we find what your sacrifice can buy us."

Chapter II

The ship rode an ascending whine into the sky, melting after a few moments into the sterile blue. Southwest, a winding dark line marked the creeping progress of the Dylaw's pack train. Aleytys shook her hair out of her eyes and dug her heels into the kaffa's sides.

The animal had an odd, loose-kneed gait that she found disconcerting, the dip and heave close to making her trail-sick. When she glanced for the last time into the canyon, then up at the sky, the ship had vanished, cutting off her retreat. She felt awash, disoriented, even a little frightened. She pinched her lips together, then sighed. Ahead, the boy's slumped shoulders were eloquent of his troubled dislike for this expedition. Aleytys caught wisps of anger and fear blown back to her like snatches of smoke torn apart by a restless wind. The silence was heavy between them, broken only by the sweeping moan of the wind, the schlupp schlupp of the kaffa pads, the creak of saddle leather.

"What's your name?" she called to the boy.

He glanced back briefly, his round face clenched in a scowl, then swung forward again without answering her.

Aleytys prodded the beast into a brief jolting run until she was riding beside the cerdd boy. "What's your name? It's awkward not knowing."

Grudgingly the boy muttered, "Gwynnor." Then had to repeat it louder, as the wind snatched the word away.

"Such anger, Gwynnor. Why?"

He stared sullenly at her.

"Don't try to tell me I'm mistaken. Look. My name is Aleytys." A corner of her mouth flicked up. "Means wanderer. Appropriate, don't you think?"

"So?" He shrugged and turned his shoulders until his back was to her. "I don't want to talk."

"You mean you don't want to talk to me."

"Yes."

"Don't be a fool. You can't ignore me. I won't let you. I refuse to ride beside a lump."

"Duyffawd!"

Her eyebrows rose. "Most impolite."

"You laugh? Ah, Mannh! What do you want on our world?"

"Nothing." She sighed and tried for a more stable position on the kaffa's limber back. "Nothing but to quit it as fast as possible."

Disbelief hung in a fog around him. "You're here."

"A waystop. That's all."

Against his will he found himself responding to her calm, friendly tone. "Why didn't you go on with the smuggler?"

"This world is as far on my way as the Captain goes. At Maeve, he circles back on the other wing of his route."

"Oh." Gwynnor starred thoughtfully at the bobbing, swaying neck of his mount. "How're you going to get off Maeve?"

She shrugged. "Bribe my way onto a starship, I suppose."

For several minutes they rode along in silence. Aleytys could feel the boy struggling to assimilate her words.

He looked back at her, his dark-green eyes open wide, the pupils narrowed in the brilliant afternoon light. "Then you're going to the city."

"I have to." She caught the sharp scent of suspicion. "Gwynnor, look! If I told the Company men I came here on a smuggler's ship, I'd be sticking my head in a shark's mouth. They'd have to sponge up what was left of me. No, I won't betray you. Couldn't if I wanted to. What the hell do I know that I could tell them?"

"About the place." He jerked a head at the dark line that marked the position of the canyon.

"Dammit, Gwynnor, Captain Arel's my friend. You think I want him killed?"

"Oh."

Aleytys shifted again to relieve the ache in her thighs. "It's been too long since I rode anything with four legs. Why hate all starmen?"

His head swung around and he stared at her, startled. Then his young face pinched into an angry scowl. "They come. Take. Take." He ran his left hand over the top of his head repeatedly. "Take and kill. Kill gentle people . . ." His shoulders slumped suddenly as he retreated into unhappy memories.

"So you want to drive the Company out."

"Yes." She felt his helpless anger. For a minute, pity stirred in her, then she pushed it away. No, she thought, not again. It's none of my business.

They rode on in silence through air thin and chill enough to make her shiver and think about untying the poncho from behind the saddle, but not chill enough to make the effort really worthwhile. The air burned her lungs and leeched the moisture from lips and nose. As her tongue flicked around her mouth, struggling to replace the moisture, she could feel hairline cracks opening in her lips. Overhead the sky was a cold blue with ragged, wispy clouds scudding across the bowl while wind down lower drove the coarse dust singing over the scarred stone. Behind her, the sun crept down in its western arc with a foot-dragging lassitude that made her feel like clawing it to a more normal speed. Each time she glanced back she had to search for the rusty disc, her body rhythms with their ingrained expectations sending her eyes automatically to the wrong part of the sky.

"Company men!" Gwynnor said suddenly. "Are you . . ."

"Huh?"

"Are you part of a Company?"

"No. Where I was born no one had even heard of the Companies. Damn! That was a long way back." Rubbing her fingers lightly over the springy hair on the kaffa's back, she stared over the bobbing head at the desolate expanse of weathered stone. "A long way back . . ."

"Why did you leave the place where you belonged?" Disapproval was sharp in his tenor voice.

"Belonged!" A bark of unhappy laughter was startled out of her. "They were going to burn me for a witch."

Her mount shied as a knobby little reptile fled in panic from under its feet. Almost immediately, a dark shadow plummeted from the sky and sailed off with the reptile wriggling in its talons. Aleytys frowned. She continued to watch a moment, then closed her eyes. The bird vanished from her senses, not even the faint flutter of awareness that proximate life usually stirred along her nerve paths unless she consciously blocked it out.

When she looked up again the black, triangular shape was soaring upward on a thermal, too high to see if the whippy reptile still dangled from its beak. "Hey!" She pulled her eyes down. "Gwynnor!" He was riding slumped over, deep in unhappy thoughts. "Gwynnor!"

He straightened his narrow shoulders and looked around.

"Is there a bird up there, or am I dreaming?"

His eyes rounded. "An eryr. Why?"

"When I close my eyes, he's not there. Why can't I sense him as well as see him?"

"You SEE?"

"If that's what you call it."

He fixed his eyes on the eryr as it sailed past the sun. "Prey animals on Maeve SEE. Most of them. So do some of the cerdd. I . . . I did once. No longer." He slid rapidly over the words, then slowed as he continued to explain. "Since they'd starve without it, some predators developed the ability to be invisible to the SIGHT." He swung bright, nervous eyes across the sky. "I was forgetting. There's worse than the eryr in these skies."

"Worse."

"Peithwyr." He shuddered. "Six meters of leathery wing and teeth with a poison sting in the tail." He dug his heels into the kaffa's side. With a snort of disgust the animal speeded up, the dip and sway of its gait increasing alarmingly. "I forgot," he threw back at her over his shoulder.

Aleytys goaded her own mount into faster movement and drew up alongside him. "I won't be able to sense it coming?"

"No." He looked around warily. "No," he repeated after a while. "If a peithwyr attacks, get off the kaffa first. Get as far off as you can the first jump. If you're lucky, it'll start tearing up the kaffa and let you get out of sight behind the first rock you can reach. Then you've got maybe a chance in fifty getting away alive."

"Why not shoot it? You're armed."

"Holy Maeve! No, Aleytys." His face was a study in consternation. "A wounded peithwyr? It wouldn't stop till the ground itself was shredded. In small pieces."

"Even if you killed it?"

"Peithwyrn are hard to kill. You'd have to be lucky. Make good an eye shot." She could feel tension mounting in him. "Where eryr are, the peithwyr haunts."

Aleytys shuddered and shifted uneasily in the saddle. "I've been able to mind-control predators before."

"Don't waste your time."

The afternoon deepened slowly. Aleytys dropped into a tired, half-dozing state, lulled into carelessness by the uneventful passage of hours. The flat stone surface stretched away to the horizon with scraggly plants here and there that were a dusty gray-green, hard to separate from the stone. Occasional reptiles scurried away from the feet of the kaffon but no eryr broke the sterile silence of the sky.

"Hit the ground!" Gwynnor's shriek sent her tumbling off the kaffa, diving for a tumbled pile of rocks, disregarding the frantic scrabble of the beast's feet. A sudden foul stench wafted past on a surge of air driven by great wings. Blackness flowed over her. The kaffa screamed, then silence filled with tearing sounds. She scrambled away. A boulder. She slammed into it. Crawled around it. Peered cautiously back.

The kaffa was down in a boneless heap, throat torn, blood

gouting in a steamy diminishing arc. Stench again. Something struck her shoulder, a numbing blow. Was gone. A scream. Cut off.

Keeping low, moving with fear-born caution, she peered around the boulder briefly. The other kaffa was down and spouting blood. The peithwyr beat its leathery wings with tremendous strokes, driving its huge hollow-boned body into the air again. It circled over the butchered animals then came plummeting at her, bloody talons reaching.

She scrambled backwards hastily, pulling at the hem of her tunic to get at her gun.

The peithwyr dropped like a bomb. Desperately, she drove her body away, still trying to get the gun free.

The peithwyr dropped, talons glittering in the russet light.

Pain. Not her throat. Her shoulder. Pain. It thrust her toward the comforting blackness pooling beneath the agony. Her shoulder was on fire. Fire spread outward from the white-hot center where a pumping artery spurted away her strength. Scarcely noticed, wings beat over her then veered off. As she faded, she heard a crunching of bones. The peithwyr crouched dark and ominous, tearing at the kaffa. Her sight blurred. Blackness was warm, the pain distant, a great grinding agony distant . . . her life spurted away through the torn artery.

Something prodded at her.

Amber eyes opened inside her head. "Aleytys!" The contralto voice was familiar . . . familiar . . . she didn't want to know . . .

Memory was a flood of agony She wanted to deny it but she had no strength. "Harskari." Aleyty's lips moved with the name. "Why?" A cone of red licking out. Killing. Killing my love. Why?

Black eyes opened. "Freyka!"

Go away. I don't want you. I won't let you . . . I won't acknowledge you . . . I won't . . .

Delicate chimes whispered around her head, delightful butterfly notes singing around the sounds from the gorging peithwyr. The amber eyes altered. A thin, dark face framed in shimmering silver hair formed around them. "Aleytys! Heal yourself. Now, girl. You can rest later."

"No." The word was harsh in her mind through her trembling lips moved with only a breath of sound. She tried to reject the presence, feeling a pain that went far deeper than the simple physical hurt from her mangled shoulder.

Violet eyes snapped with annoyance as a pointed elfin face materialized around them. Shadith's aureole of coppery curls quivered like tiny springs. "Move ass, Lee. You can wallow in self-pity when you've got the leisure for it. Come on, let us help you. Lean on us. Reach out for your river. Come on, dammit! Reach!"

Cool, ironic black eyes slanting down at the outer corners set in a rugged, intensely male face, Swardheld grinned at her. "Glad to see you with us again, freyka. Now!" He narrowed his eyes, then bellowed, "Move it, woman!"

Prodded by the phantom images in her head, Aleytys focused her mind on reaching for the black river that fed her talents. And as she reached, she felt phantom arms cradling her body, lending her the strength she lacked. She shuddered with that wrenching psychic pain inflicted by the memory of love and death. Weakly, she tried to push the memory away, shutting out the three in her head along with it. For a moment the hands supporting her faltered, seemed to retreat. No. The word roared at her. No. Don't shut us out. Not again.

The black water came pouring over her. She writhed and shrieked . . . pain . . . pain . . . tearing at her . . . and worse . . . tormenting itch as the torn flesh grew back. As blood cells doubled and redoubled. Then the thunder of the water died to a whisper.

"Aleytys." The quiet word vibrated through her head. "Remember Irsud. Remember that ill-fated world. Remember Burash, your lover. Face your anguish. Don't run away from it again. You're a woman, not a child."

"No . . ."

The peithwyr beat its way into the sky, sending great gouts of wind to batter her. Then it dropped again, talons reaching for her, screaming, a battering of sound that shocked thought from her head.

The diadem chimed, and the air turned stiff. Aleytys shuddered as dead men's faces came tumbling back, triggered into consciousness by the sound. And Swardheld shoved her aside, knocking her loose from her body, shouting, "Verdamn, freyka, move over!"

He flipped her body over the nearest boulder, diving with a

smooth continuation of the movement to end on his feet behind the plummeting bird. The diadem chimed again.

The peithwyr squalled with rage and muscled its great body around.

Swardheld cursed and jerked the tunic up, snatching the energy gun from the waistband of her trousers. As the monster dived toward him, he cleared the sensor and sent the thin red beam searing first into the chest region, then, with his usual calm accuracy, he sent the ruddy beam into the mad eyes of the beast. Immediately, he leaped the body back, wheeled it, put six meters between body and dying bird, dropped body behind one of the piled boulders and waited.

The peithwyr tumbled out of control, cracking the air with shrieks of pain and rage. Then it fell onto the rock and writhed, snapping haphazardly, tearing at its own flesh. Grinning his triumph, Swardheld let go his hold on her body.

With the weakening cries behind her, Aleytys slid back into control and tried to get to her feet. Her legs were so weak she fell, bruising her knees. She felt sick.

Shaking, she pulled herself onto the boulder, pushed her legs back against the stone and leaned forward, resting her head on her hands, elbows pressed against her knees, breathing in great shuddering gasps that wrenched her body. Gentle hands, immaterial hands, moved over her, comforting her.

Harskari materialized in her head. "Aleytys, look to the boy. He might be still alive."

"Ahai Madar!" She pushed up on wobbly legs and stumbled across to the second kaffa.

The cerdd was crouched behind his mount, blood seeping sluggishly from the shredded flesh of his back. He lay very still.

Grimacing with distaste, Aleytys knelt beside the pool of blood and touched him. Life beat faintly under her fingers. Arching her body over the blood to keep the sticky mess off herself, she placed her hands on the cerdd's back and let the healing power flow.

After awhile, back aching from the unnatural position, she straightened. Gwynnor's flesh was whole again, the only sign of the savage wounds a faint pink tracery crossing the thick, grayish fuzz growing on the pale skin of his body.

He blinked and sat up, looking at her, eyes staring wildly, he quickly focused on the gelatinous blood pooled around him. He tugged at his tattered tunic and glanced briefly at the bloody rags that barely covered her torso.

Uncomfortable in the silence, Aleytys said abruptly, "I heal."

"So I see." He chuckled, a sudden flash of humor born from his near-brush with death. "The peithwyr?"

Aleytys jumped up and looked back across the stone. "Still dying."

Holding onto her, Gwynnor pulled himself onto his feet and stared at the slowly writhing form of the killer bird. "How?"

She touched her waist. "Energy gun."

"Come on." He scrambled over the corpse of the kaffa and began tearing at the saddle bags.

"What's the hurry?"

"Its mate. We might not be lucky a second time." He pulled the knots loose and swung the waterskin over his shoulder, the bags over another. Aleytys hurried to follow his example.

As they moved along a path, clinging to the side of a ravine that opened out a few meters from the battered corpses of the kaffan and the still struggling peithwyr, Aleytys glanced nervously at the sky. "You think the peithwyr won't see us down here?"

Gwynnor shrugged, then edged around a curve, pressing his body tight against the side wall. His voice came back to her. "Be careful. The stone is crumbling badly here."

After they negotiated the dangerous area, Gwynnor said suddenly, "Their wing spread's too great. We should be safe as long as this keeps going in the right direction." Then he added, "I think."

She looked back at the sun, still stubbornly high above the western horizon, fully visible even from the depths of the ravine. "How long till sunset?"

"Four, five more hours. Why?"

"I'm about out of push. My home world has a shorter day. And the standard one I've got used to since is shorter than that."

"Oh."

A shattering scream battered at them. The peithwyr's mate, wings folded back, plunged at them in a steep suicidal dive.

"Swardheld." Aleytys surrendered her body, scarcely waiting to be sure he heard. Black eyes blazing, he took her body, snatched the gun from her trouser belt. An eye shot. Then he scrambled back frantically to avoid the plummeting body.

Breathing hard, Gwynnor and Aleytys stumbled around a bend in the ravine, the screams and papery rattle of the dying bird following them.

Gwynnor eyed the blunt, ugly gun with a touch of envy. "If we had those instead of . . ." He flicked contemptuous fingers over the butt of the darter shoved behind his belt.

Aleytys shuddered, still loathing the feel of the deadly thing. She thrust it away and pulled her tunic down. "The Captain couldn't sell them to you," she said quietly, absently. She breathed a swift flash of gratitude to Swardheld, felt his answering grin, then moved away from the wall and continued along the bottom of the ravine. "The Company men would hunt him down without mercy if he did that. You, too, and your companions. So be grateful the situation is as it is."

"Tchah!"

Behind them, the peithwyr tore at the stone and groaned as it fought death fiercely. The sound lessened and died away as they turned more corners in the torturously winding ravine.

"Will we reach the edge of the plateau anytime soon?"

"No." He stumbled, caught himself, then rearranged the straps of the waterskins and the saddlebags. "We have to change the plan. There's not enough water to go the way you wanted. And we can't move as fast as the kaffon. So we head due east. Should get to the edge in a couple of days. Can you climb?"

Aleytys was silent a minute. She let Gwynnor draw ahead, then narrowed her eyes and unfocused them. "Harskari. Shadith. Swardheld."

Three faces blinked into being. Harskari looked a little impatient. "What is it?"

"Any of you mountain climbers?"

Swardheld grinned. "I was born in the mountains, Leyta. Remember? No damn rock I can't climb. Once . . ."

"Heaven forfend we hear another of your stories, old growler." Shadith's voice was gently mocking.

Harskari turned cool, amber eyes on her companions and they quieted immediately. "Why, Aleytys?"

"Though I was born a mountain girl, I never climbed anything. Raqsidani women weren't allowed to. Now it looks like I'll have to go down a cliffside."

As Gwynnor walked along waiting for his answer, he realized that the silence had gone on too long. He looked around. The star-woman was standing slumped against the side of the ravine, her eyes half shut, her mouth moving soundlessly. Talking? To someone? To something? He shivered in sudden, superstitious fear. Reluctantly, he edged closer.

She opened her eyes and smiled at him. "Yes." Her voice was a warm contralto that he found gentle on his music-starved ears. "I can climb." She pushed away from the wall of rock. "I was born in the mountains."

She walked beside him, her stride long and free, one accustomed to walking, not like those feeble types from the city. More and more he felt confused by her. He couldn't fit her anywhere among those in his experience, not as enemy and certainly not as friend. And how could anyone be neutral about her? The wind blew over her and brought him her complex scent, a tart-sweet smell that disturbed . . . excited . . . She was taller than he was, had a look of completeness about her, of knowing who she was and what she was, needing no one, nothing. He envied her and distrusted her. Wanted her. Despaired. She seemed to point up all the things he found wrong in himself. Sunk in the melancholy gloom that was the curse of his temperament, he plodded wordlessly beside her.

"Any more of those devils about?"

He looked at her, startled to hear her break the silence. She smiled and the knot began dissolving inside him. Tentatively, he smiled back. "They have a kind of nest-clan arrangement. Several pairs together. So we'd better keep watch. Holy Maeve be blessed, they don't fly about after dark."

"That's a relief." She raised her hands high above her head, stretching and twisting to relieve muscles held too taut too long. "I wasn't looking forward to shivering under my blankets waiting for old big mouth to descend on me." A sudden thought sent her eyes to his. "Or do you have worse mouths that inhabit the night?"

He grinned at her, obscurely pleased by this evidence of her mortality. "Only snakes. They like your body warmth and crawl under the blanket with you."

"My god." Shaking her head, the starwoman shortened her stride to match his and paced down the winding and deepening ravine toward the haunt of the rising sun.

Chapter III

The meager fire glowed red and gold in the blackness. Aleytys felt its gentle heat bathing her face as she stared at the constantly altering patterns of dark and light.

"There's no need to keep watch."

She looked up. Gwynnor's eyes shone phosphorescent green in the firelight. She smiled. "Your night's too long for me. I need to do some thinking before I sleep."

He lay down and pulled the blanket over his head, his feet pointing toward the fire. Almost between breaths he was asleep.

With a sigh, she tucked her blanket around her and hugged her knees, staring into the flames, hypnotized into mind blankness until she shrugged herself out of the haze. "Harskari," she whispered.

Amber eyes opened, blinked, then the thin, clever face smiled out of the darkness in her mind. "Aleytys."

"I've been remembering."

"I know."

"Why did you all stop talking to me?"

The wind was strengthening, whispering across the coals and blowing alternate gusts of warm and cold air past her face. Small pieces of grit pattered against the blanket.

Harskari shook her head, her white mane shifting like silk. "We didn't. You were so hurt by the nayid male's death that you couldn't handle it. You transferred the guilt you felt to us and took the only revenge you could by totally denying our existence. You forgot us and sealed us off from contact at the same time. I don't think you know your strength, Aleytys."

Aleytys dropped her head on her arms, burying her face in the folds of the blanket, grieving because she was not grieving. But too much time had passed. Once there had been first affection, then a deep love shared. Now there was only a

26

faded memory as if all that had happened to someone else. Was this all love came to? She tried to find a trace of that tumultuous warmth in herself, but there was nothing. Too much time. She sighed, brushed a hand over her face, and stared back into the glowing coals. "So when I was close to dying, you could get through again."

"Yes. You needed us."

"I've just about got straight in my head what happened since I left Jaydugar. What about you?"

"To see your world, we look through your eyes. But there are other worlds and other ways of looking."

"Oh." Aleytys glanced briefly at Gwynnor's sleeping form, then lifted her eyes to the brilliantly lit sky. A huge pale moon thrust up over the eastern horizon, filling half the sky with its milky glow. The air was cold, thin and sharp and invigorating, biting the fog out of her mind. "That doesn't really answer my question."

Harskari chuckled. "Yes, young Aleytys, we know what you've been doing."

Abruptly, Aleytys felt very good, her body ticking like a fine watch. She laughed and patted her mouth as the laugh turned into a yawn. "Harskari?"

"What is it?"

"On Jaydugar, we made a mess of the nomad clan. On Lamarchos, I got involved with Loahn and the Horde, Kale and his complicated plots, until the whole damn world was crushed under dead bodies. On Irsud, I stuck my nose into the hiiri's fight with the nayids, though the nayids asked for it. The outcome was that I destroyed a large part of the nayid population. So here we are on Maeve, in the company of a cerdd who is helping wage an undeclared war. Makes you think."

"It does, indeed," Harskari chuckled, a gentle affectionate sound, "considering past performance."

"Damn." Aleytys yawned again. "I'll probably have nightmares."

Chapter IV

"How the hell are we supposed to get down that?" Aleytys muttered. Stomach pressed against the rock, she lay with her head over the cliff edge, looking down, down, dizzyingly down to a mossy green carpet marking the tops of trees far below. Warm updrafts sweeping up the face of the slope brought scent loads slipping past her face, a complex melange of smells that tickled her nose and intrigued her mind, surprising her with its strength here, so far above the forest below.

The face of the stone slanted outward. Rough and craggy with plenty of hand and foot holds, it didn't look especially hard to climb, but it went so far down. Aleytys closed her eyes. "Swardheld, you weren't just bragging, I hope. You better be able to manage that."

Swardheld's face laughed out of the darkness at her. "That? Freyka, that little slope's almost flat ground compared to some mountain faces I've climbed. Look over the edge again."

Aleytys opened her eyes. The ground below looked farther away each time she glanced that way. "Blessed Madar!"

The black eyes narrowed in shrewd appraisal. "No problem at all, not if you've got any spring left in your legs, Leyta."

"Oh, fine." Scrambling to her feet she met Gwynnor's puzzled gaze. Flicking a hand at the cliff, she said, "You sure this is necessary?"

He dropped the coil of rope and held out the waterskin. "Drink."

She lifted the bag and caught the last stale drops on her dry tongue. She slapped the stopper home and handed the limp skin back to him. "You make your point."

He nodded briefly and picked up the rope. "Do you know the climbing knots?"

28

Gwynnor had watched the starwoman look toward the distant western horizon, eyes unfocused, face slack. Talking to her spirits again, he thought, and felt a tightness in his chest.

"I'm afraid of her," he whispered, the soft words hidden in the soughing of the wind.

As he handed the rope to her, her body straightened, altered its posture slightly with a new way of holding her head. Eyebrows lowered over the narrowed green-blue eyes, mouth hardened, her voice was deeper than usual when she spoke. "The knots?"

He watched as her fingers moved with sure knowledge, making a knot that held firm but could be jerked loose in an emergency. The knot was done with enough mastery to reassure him. "Good. Who goes first?"

"I do." The words were sharp, clipped, with a weight of authority unlike her usual friendly, offhand style. It was as if another personality inhabited the familiar flesh. Gwynnor felt a squeezing of his stomach as he contemplated that terrifying idea. Then the starwoman spoke again. "You climbed this spot before?"

"No."

She stepped briskly to the cliff edge. "Then we go over here. Follow that crack down to there." She pointed to a place where the stone broke into a deeply weathered washboard. "How friable is this rock?"

"Your eyes seem as good as mine." He shrugged.

She nodded briskly. "I see." Knotting the rope around her waist she waited for Gwynnor to follow her example. "Don't kick rocks on my head." She grinned at his indignant exclamation. "Let's go!"

Aleytys stamped her feet briskly, putting her body back on like a pair of too-tight boots. Looking back at the stony slope, she wrinkled her nose and shook her head.

Gwynnor wound the rope between hand and elbow while the straightening twist sent the free end leaping about. "You came down fast."

"Sooner off the rock, the better." She sniffed at the soup of smells slopping about her on the edge of the forest. "What a stink."

The soil under her boots was heavy and black, damp enough so that she sank inches into it. There was a waiting quality in the heavy humid air that hung so still and quiet around her. Not a sound, no insect noises, no birdsong, not even a rustle of leaves. Only the scent, strong enough to start her head aching. She scuffed her feet in the soggy earth, reluctant to get mud on her clothing. The waiting silence tugged at her nerves, reminding her that she needed to make her peace with the elementals of this world. "Is there some water around here?"

The tip of Gwynnor's longish nose twitched fitfully as he watched her. "I saw a shine of water that way," he pointed.

The rusty sun sparked orange glints from the narrow stream. Aleytys leaned against a tree and pulled her boots off. The scent from the tree was almost overpowering, cloyingly sweet with dusty undertones, though where dust would come from in this saturated atmosphere Aleytys couldn't begin to guess. She glanced at the silent cerdd, shrugged, and broke the magnetic closure on her trousers. Tiredly, she stripped, and tossed the worn clothing over a low-hanging limb. Then she picked up the boots and carried them to the water. Kneeling on a half-buried rock, she ran her hands over the mud-crusted leather, washing them clean. She looked up and met Gwynnor's astonished eyes. A grin on her face, she shook her head. "I haven't lost my mind." She splashed her hand in the water. "And I'm not trying to seduce you. Ride with it and be patient. I'll be finished in a minute."

She knelt on the damp earth, resting her hands on her knees. Closing her eyes to slits that let light in but screened out distraction, she began the breathing discipline that slowed her body and let her mind reach out and out to touch the places where the world's elementals rested. "Gweledi dayar," she murmured. "World spirits, I cross in peace, seeking nothing more than passage from one place to another."

She felt a stirring, a formless flow in the earth beneath her. Bending forward, she placed her hands on the ground, fingers splayed out like pale five-pointed stars. Tendrils of warmth tickled along her veins. Momentarily the scents around her increased a thousand-fold in strength so that she nearly fainted under the burden on her senses. Through the bombardment she felt a sluggish curiosity, a measure of interest, a question, then acceptance as the tendrils withdrew.

Sighing, she sat back on her heels and grimaced at her muddy hands. Around her, the tension was gone from the air. Small, homey sounds filled the gaping silence so that the world under the trees hummed with life once more.

Gwynnor stood on a boulder in the center of the stream where the sun trickled through the leaves, feeling more comfortable when he could still see fragments of sky. Briefly and repeatedly he glanced at the pale body of the woman crouched on hands and knees on the black earth.

When the normal forest sounds began, he started and nearly fell off the rock. He felt the forest reach out and enfold them and he shivered, clamped his teeth onto his lower lip, fighting fear that nibbled at him like a hungry rat. Silently, she came back to the stream and knelt on the stone, washing the mud off her body.

The heavy smells around him bothered him a little. It was too much. And there was too much life here. He couldn't sort out the complexes as he was used to doing on the maes. Not yet, anyway. Sweat oozed down his scalp under the clustering gray curls. He didn't like the forest. He wanted to leave it. Now. Or as fast as possible.

The starwoman dressed briskly. She brushed back wispy red-gold curls that escaped from her braids and formed a fragile halo about her face. A relaxed, smiling face.

She turned to him. "Where do we go now, Gwynnor?"

He glanced around uneasily, not liking to hear his name spoken aloud in this place.

She sensed his unease and laughed, a warm sound that poured like honey over his quivering nerves. "Your name is not you, my friend," she said gently. "Besides, you're with me."

Growing calmer, he dug in his mind for a logical answer to her question. "Three days to the north . . . three days on kaffa back, I mean . . . I don't know how long it might take in that." He swung a hand at the forest. "There's a river, the regular trade route from the maes. It leads to the sea where you wanted to go." He pointed up at the sun then brought his hand down, moving fingers to indicate the flow of the stream. "This stream seems to be moving toward the river. We could follow it. On the other hand, the sea is straight east from here. But I've never been over the ground between here and there."

"Mmm." She stretched and yawned. "I'm not pressed for time. Not that much, anyway. We'd better stick to the stream as long as it goes where we want."

Chapter V

Gwynnor knelt beside the smoky fire, automatically moving to avoid the straying aromatic puffs of smoke billowing from the damp wood. He watched the starwoman groan as she sat up, throwing off her blanket and stretching, yawning, running hands over her rumpled hair. Then her face went slack as her attention was directed inward.

"On your feet, freyka." Swardheld's black eyes snapped good-humored command at her.

Aleytys stifled another yawn. "What the hell . . ."

"Your training starts today." The face floating in the blackness scowled at her. "We barely made it down that mountain. You're soft as butter, Aleytys."

Groaning as sore muscles protested, Aleytys staggered to her feet and kicked the blanket aside. "I know you mean it when you use my full name. What do I do?"

"Warm up first." His voice was a comfortable burring in her head. "Then we walk through a few exercises. You need to build up arm and leg strength. And flexibility. And wind, love."

Gwynnor watched as she bent and strained, hopped and swung, pressing her body through a series of gyrations that poured sweat down her face and breath whistling through her teeth. Then the cha water boiled. He snatched the pot off the fire and poured the steaming water over the curling cha leaves. Then he watched her again, wondering again why she did it. She was flat on her back, arms stretched out straight from her shoulders, then she wrenched her body into a vee, fingers reaching to touch toes, with her buttocks as fulcrum. It made his middle hurt just watching. Shaking his head, he poured the cha into two mugs.

Aleytys came over to the fire, rubbing her arms. "And I

have to walk after all that." She accepted a cup and gulped gratefully at the hot liquid.

"Why do it, then?" As she drank more cha he unfolded waxed cloth from around some loaves of waybread. "Why tire yourself out before a long day even begins?"

She rubbed a finger beside her nose. "Have to get my body back in shape. A couple of times on the cliff I didn't think I'd make bottom."

A large insect with greenish-gray wings flapped unconcernedly past her shoulder and landed on a waxy knob surrounded by a star-shaped complex of leaves. It settled close to her shoulder, head-high. She tore off a chunk of bread and chewed at the resilient mouthful while she watched the insect poise on black-thread legs and nuzzle at the bud.

Its wings had a dark green base with a gray flaky powder spread in concentric whorls over the top surface. On the side of the bulbous head she saw two deep pits that at first she mistook for eyes. But they were sensory patches filled with thousands of fine, fine hairs. As she watched, the side-moving jaws pierced the bud, letting loose a flood of spicy scent. She bent closer. "Gwynnor?"

He dumped water on the coals, then scraped dirt over the fire, meticulously returning the forest floor to its natural state. When he was quite ready, he walked across to her where she fidgeted, bending over the opening-closing wings as the bug sucked greedily at the strong-smelling fluid oozing from the pierced bud. "We should be starting on," he said, voice low and unhappy.

"Look. It doesn't have eyes."

He looked instead at the solid canopy of leaves that kept the forest floor in a constant state of greenish twilight, keeping out the clean, honest light of the sun. "What's to look at in here?"

"This." She curved her hand over the bug. "What is it?" As she asked the question she turned her head, wondering what had brought on his fit of sullens. She saw him staring upward hungrily. Maes, she thought, that means plains. I suppose this place gives him claustrophobia.

He bent closer, finally looking down at the insect. Then he straightened and shrugged. "I live on the plains," he said, unconsciously echoing her thought. He broke the branch free from the bush and flipped it and the bug into the gloom under the trees. "It's just a bug. What does it matter what it is?"

Aleytys pulled back the hand that had gone out to stop him. Anger flared in her at the thoughtless destruction, and blasted out from her like flame.

Gwynnor saw the starwoman's face redden then turn pale, eyes blue-green ice glittering, then flames red and blue licked out from her, leaped at him, seared his body. He shrieked, batting at his face and body with frantic hands.

Hastily, Aleytys wheeled, turning her back on him until she could control herself. When she turned around again, his face still twitched with the memory of pain. "You're all right," she said coldly. "I suppose I should be sorry."

"It was only a bug."

She sighed. "Never mind. Just don't do that again."

They followed the stream. Over the water, the leaves were a little thinner, so the walking was easier because it was easier to see where to put their feet.

Aleytys stooped down and put her hands flat on the earth in front of her toes, then she straightened and flung out her arms, then swung her body vigorously, first to the right then to the left. Meeting Gwynnor's startled gaze, she smiled. "I'm not crazy. Just stiff with walking."

He shrugged and was silent, waiting for her.

"You're quiet today."

"I've got nothing to say."

She dropped on a tree root. "So you say nothing. How wise. Let's stop awhile." She leaned back against the tree. "Your days are too long for me."

"You said that before. Several times." Gwynnor sat some distance from her, staring into the hurrying water, cool green tumbling down small steps with a muted musical murmur. "Why did you have to come here?"

She scratched her wrist while she watched her toes wiggle. "Haven't you ever stopped in a place where you didn't mean to stay, a halt, say, where you change from kaffa to boat?"

"Yes."

"The smuggler captain brought me as far as he could on my way. Now he goes back and I go on." She moved lazily, her shoulders grating against the grainy bark. "I told you that."

"I know."

"I appear to be fascinating you with my conversation."

His head turned quickly toward her, then away. "So you go to that place."

"Huh?"

"Caer Seramdun. That city."

"I don't know how else I'd get offworld."

"You told Dylaw you wanted to go to the sea."

She sighed. "Gwynnor, it just seemed simpler. You wouldn't go to the city anyway. So why ask?" She stood up and was beside him before he could move. "Take my hand."

He shied away from her, shaking his head in quick denial.

"Take my hand!"

Aleytys sighed at the queasy mixture of terror and repulsion that flooded from him. "I don't bite. And my flesh won't leave a stain on you."

Gwynnor trembled, frightened and angry at himself for wanting to touch her. Her scent billowed around him until he felt close to drowning in it. He saw her again naked, kneeling in the mud, her hair loose like a flow of silk. And he saw her slack-faced, talking to her demons, and he saw the demon taking her body. Hand shaking, despising himself for being afraid to touch her, he reached out. Her fingers were warm and vital, smooth and strong, closing around his with a firm grip.

Aleytys almost dropped the hand, but hung on and felt the painful confusion finally diminish. Felt something else. "You're a sensitive?"

"What?"

"You *see?*"

"I did. Once."

"It's not something you lose, like your baby teeth."

He moved his hand but didn't quite jerk loose. "I lost it," he said tensely.

"Hai Madar." With a sigh she gathered the remnants of her patience. "It doesn't work."

"I told you."

"No, no. What I meant was you can't deny what you are. I tried it and I know. Never mind. Gwynnor, I swear to you I will say nothing of you or your people or the smuggler or the weapons or anything at all that could bring harm to you." She concentrated on projecting her intense belief in that.

This time he did snatch his hand away. He jumped to his

feet. "Don't." After putting a couple meters between them, he said hoarsely, "You rested enough?"

"Just enough to get stiff again. I'll be all right once we start moving."

"It's another two hours till noon." He walked nervously on without waiting for her answer.

Aleytys rubbed her stomach. "Damn. I could eat now." She followed Gwynnor along the stream, keeping as close as she could to the water's edge. The going was difficult, tree roots bursting from the soil at irregular intervals, the awkward spaces between the rocks threatening to trap a foot or break an ankle. When the banks were wider, there was grass and the walking was easier. By the time the position of the sun announced the noon hour, Aleytys was too exhausted to bother about Gwynnor's puzzling reactions. She dropped onto a patch of grass and pulled her boots off. As she sat rubbing her numb toes, he stopped and came back. "Can you go far-ther?"

She stretched her feet out in front of her, wiggling her toes as she frowned at the constricting boots. "Give me awhile. I have to think."

He scowled, then sat down some way off, turning his back to her as if he was unwilling to look at her.

Aleytys closed her eyes. "Harskari?"

The narrow, pale face with the big amber eyes developed from the darkness. "What is it, Aleytys?"

"I just wanted to see a friendly face."

A thin eyebrow flicked up toward the tumbling silver curls. "So your little friend doesn't appreciate you."

Aleytys frowned. "I pushed a wrong button somewhere. I wish I knew what I said. Or did."

"Give him time. He's in a strange place and uneasy about it."

Aleytys rubbed her nose thoughtfully. "And he doesn't like any of us starfolk." She chuckled. "My god, Harskari, did you hear what I just said?"

"A truth you've taken a long time to acknowledge." Harskari hesitated, her amber eyes narrowing. "You're still dreaming of going back to Vajd."

Aleytys fidgeted. "I don't want to talk about that."

"Obviously. However, you'd better think about it." The face faded and she was alone again.

Stretching her aching limbs, Aleytys leaned back against

the tree, letting the black waters of her symbolic river run in healing waves over her, working out the poisons of fatigue, washing away the muscle aches. The soothing water ebbed and she jumped to her feet, yawned, grinned at Gwynnor's stubborn back. "I'm starved."

He rose and walked silently into the forest, leaving Aleytys staring in surprise. As she was making up her mind whether to follow him or wait by the water, he came back to her holding out a large green fruit with a thick, pithy rind. Tentatively, he smiled, a mere twitching of his lips. "A few minutes ago you couldn't move."

After tearing the rind off the fruit, she sank her teeth into the juicy pink-crimson flesh. She smiled with delight at the taste. "This is good, Gwynnor."

"We call it chwech."

"So, you're talking to me again." She wiped away the juice that trickled down her chin, then rubbed her hand clean on a thick patch of grass by her feet. She sat. "Come here and tell me about your maes."

After a half-hour's rest they went on. Sluggishly, the sun crept down toward the western horizon, its descent marked by a dimming of the greenish glow and the gradually decreasing brightness in the bits of sky visible over the center of the stream. They seldom spoke but shared a kind of tentative friendliness that made the going easier. Aleytys burned with curiosity to know why he'd changed so oddly, but she liked the results too much to wish to initiate another alteration in his behavior.

She looked around curiously and found what seemed a safe subject. "Does anyone live here or are the trees left to themselves?"

"The forest people. Call themselves cludair. We trade with them a little. Cloth and metal goods for spices, perfumes, scented woods, beads and carvings."

"What do they look like? Like you?"

"No!"

Before she could pursue the cause of his indignation, a crackling, crashing sound brought her head around. She heard a scream and caught hold of Gwynnor's shoulder. "What was that?"

She felt his muscles shrink from her rough touch. "It's none of our business. All we're here for is to get to the river."

"Sounds like someone's hurt." Ahead and to the right she heard a frightened wailing. "A child!" She ran toward the raw blat of pain.

Gwynnor heard the scream and the whimpering but shrugged it off. In the forest, bad things were always happening. Too many secret things here. But, at least, no cerdd was hurting. This wasn't like the maes where men saw each other's faces open under an honest sun. Reluctantly he went into the forest, following the crashing of the starwoman's reckless plunge. She gets involved with anyone, he thought. No discrimination. Whore! No. That's not right. I don't know. A low limb smashed into his head, knocking him out of his abstraction. Moving more warily, he followed the sound of the moaning.

When he came up with her, she was bending over the tumbled stick figure of a cludair child whose greenish-brown fur was matted and bloody, its big red-brown eyes glazed and lifeless. The starwoman had one hand pressed against a deep wound in the child's lower abdomen and the other hand curved around its head where blood was gushing out, staining her fingers. Her face was black with the intensity of her concentration. The air steamed around her, shivering at the power pouring through her. Gwynnor felt it tremble along his nerves, opening doors in his mind he wanted closed. He looked away from her.

The corpse of a greenish furred cat lay sprawled beside the intent pair, the rosettes of darker green spots making it still hard to see. He caught hold of the beast's hind leg and dragged it deeper into the darkness under the trees. There was no blood, just a small scorched puncture wound drilling through the round, blunt head. Once again, he felt a frustration close to anger at not having access to those powerful energy weapons.

Then he came back to the small open space. Under the starwoman's bloody hands the grisly wounds were healing, the new flesh growing visibly to fill the torn places. The small contorted body was slowly straightening, the taut knotted muscles relaxing as the pain went away and strength flowed back.

Aleytys looked up as she pulled her hands away. Gwynnor stood beside her, dart gun out, eyes warily searching the shadows under the trees. "Thanks, friend."

At the sound of her voice he started and turned to face her. "If you're finished, we'd better get moving." Without looking at the child, he said, "It's healed. It'll be all right now."

"He," she corrected quietly. "I still have to fix his leg. It's broken. Help me hold it straight while I heal the break."

Reluctantly, Gwynnor thrust the gun behind his belt and knelt beside the child who was awake, staring at them out of frightened, unblinking eyes. Aleytys frowned at the top of Gwynnor's curly head, worried now about his instinctive repulsion when he touched the cludair child.

He swallowed his disgust and did what she asked, quietly and competently, straightening the leg carefully, gently, firmly, holding it still when pain made the child cry out and try to twist away from him.

Aleytys set her hands on the break and called down the healing power.

When she raised her head again, she looked into a ring of stern faces covered with the fine mottled greenish-brown hair. The tallest male wore a leather loincloth and held a short bow with arrow nocked and ready to shoot. He advanced to stand in front of her.

"Ineknikt nex-ni-ghenusoukseht ghalaghayi."

Aleytys heard the sounds as a string of nonsense syllables, then a knife pain stabbed through her head and the meaning slid like white beads on a string against the blackness in her mind. *The people do not know your smell, younger sister of fire.* She nodded quietly. "I pass through your world, father of men."

"The child." He pointed a long, thin forefinger at the small version of himself now crouched on the earth. "It is son to me."

"I heard a cry and came to see if help was needed. A woodcat had attacked the child. I am healer. I must heal." She flipped a hand at the big-eyed child. "Ask."

He dropped with easy grace beside his son. "Little brother, what happened?"

"Father of men, the gasgas sang to me of strangers in the forest. I came to see." Sheepishly, he dug at the gritty soil with long, double-jointed thumbs, eyes avoiding his father's stern face. "In coming . . ." He hesitated, fingers twisting in the sparse grass. "In coming I was careless and let the cat get above me. Sister of fire was bending over me when I woke. I was hurting." He touched his stomach where the fur was gone, showing the pinkish silver of the bare flesh. "I was torn here, my entrails coming out through the hole. And here," he touched his head, "there was much pain. At times, I saw two of everything. And my leg was broken below the knee, the bone a white stub sticking through the flesh. Sister of fire put her hands on me. Fire came and burned me but it burned the pain out of me and drove the death snake back. Then the plainsman came and took hold of my leg. Sister of fire put her hands on me again. And see, my leg is whole. It is a great mystery, father of men."

The male's round dark eyes lifted to Aleytys. "I am healer," she repeated quietly. "Where there is need, I must heal."

He stared at her a moment, the nostrils of his long nose moving rapidly in and out, measuring her odors, testing for truth in the scents her body released into the air. After a minute, he dropped his eyes and inspected the boy's stomach and head where the hair was gone, then felt along the leg, grunting as the strong slender bone slid under his fingers without a sign of a break knot. He stood. "Get you home, fingerling, and take more care this time."

In seconds, the boy had vanished onto the woven way high in the upper sections of the trees. Aleytys watched with astonishment. She had noted the presence of the vine complex but thought it a natural formation. Now, as the boy darted silently and invisibly away, she realized that the vine trail was part of a complex of ways that webbed the upper levels of the forest. She turned back to face the cludair.

Eyes gleaming a dark red-brown snouted, nearly chinless, face intently serious, he stared gravely at her. "Sister of fire, my gratitude you have earned. What I have is yours without measure."

She shook her head. "You owe me nothing."

He looked down at his hands clutched tightly about the limbs of his short bow, showing a hesitancy clearly foreign to him. After a short, tense silence, he said slowly, "Will you come with me, sister of fire? Only the great need of my people can justify my breaking of courtesy to one of great power and great heart. The house of cludair is being destroyed and we are powerless to stop it. As father of men, I must seize on whatever might be able to help us."

Chapter VI

The noise was deafening. Trees crashing, saws whining, wood screaming under lathes—slaughtered trees evaluated as worthless, chewed into chips and spat out behind. The squat, ugly machine ate at the forest like a monstrous locust.

A skimmer hovered over the anal orifice of the metal locust, scooping up the end products of the machine's digestion, hanging the processed lumber in a bulbous cluster beneath its flat bottom. As they watched, it reached its lifting limit, rose, and darted off to the south. The machine inched along without taking the slightest notice of this visitation.

Tipylexne touched her on the shoulder. When she turned, he bent down so that his mouth was close to her ear. "You see, fire sister?" She could barely hear the words over the raucous din from the machine. "That thing," he went on, "has been eating at the forest for the past year." His face pinched with pain as if the devastation before them was perpetrated on his own body. "This is the second time it has passed, leaving dead land from sea to stone."

Aleytys nodded, got silently to her feet and followed the cludair back under the trees. As they moved away from the clearing, the forest blocked out some of the noise so that it was possible to talk. She thought over what she had seen as she followed the silent, grieving forest man. Then she quickened her pace until she was walking beside him. "I suppose you tried driving it off."

"Too many died. Uselessly." She could hear the pain in his voice. "We couldn't touch it."

Aleytys frowned at the leaf-padded earth that muffled the sound of their feet. "I see. You want to know if I might have a way to kill the machine." She rubbed her throat and considered the problem. "I think I do. They'd repair it, you know." She shook her head as he caught eagerly at her arm. "They will repair whatever I do. And they'll retaliate, hunter.

41

Are you ready to face what that would mean for your people?"

His first elation faded, replaced by a thoughtful optimism. "The forest is large. And you can break the machine again."

"I don't know this Company, Tipylexne. They might keep fixing the machine for months. I can give you a little of my time but I can't stay forever."

Tipylexne nodded briskly. "I understand. The council will consider."

Gwynnor watched the two emerge from the shadows, walking quickly together in quiet companionship. He clenched his fingers into fists until his knuckles ached, wanting to drive them into that exotic face, wanting to hit hit hit the starwoman until she lost that bone-deep certainty that marched her imperiously toward some goal; that gave her power over men who fumbled about in pain and confusion for the little self-knowledge that life seemed willing to allow them.

Unconsciously, he drew his body in on itself, wrapping his arms around his knees, untying his fists and wrapping hands tautly about his calves, pulling himself as far as he could from contact with the silent cludair beside him. The slight, sweet oily smell of their mottled fur nauseated him. He tautened the muscles of his throat rather than humiliate himself by vomiting in front of them. He pressed his face against the hard bone of his knees and cursed the peithwyr whose attack had forced them off the plateau into this mess. A sharp spasm of shivers went through his crouching body and he wanted desperately to be back on the open plain, the gentle welcoming maes where yellow broom glowed like butter tucked in amid the grassy swells.

The forest men drifted, silent as motes in a light beam, to cluster around Aleytys and Tipylexne. They spoke briefly, then Aleytys moved past them, coming to stand over him, eyes irritated, amused, understanding. He resented her understanding even while he desired it. The ambivalence she generated whipped him to and fro.

She spoke. "You can return to your people, Gwynnor, if you want to." Her voice caressed his ears. Again . . . again . . . the tart sweet fragrance from her body nearly brought him to sexual readiness. In a total embarrassment, tears gathering in his eyes, he fought for some kind of equilibrium. Leave her . . . leave . . . go back to the simple, uncomplicated life on the plains. Or stay . . . and endure the continual vertigo from having his world turned upside down repeatedly . . . and suffer . . . continual uprootedness as his certainties were undermined. Go? He struggled with the idea until he knew that there was no way he could force himself to do what he knew he should do.

Aleytys looked down into the flat green eyes, all surface with no depth to them. She sighed, annoyed by his persistent abhorrence for living beings other than his own cerdd. Even her empathetic outreach that brought his stomach churning, disgust vibrating into her nerves along with his alternating surges of desire and despair, didn't help her understand what created this furor in the cerdd. She felt his head jerk as she touched him. Letting her fingers move down over his ears to his neck, she wondered if she should try to heal that sickness in him. Then she looked into his eyes again.

He watched her with a kind of puzzlement in his face, the brief sexual response dying with the anger it provoked.

She pulled her hand away, shaking her head with disgust at herself. What right did she have to rearrange his personality without his consent and understanding? She stepped back and rubbed her hands down the sides of her tunic. "Well, if you want, come with us." She jerked her head at the waiting cludair. "There's a problem with starmen from the city. I think I can help. So. We go to talk over the implications of interference." She smiled at him. "You've done all you need for me, my friend. I know you don't like being here."

"You want me to go?" In spite of his obvious effort to speak calmly, his voice shook. She had to block out the blast of anguish flooding suddenly from him.

"No. Of course not," she said quickly. She dropped to her knees so that her eyes were closer to a level with his. "Gwynnor, I have to admit I don't understand why you want to stay since you don't even like me and you find the cludair repulsive." She stared into his unresponsive face and shook her head. "Gwynnor, they're people. Like you and me. People. Not animals."

He wrenched his eyes away. "They smell bad," he muttered.

"Damn." Aleytys dropped back onto her heels. "How do I deal with that?" His sense of smell was considerably keener than hers. She glanced over her shoulder at the cludair waiting patiently for her. Their noses, though broader and less defined than Gwynnor's suggested that they, too, had a strong dependence on odor for information. She sighed, recognizing her inability to understand a world where the nose was as important as the eyes in making value judgments. "It's up to you, Gwynnor. I'll be sorry to see you leave, but if you can't endure these people, it would be better for you to go."

Gwynnor hugged his knees tighter. He felt hunted. He couldn't explain to her that he wanted desperately to go away, but knives turned inside him whenever he thought of leaving her. Biting his lower lip, he turned his head and met the eyes of one of the cludair males. He jumped up. "I contracted to take you to the sea, gwerei. A matter of honor."

The starwoman stood. "I see," she said. "If you think you can manage." She nodded at Tipylexne. He turned and strode arrogantly down a nearly invisible trail, his hunters falling into line behind. As they followed, the starwoman turned to him. "Remember, my friend, I'm a healer. If this gets too bad, I can help."

He shivered and walked faster.

"Gwynnor."

"What?" He threw the word back over his shoulder without slowing. He didn't want to listen to her.

"Smell works below the level of consciousness so you'll be feeling queasy awhile."

"Huh?" Distracted, he tripped over a root and nearly fell. She caught hold of his arm, steadying him on his feet. Embarrassed, he walked beside her, staring fixedly at the green haze that shrouded everything more than a few meters off.

"What I'm trying to say is you'll get used to these strange smells quickly if you don't keep tensed up all the time. Let yourself relax. Remember, even though you're a stranger here, the cludair accept you."

"Because of you."

"So?" She chuckled suddenly, the sound startlingly loud against the background of small constant rustlings. "You ought to be cheering the cludair on, Gwynnor. They want to get the aliens off Maeve as much as you do. Maybe more."

He looked thoughtfully at the back of the cludair just ahead, feeling a little lightheaded as she forced him to examine once again the beliefs that ruled his life.

Silence settled thickly around the line of walkers.

Chapter VII

"I see them, Lee. Give me time, will you?" Shadith's purple eyes narrowed in a thoughtful frown. Using Aleytys' farseeing gift, she probed into the machine as it ate slowly through the forest, spewing out lumber and debris. The saw-teeth ripped through the scent glands in the wood, releasing gouts of odor until the stench was as overwhelming as the noise.

Aleytys followed Shadith's exploration, understanding nothing, feeling bewildered and lost in the complex of lines and forces the singer was sorting out to her obvious satisfaction.

Shadith's laughter gently mocked her. "I call them, you pull them, Lee. You don't have to worry why."

"Huh." Aleytys shifted on the uncomfortably knobby branch, looked briefly at the ground, shivered and wrenched her eyes away. "Well?"

"Just be a good girl and listen."

"Girl!"

Shadith sobered. "Look. There. You can see the power flowing like thin lines. Very close but not touching. All you have to do is force a conduit from one to the other. Then, whoosh! Pieces of machine raining from the sky. I'll pick the spots. Mmmm. At least two, I think."

Aleytys wrinkled her nose. "It seems such a tiny thing to stop that monster."

Shadith's laughter was full and warm. "Lee, a short between power lines carrying that load! Well, it'll be effective. Believe me. You won't be disappointed."

"If you say so." Aleytys backed carefully down the limb to the trunk, then swung down to the forest floor.

Qilasc fingered the nine rule-beads laced on a heavy thong that hung between her high, shrunken breasts. Tipylexne, reserved and impassive, stood beside her, hands tight on the short powerful bow that was the sign of his manhood. Behind

45

him, six nameless cludair squatted calm and ready, expert hunters, with only their skills to worry about, not the life or death of a people.

To one side, Gwynnor waited, back pressed against a tree, unhappy and tautly nervous. She smiled at him and, by effort of will, he produced a twitch of his lips in answer. Slowly, with her help, with the healing effect of the passage of time, with the growing familiarity with a naturally dignified and open-hearted people, he was breaking free from his instinctive revulsion for the cludair. Teaching the cludair boy, Ghastay, the first steps in playing the flute was helping the alteration in his attitude move faster and a good deal more easily. Aleytys' smile widened as she saw him fingering the flute. She gazed thoughtfully at the finely crafted instrument, remembering the meeting in the long house . . .

"I can't be sure yet," Aleytys said.

The calm, strong face of the old woman was undisturbed by her uncertainty. Qilasc nodded. "Sister of fire," she said quietly, looking once around the still faces of the women to gather their agreement for her words. "You can injure the harvester. I know it. And I know that we wish this."

"There's something else to consider. Have you thought about reprisals?"

Qilasc frowned, her hand going automatically to the heavy wooden beads. "The forest is big. What could they do? Attack women and children?"

"The Company men have the morals of a starving wolf. Or worse. If you hurt them badly enough they might quarter the forest with their energy weapons until there was nothing left but ash."

"What choice have we?" The old woman shook her head. "Better to die in struggle and free than to lie down until we are nibbled to death." She turned her head slowly around the silent circle of women. Each in turn nodded agreement. "Father of men?"

Tipylexne nodded shortly, not wasting breath on unnecessary speech.

A sigh exploded out of Aleytys. She rested her hands lightly on her knees. "I can't stay too long with you. I'm on quest. My baby son was stolen from me by a crazy woman and I now travel in search of him." She sat very straight, her face stern. "As you must see, people of the forest, I can let nothing hinder me."

"I understand." The beads clacked again as Qilasc settled back to listen.

"Eventually you'll have to make some kind of bargain with the starmen. In the meantime, I need a distraction, something to mislead the Company men when I do my bit with the machine. One thing I've learned in my travels—starmen are bundles of superstition where groundings are concerned. Anything that smells of native magic scares hell out of most of them."

Qilasc stirred. "The only magic we know is that of fostering, the magic of growing things."

Aleytys smiled briefly. "I thought so. The spirits of the earth on this world are gentle and lazy. But the starmen don't know that." She snorted. "Anyone who'd ravage a forest with that hideous creation has the sensitivity of a . . ." As she sought an adequate comparison, she glanced at the somber faces around her, halting at Gwynnor who sat huddled near her in one corner of the torchlit house. "Of a peithwyr. So I suggest we play on the fears they already have. The physical they handle with contemptuous ease. As you have already seen. Shall we see what magic can do?"

Qilasc frowned. "I don't understand."

"I don't mean real magic. I mean tricks. I do my tricks with the machine and you provide a cover that should convince the Company men that you're doing the things I make happen."

"How will that help?"

Aleytys sighed. "From my experience," she said patiently, "the only thing some Companies respect is power. If you bargain from a position of power, then you have a chance of getting what you want. Otherwise, they're likely to ignore you."

A sudden smile lightened Qilasc's straining face. "Like facing a rutting bull weywuks. You don't argue about who rules the path unless you have a spear in the throwstick."

"Right." She frowned. "I don't find a word in your tongue for . . ." After struggling for a way to say what she meant in the limited tongue of the cludair, she went on slowly, "for the making of pleasant sounds like bird talk."

"Bird talk?"

"Damn. That's the closest I can get to . . ." She shook her

head. "Though one can scarcely say the birds here make a pleasant noise."

"I don't understand what you're trying to say."

"And I'm explaining badly. Never mind. Showing's better anyway." Aleytys turned to Gwynnor. "You carry a flute with you. Do you play it?"

He nodded mutely. Then he shook his head. "I did," he said, his voice barely louder than a whisper. His fingers fumbled with a thong crossing his shoulder, and pulled the instrument around in front of him. As he spoke, he ran trembling fingers up and down the slender length. "I don't anymore."

Aleytys moved over to kneel beside him. One hand touched his face. "I need you," she said softly. "The cludair don't know music and I need music. I need you."

His mouth worked nervously. Then he stammered, "I can't, Aleytys. Ay-aiiii . . . don't ask me."

"You still have the flute. You haven't thrown it away. I think you remember how to play it. Gwynnor, you'll be fighting men you hate, fighting the Company men. Play a few notes for me. Please?"

He licked his lips, glanced around uneasily. Then he raised the flute. At first, the sound that came out was harsh, cracked. Qilasc grimaced, made an impatient movement. This brought anger glowing in the boy's eyes. He licked his lips again and stared blankly into the darkness at the curving top of the long house. When he played again, the sound steadied to a gentle lilting tune that rippled through the dim torchlit council house, startling grunts of delight from the councilors.

"Gwynnor."

At the sound of Aleytys' voice, the cerdd broke off his playing, looked uncertainly around, then stared down at suddenly shaking hands.

"That is what the cerdd call music. The sound Gwynnor made with the wooden tube. On many worlds music is used to accompany magic, expecially the greater magics. The starmen will expect it and it will cover the reality. What I do is not magic, Qilasc, at least . . . I don't know, I'm not really sure what people mean by magic anyway . . . this I do know—if they suspect what's really happening, they have ways of detecting me. Now. Even if you don't have the word for that," she waved a hand at the flute, "have you anyone who makes sounds like that?"

The old woman sighed. "We're a silent people, fire sister. This is a new thing."

Aleytys frowned. "Does the sound offend your ears or your beliefs?"

"No." Qilasc looked vaguely wistful. Once again she glanced around the circle of women, checking their agreeing nods. "It is pleasant."

Turning back to Gwynnor, Aleytys chewed on her lip a moment, looking thoughtfully from his instrument to his face. "Think you could teach one of the cludair to play a simple tune?"

Gwynnor shrugged. "Depends on aptitude."

"How long did it take you to learn that thing you played?"

"My life." His mouth twitched into a brief smile at the shock in her face. "There are lesser degrees of proficiency, Aleytys." Sadness darkened his young face. "I was apprenticed to a master eileiwydd—a maker of songs—when my gift was found at the Discerning. But . . . ," the words stumbled painfully from his lips, "he was killed a year ago by the Company men. They came hunting maranhedd and hit the caravan we were traveling with. He . . . he fell on me . . . protected me by his body . . . died as he lay over me . . . I felt his body shudder . . . after that I . . . I couldn't go home . . . I joined Dylaw. I haven't played . . ." He dropped into silence.

Aleytys rubbed her finger along the crease beside her nose, then dropped her hand to cover his when she made up her mind. "We need you. Will you try?"

After a minute he lifted dull eyes. "I don't want to."

"If it would hurt the Company men? Hurt them where they'd really feel it, in their profits?" She felt anger flare in him, partly directed at the Company men, but partly at her for forcing this painful decision on him.

"I'm going to try to teach them to respect the cludair and their forest. I'm going to make them feel cold fear run along their bones whenever they hear the sound of your flute. I want you to wake such terror in them that they'll turn tail and stampede. Will you help me?"

His face flushed then paled. Unable to speak he nodded once. Then nodded again, the hunger in him so intense it battered at her. She clutched at her sliding senses and raised her shields. "Good. How long would it take to teach a cludair a simple tune?"

"Given a youngling with some shade of gift willing to put in a lot of tedious practicing, about a week."

Qilasc stirred impatiently, pulling Aleytys from her reverie. She looked rapidly around again.

Ghastay squatted beside Gwynnor, stroking his new flute, his fingers moving repeatedly from hole to hole, silently practicing the fingering of the tune.

Aleytys felt a quiet satisfaction that had nothing to do with her purpose here in the forest. A week ago the plainsboy couldn't have come close to the forest boy though they were near matching in age. But the teacher-pupil relationship had insensibly altered Gwynnor's prejudices. Now he had a proprietary attitude toward Ghastay that made Aleytys want to smile. She repressed her amusement, granting him the dignity he needed. "You ready?"

He touched the dart gun at his waist, then the flute, then smiled, a fierce, savage baring of teeth. "When you give word, Aleytys."

"Remember. When the machine stops, play on a few minutes, no more. When you go, go away fast. Both of you."

"You think they'll come into the forest?"

"I have no idea. If they do, that's what the hunters are for." She jerked her head at the squatting cludair. "You and Ghastay take off. I need you both to work up a good healthy terror in those bastards. If you get yourselves killed, you waste a good plan. You hear me?"

Gwynnor grinned at her. "I hear."

"Ghastay?"

The cludair boy twitched his nose and shook his shoulders, his thin lips curling up with excited glee. "I hear."

She looked up at the tree and sighed. "Give me a leg up." Stepping briefly onto Gwynnor's knee, she sprang up and caught hold of the lowest limb. As soon as she was straddling it, she called down, "Begin playing when I whistle."

"We know, Aleytys. We know. You only told us half a dozen times."

"Huh." She clambered laboriously up the trunk then pulled herself out onto the familiar limb until she could see the top of the machine. As soon as she was settled, she whistled briefly.

Below, the eery, jarring music trickled up through the thick cover of leaves and wound through the noisy clatter from the machine. It made her head ache. My god, she thought, Gwynnor was right. He knows his music. It doubled its impact as it wove in and around the harsh grinding roar of the locust machine. She saw the harvester slow to idle. A dark head came out of the cab, looked around. She could see the frown drawing the blunt features of the man's face into a concentration of disgust. Then armored figures came lumbering around the back of the machine, energy rifles resting lightly on glittering arms, visor-protected eyes moving with trained skill along the deceitfully tranquil face of the forest.

"All right, Shadith," she whispered, "here we go."

Together they reached out, found the vulnerable places. One. Two. Shadith bubbled with glee and chose a third. Then Aleytys opened a pathway between the wire shapes. One. Two. Three. Whipping from point to point with the speed of thought. Not needing to hold because the damage was done instantly when the two lines touched.

There was a spectacular crashing and roaring behind her as she slid recklessly down the trunk in a controlled fall. Small fragments of metal came pattering through the canopy of leaves. One struck her on the shoulder, drawing blood before she brushed it away. The jarring music went on as she ran past the boys, glaring at them. The music cut off as Gwynnor dropped the flute, grinning fiercely at her. Aleytys sighed and trotted off toward the village.

Running easily, feet nearly silent on the leaf-padded ground, Gwynnor and Ghastay caught up with her. Once again, Aleytys felt a small triumph as she felt the growing ties between the two boys.

Then Tipylexne came to join them, his hunters silent and disappointed behind him.

"They didn't come?" Aleytys slowed to a walk.

"Not this time." Then he grunted with satisfaction. "The machine has stopped. You killed it."

She shook her head. "No. They'll fix what I did."

"You'll stop it again?"

"I'll stop it again."

"They'll begin to be afraid?"

"I think so. I don't know. Depends on their leaders. But frightened men often do stupid things. You'll have to take care."

"At least that thing will eat no more trees."

Chapter VIII

Nine days later, wisps of smoke drifted in slow circles over the harvester as it lay in its own debris like a squashed bug. Armored men climbed down from the crawler and formed a circle, facing the sharp-cut perimeter of the forest, energy rifles held at ready.

Aleytys swung down to the closest limb and leaned out to nod at Gwynnor. He jumped up and ran off, Ghastay following close behind. When they were safely out of sight, she pulled herself back up until she was hidden by thick patches of leaves.

As soon as the eerie tune died, the leader of the guards barked a command and led his men at a trot into the forest. Hidden above their heads, Aleytys watched them tramp past, moving with a heavy efficiency she hadn't expected from the city bred. A few meters into the green gloom they broke into twos. Swinging energy rifles through fan-shaped spaces, the pairs trotted off in the beginnings of concentric circles with the collapsed harvester as their common center.

"Time to shift out of here, Lee." Shadith's purple eyes snapped with excitement. "They've got heat-seekers mounted on those guns. Thank god, they haven't thought to look over their heads."

Aleytys slid down the trunk again until she was hanging from the lowest limb. Then she dropped to the forest floor and ran lightly on the camouflaged path that led to the cludair village.

Perched in an offshoot of the vineway, Gwynnor watched her until the last bright gleam of her hair vanished. Ghastay pulled him around and jerked a double-jointed thumb after the thudding guards. "Come on. I want to watch the hunters."

Gwynnor hesitated. "Aleytys told us to get back to the village."

"We will," Ghastay said impatiently. He tugged at Gwynnor's arm. "Come on, friend. We're missing all the fun."

Uneasy but intrigued, the plainsboy followed the forest boy down the nearest tree and through the gloom under the canopy, the two of them sliding through brush like a mottled green-brown shadow in company with a silvery ghost.

They flitted through the brush and caught up with two guards. The men in the silvery, flexible armor, alien, like mobile units of the dead machine, ran lightly, absurdly lightly, with power-assisted legs to a faint sweet hum of machine noise—man-machines under the silent, aloof trees. One rested a gun lightly on a forearm, ready to fire at the slightest sign of life while the other watched the readout of the heat-seeker, fanning the directional instrument in a wide arc before him. Neither one bothered to examine the forest above eye level.

Without warning, the net dropped.

Tough, sticky strands wound around arms and legs as the guards struck out against the billowing folds of the net. Greenish-brown shadows dropped immediately after, leathery palms glistening with cuyen oil, applied to keep the sticky substance on the net off their hands. One of the energy rifles flared briefly. A cludair grunted and clutched at his side where the edge of the beam had sheared away his harness and bitten into muscle. Before the gun could fire again, another hunter kicked it from the guard's hand.

The four cludair still standing caught the net and tugged at it. In minutes, the armored figures were wound in its sticky strands like flies in a spider's web. As soon as the leader worked a polished pole through the web, three of the hunters shouldered the pole and trotted their burden deeper into the forest. The fourth helped the wounded cludair hobble toward the village.

Gwynnor watched both groups disappear. "What are they going to do with the guards?"

"Come see." With a ghost of a laugh, Ghastay ran after the burdened hunters.

Five minutes later they watched the hunters drop the hardening lump on the ground with a careless thump that jarred the helpless guards till their teeth ached. Grimly, the leader rubbed the aromatic oil on his knife. Ignoring the frantic twitches that were the only movements the imprisoned men could make, he cut their heads free from the net, pulling the knife across the face-plates with a shrill nerve-rasping screech until they were clean. Then the knife poked and prodded at the plates until the point suddenly tripped the latch. The guards drank in gulps of the hot, humid air, then glared at the mottled face of the native bending over them.

He stepped back, gestured briefly. A second hunter brought a green glass phial from the pouch at his belt and pulled the rolled leather stopper out. He thrust a finger deep into the phial and brought it out covered with a viscous amber liquid. Carelessly, with brisk economy of motion, he wisped his finger across a guard's face, leaving behind a trail of sticky sweetness. He repeated the action with the second.

In the brush, Ghastay clapped a hand over his mouth, smothering a slight fizzing of laughter.

"Why'd they do that?" Gwynnor whispered.

Ghastay pulled his hand down. "That dead tree the Company men are up against. You see?"

"So?"

"It's an ant tree. Get it?"

Gwynnor stifled a gasp, shoving his fist against his mouth. "Cwech arteith!" he muttered as soon as he had control of his speech. "The hatchlings have just cracked shell if they're the same as ours."

Ghastay nodded, his young face turned grim. "The Company men want to eat the forest; well, turn and turn is fair. Let the forest eat them."

A second pair of guards dangled, turning and twisting as hundreds of needlebirds darted at them in swooping dives. Only small crimson and blue bundles of feathers, their darting rushes sent the mecho-bodies at the end of the nooses swinging in erratic, sickening circles. The birds couldn't get at them but the faces inside the helmets had a greenish tinge that owed nothing to the verdant light filtering down through the canopy of leaves.

Ghastay and Gwynnor crept very carefully past the tree with the strange fruit. Very carefully, to avoid attracting the attention of the glittering swarm.

Safely past the danger, Gwynnor peered through bush leaves, his movement crushing the delicate fuzz on the leaves, loosing a stiffling cloud of oil droplets around his head.

Ghastay jerked him away impatiently. "If you call out a swarm of needlebirds. I'm going somewhere else."

He ripped a handful of purple leaves from a small vine crawling along the ground at ankle height. "Take this. Wipe the oil off your head." He glanced around apprehensively. "Those damn birds make welts the size of your thumb. That oil pulls them in for miles."

"Sorry about that." Gwynnor rubbed the leaves over his upper body, wrinkling his nose at the fetid stench rising around him. "This is better?"

Ghastay grinned. "You ever been swarmed by needlebirds, you'd rather sit behind a bull weywuks with diarrhea."

As they trotted on to intercept the third pair of guards and their ambushers, Gwynnor jerked a thumb back over his shoulder. "Will the birds get inside the armor?"

Ghastay shrugged without breaking stride. "Probably not, but those kiminixye will be pig-sick before they're cut down."

Loops flicked out silently and dropped over nervously swivelling heads. Strong arms lifted briefly, then relaxed, swinging the startled guards into the center of a plant with leaves wider and taller than a man. Tentacles tough as wire cable snapped out and whipped around and around the struggling starmen. As Gwynnor and Ghastay slipped up to the edge of the clearing, a blue-edged ray of killing light sliced briefly through the leaves, burning a part of the plant away.

The thick serum in the succulent leaves quenched small flames that died into a smouldering stench while the wiry tentacles closed tighter, knocking the long gun out of the guard's straining hand.

Gwynnor stared as the remaining leaves began folding with a terrible, slow inevitability over the metal figures. "What's that?"

"Kalskals. A good thing to keep away from. Look." He pointed at the knobbly white threads raying out from the base of the plant. They were visible over the short velvety grass only because they were twitching wildly as the plant struggled to deal with the metal covering its prey. At rest, they would be well-hidden by the grass. "Whenever you see those red-veined leaves, you look down fast. Those false roots carry enough shocking force to knock you out so you'd wake up down the kalskals' throat half-digested."

Gwynnor shuddered. "You think it can eat through that armor?"

"One way or another. Come on. And watch out where you're stepping."

The sticky net swooped down, tangling the last pair of guards in an awkward knot of arms and legs. A grinning adolescent hunter plunged in a controlled fall down the rope, checking himself with proud skill, one hand opening and closing so that he came to a smooth stop, kicking the gun loose before the guard could fire it.

The knot was secured and the pole thrust through. Then the cludair trotted off, pole slung between two shoulders, the other two running guard beside them.

Gwynnor watched. As Ghastay started to follow, he stopped him. "What are they going to do with those?"

Impatiently, Ghastay pulled free. "They go back to the machine. Hurry up. We have to play the music when they throw them back like inedible fish."

By the clearing where the machine huddled, still sending up occasional spurts of pungent blue smoke the cludair, with swift efficiency, knotted ropes to the hardened web and pulled the pole free. As Gwynnor watched they swarmed up the tree, the ropes jerking behind them.

The webbed knot, with the two guards forced in contorted embrace by the hardened exudation, rose rapidly as the hunters hauled on the ropes. Then it began swinging in an increasing arc until, at the end of the swing, the cludair let go of the ropes. The knot flew into the clearing, landing next to the machine with a heavy metallic clang.

Several startled offworlders dived down behind the bulk of the tracks, then, after a while, emerged cautiously, wincing as the eerie music frazzled already jangled nerves. As they discovered the guards inside the glassy webbing, their startled exclamations cut through the thread of sound. Ghastay's dark-reddish eyes caught Gwynnor's. His hairy, mobile brows dipped down then up in humorous appreciation.

Aleytys lifted her hands and inspected the cludair's side. The skin was a grayish-silver where it was denuded of hair by the burn. She patted the young men on the shoulder then looked up to see Tipylexne watching her.

"That's it?"

He nodded briefly. "There was only the one who got hurt."

"You got all the guards?"

"Yes. I don't think they'll send after us again."

Aleytys frowned. "No. But now they know the danger comes from the trees. We've lost that advantage." She rubbed her thumb beside her nose. "I don't know enough. I don't know how they'll react to this."

Tipylexne shrugged. "You've bought us some more time, fire sister."

She stood up, staggering a little as her knees locked briefly. "Time. Damn. Knowledge is what I need."

His face twisted in a thoughtful scowl, Tipylexne flexed his double-jointed thumbs. "We left two of them alive. Want us to bring them in for you?"

Before she could answer, Gwynnor and Ghastay slid into the circle of hometrees. The two boys were immediately surrounded by children clamoring to hear what had happened. The noisy group swept away out of sight.

"We've brought change." Aleytys touched Tipylexne's shoulder, feeling the warm plush of his fur, the swift throb of life under his skin. "Do you mind?"

"All things change, flower to seed to plant to flower." He laid his own long-fingered hand over hers. His body temperature was higher than hers and the warmth was comforting. He went on, eyes on the vaulting arch where the boys had disappeared. "Hybrids grow and sports come as they of the earth play with destinies of plants. If the sport is strong and life-giving, it survives. If not, it dies. If this change is good, it will last."

Aleytys smiled wearily. "You're a wise man, my friend. Thanks." She stepped away from him, running hands through her loose hair. "I think I want a bath."

He shuddered. "Water all over. Even thinking of it. Hah!"

With a chuckle, she moved off. "I like it, Tipylexne. Remember, I haven't fur to groom like yours."

"You miss a quiet joy, fire sister. Sitting of an evening, my wives grooming me, their slim fingers hunting through the fur on my back and head. Ahhhh . . ." He shivered with pleasure.

She laughed. "To each kind his own kind of joy. The council meets tonight?"

"Yes." His ugly, friendly face puckered. "After your bath."
She laughed again. "I'll see you then, my friend." Still chuckling, she vanished under the trees.

Chapter IX

A tree cat somewhere to the south howled in frustration, the wavering shriek jerking Aleytys out of her uneasy sleep. The darkness inside the guest house was stygian, stifling, quickening an urge to get outside. She pulled a tunic over her head and stumbled out of the swaying tree house.

Below, a faint red spark marked the coals of the community fire, the glow thickening the blackness under the trees. Cautiously, she edged along the broad limb, stepped over the poison-tipped wirebush and climbed swiftly down the trunk, feet moving from loop to loop of laddervine with the blind eyes of habit.

A thread of music broke the silence. She followed the sound and found Gwynnor sitting on a grassy tongue of earth thrust out from the woods, forcing the stream to swing wide at this point. Here the sky was almost clear of leaves and a scattering of stars was visible. He lay on his back, listening to the song of the water and staring hungrily at the open patch of sky. The flute lay on his stomach and his hands were clasped behind his head.

Aleytys sank down beside him. His eyes twitched to her then went back to the sky.

The silence drifted along, filled with the music of the water and the rootless directionless night sounds coming from the darkness under the trees.

Gwynnor sat up, catching the flute as it rolled off his chest. "I have to thank you, Aleytys."

"Why?" She yawned and hugged her knees, her head turned toward him.

"I've been sitting here for hours. Thinking. Playing this." He touched the flute. "Really playing. I think . . . I think I'll go back to the maes and hunt another teacher. The pain here," he touched his chest, "it's not completely gone. But I can live with the memories now." He lifted the flute to his lips and began playing.

Aleytys lay back on the grass and let the melody play over her, blending with the night sounds to evoke a mood of magic, gentle happiness.

Chapter X

Gwynnor came hesitantly into the council house. Qilasc looked up, frowning. "The council is meeting, tkelix."

"A skimmer from the city. Flying over. I thought fire sister ought to know."

Aleytys jumped up. "I'd better go look. You don't need me anymore." She wrinkled her nose at the dazed, slack-mouthed guards. "You know what to ask them."

Qilasc nodded. "You think this is reaction to what we did at the machine?"

"I don't know." She shrugged. "You might add that to your list of questions."

Outside, Aleytys glanced thoughtfully at the canopy of leaves. "How'd you spot the skimmer?"

"The stream." With Aleytys following close behind, he trotted down the path. At the edge of the clearing he stopped and pointed at a tree. "I was up there. Looking at the sun."

Aleytys glanced up. "I suppose I have to climb it." She rubbed her hands down her sides then reached for the lowest limb.

As they reached the twin forks at the top of the tree where the leaves were thin enough to make large portions of the sky visible, a skimmer passed overhead. Off toward the eastern horizon, another moved slowly over the tree tops. A third circled to the south.

"What do you think?" Gwynnor frowned anxiously at the skimmers. "They aren't attacking, just flying around."

"I can see that," Aleytys said absently. She closed her eyes. "Shadith," she whispered.

The elfin face with its aureole of coppery curls materialized against the deep black of her mind. "Problems, Lee?"

"What are they doing?" Aleytys opened her eyes and focused them on the approaching skimmer. "Do you think they're dangerous? Should I try bringing them down?"

Shadith frowned. "It looks like a mapping pattern. What do you say, old growler?"

Swardheld's face developed from the darkness. "About what?"

"Them."

It was as if he tilted his head, leaned against a wall, and watched the circling skimmers. "Search pattern, looks to me. I'd say they've got personnel locators onboard. Next time we hit the harvester, they hit the villages."

Gwynnor watched, feeling a thrill of fear. She sat loosely erect in the fork of the tree, head following the movements of the skimmers, eyes blank, lips moving in a silent parody of speech. He could almost see a halo of spirits circling her bright head, glittering sparks like jewels in an invisible crown.

"Should I do something?" Aleytys whispered.

Shadith compressed her lips. "I don't like this," she muttered. "If they're plotting the location of cludair villages . . . might be a good idea to stop this now."

"Bring the ships down?" Aleytys asked sharply.

"No. That's not what I mean. Maybe you shouldn't wreck the machine again."

"I can't stop now."

"Don't fool with the skimmers, freyka." Swardheld's deep rumble interrupted the exchange.

"Huh?"

"Bad idea. Provoking."

"And busting their harvester isn't?" Shadith snorted.

"I think Lee's got one more go at the machine," Swardheld said. "We'll see what Qilasc got from the guards to find out for sure."

"Even so, what does Lee do about the mapping out there?"

"Nothing." He grinned at the disgust on Shadith's face. "Warn the council and let them handle it. The threat isn't bad enough to bring hell down on their heads before they're ready."

Aleytys nodded. "I agree. So I bust the machine again and look for some kind of opening."

"You'll have to make your own breaks, Lee." Swardheld frowned. "You might think about taking the fight to the city. I don't see them giving up. Too much power."

Aleytys sighed. "Damn. How do I get myself into these things . . ."

She opened her eyes. Smiling at the question in Gwynnor's face, she shook her head and dropped down the tree until she stood with her back against the trunk watching the water flow past her feet.

Gwynnor dropped beside her. "Well?"

"I think they're using personnel locators and mapping the locations of the cludair settlements."

His face flushed, then paled. Involuntarily, his hands reached up and closed hard around the flute. "Not again."

She caught a hand, lifted it to hold it briefly next to her face. "No. No death coming from the sky. I'll crash every damn one of them before I let that happen." A sudden fierceness sharpened her voice, then the fierceness died to weariness. "But the cludair can be warned to get out of their villages." She paused and stared thoughtfully at the scattered bits of blue visible overhead. "This is a mapping pass, not a raid. Time to watch out is when I crack up the tree-eater." She moved restlessly. "I'm going to shred that machine this time."

Gwynnor looked down at his hands. He uncramped his fingers and flexed them slowly.

Aleytys settled on a tree root and he made himself comfortable beside her. "Funny."

She raised her eyebrows. "What?"

"Six weeks ago I was miserable."

"Do you want to stay here? Tipylexne can get me to the river."

"No. I'll miss Ghastay and the others, but . . ." He put his hand on her knee and smiled up into her face. "Thanks to you I'm going home."

"Then you won't be going back to Dylaw."

"I was getting fed up with him before you came." He laughed. "I've found out again that I'm a song-maker. That time with Dylaw, a detour and not very profitable however you measure it."

"You've changed."

"I suppose so." He yawned. "You're not going to let the Company men hurt the cludair?"

"Not if I can help it."

"I remember telling you they smelled bad." He chuckled, then yawned again. "I remember your singeing me when I threw the bug away. I suppose you were trying to tell me all life has value, even a starman's." He grinned at her.

"Now that's a leap."

He lifted the flute and blew a rapid, happy dancing little tune that made her laugh in spite of the problems hanging over her head.

When he finished she shook her head. "Gwynnor, I wish it was really like that. I'm glad you've . . . you've found a new center for your life. But there's something . . . I don't know . . . there's a kind of coldness I feel. It's connected with the Company . . ." Once again she shook her head and fell silent.

The water susurrused past, a brushing murmur with a melodic descant where rocks created miniature whorls and waterfalls. A red-crested insect-eater skimmed along the surface of the water, picking gnats from the wavery air. Gwynnor put the flute to his lips and let a dreamy, drifting melody float and mingle with the gentle rustle of the leaves and the sound of the water.

Aleytys stirred restlessly, the music suddenly an irritation. "You said your master was killed. Recently?"

"Not quite a year."

Aleytys paused while she struggled to organize her thoughts. "A raid, you said. For maranhedd. Did the Company always do that?"

Gwynnor frowned. "No." His fingers tightened on the flute and stared blankly at her. "I never thought of that. No. When they first came here, about a hundred years ago, they set up a system of tribute. So much maranhedd delivered at such and such a time. They even paid for it. They only started raiding about a year ago. My master was killed in one of the first raids."

"You're sure they were Company men?"

"They were in Company skimmers and they had the look. You know, like those guards."

"So something happened to make the Company change policy. I wonder what it was." She tapped her fingers on her knees, then shrugged. "I wonder if I'll ever know." She leaned back against the tree. "So you're coming with me."

"All the way to Caer Seramdun. It's on my way. Going home," he smiled up at the sky, "where I can see the whole face of the sun."

"I wish that was a mountain river," Aleytys said suddenly.

"Huh?"

"Damn. I can't get a focus. Gwynnor!"

The sharpness in her voice startled him. "What?"

"There's something wrong in that city," she jumped to her feet and began pacing back and forth over the short, tough grass, "and I'm up to my ears in the mess. Damn. Damn. Damn. Why can't I simply march straight across a contented world, take ship, and leave it behind untouched and untouching?"

He laughed. "There isn't any such place. Besides, you can't help it. Look what you did to me."

She dropped onto her knees beside him. "I know. When I'm in trouble I . . . well, I commandeer help. You remember back at the ship?"

He nodded, eyes squinting thoughtfully at her. "I volunteered to guide you."

"Volunteered!" She moved her shoulders restlessly, then ran her hands through her hair. "I'm a leech."

"It worked out fine. I was a miserable little rat, but look at me now."

"Ah!" She jumped up. "I've got to get back to the council. Coming?"

He fingered the flute, then shook his head. "No. I'll stay here a while."

Chapter XI

Aleytys tugged at a lock of hair hanging forward over her shoulder. "Tipylexne. Gwynnor. Ghastay. Damn. There are too many variables."

Tipylexne touched her shoulder. "The council decided, fire sister. We're ready for whatever's going to happen."

"You hope so." She sighed. "I wish you all would go back to the village."

Tipylexne shook his head. The others echoed his silent refusal.

"All right. It's your life. Gwynnor!" She sprang from him and caught hold of the branch. Grunting with effort, she pulled herself up to the broad limb, tongue caught between teeth, then ran out along the limb and settled carefully behind a forking secondary branch. Her weight pulled the limb down slightly, opening a hole in the foliage she could see through.

Beside the harvester a man straightened, wiping his hands on a soft red cloth while he pursed his mouth at the complex array of components. Stuffing the rag in a back pocket, he snapped the cover into place. Stepping back once more he glared at the forest then vanished inside the machine.

The harvester sputtered briefly, then began a whining roar.

Aleytys frowned. There was a peculiar uncertain flutter that rippled up her spine and flashed across her breast. Then she shrugged and whistled.

As the first notes of the flute sounded below her, she reached out to touch the power lines within the machine. This time, the shielding was fierce. It took her several minutes to wriggle a probe past the force screen, but once her fingers reached inside, opening the short was a second's work. She grinned and began drilling a second hole in the shielding.

There was a loud *whump!* and several spurts of blue smoke

blew from one side of the machine. The harvester sprayed out fragments of metal. Aleytys smiled and began poking at the screen for a third hit.

The last thing she heard was a loud explosion from the cutting arms of the machine.

Chapter XII

"Aleytys!" The amber eyes shone furiously. "Wake up!" The contralto voice nudged at her, broke through the daze blocking coherent thought. "You were stunned," Harskari went on more calmly. "They didn't bother trying to locate you, just swung a heavy-duty stunner over the face of the cut. Like squirting water from a hose." She closed her eyes and firmed her mouth into a thin line, disciplining herself back into her usual calm. More quietly, she said, "Then they carried you and the others here."

"The others . . ." The thought drifted in her mind but her mouth made no sound. She could feel nothing, see nothing but Harskari's tiger eyes. After a moment's slow reflection she began to panic.

"Quiet, Aleytys. Don't be stupid. Your body is still stunned. You have another several minutes before the effect begins to wear off." She was silent for a moment. "Look along yourself, Aleytys," she said after her first words had had time to sink in. "Your body was damaged when you fell."

"Fell . . . I fell?"

"You were in a tree, remember? When the stunner hit, you fell. You hit the ground hard, Aleytys."

Aleytys groped for memory but dropped the search when she found nothing but fog. She scanned along her body. Damaged. My insides are a mess. Lung punctured. Broken arm. Broken shoulder. Cracked pelvis. Right leg fractured in two spots. I wonder they thought it worthwhile moving me. Reality bloomed slowly in her. "Moving me? Where am I?"

"Inside the machine. Although the stunner shocked you

into overload so that you can't feel pain, Aleytys, your life force is draining away. Unless you want to join us prematurely you'd better get busy healing yourself."

"Hmmm." Aleytys drowsed through the evaluation of her injuries. "My leg and arm, I can't do anything about those until they're set."

"Yes, Aleytys."

"I can stop the bleeding . . ." She reached lazily for the black water and let it play over her ruptured organs, over cracked ribs, over the cracked pelvis. Arm and leg . . . sealed the cuts but not the breaks. She let the roar diminish to a trickle and drifted sluggishly on the shrinking film.

"Aleytys!"

She sighed mentally and let the comforting water sublimate. "What is it?"

"I think you'd be interested in the engineer's conversation."

"Engineer . . ." She turned her other sight on the life source at the other end of the room.

The man was long and narrow, dressed with a mannered elegance that emphasized his really beautiful hands and his hollow-cheeked scholar's face. His eyes were very dark, slanting upward over high cheekbones. His hair was straight and black, worn long, clipped at the nape of his neck into an elaborate bronze clasp. His skin was a pale ocher with olive-green shadows.

With an effort Aleytys pulled her mind from his appearance and struggled to hear what he was saying. After the usual stabbing pain, the translator functioned efficiently.

"Yes, yes. The stunner worked. We managed to collect four individuals. A very interesting assortment."

"Yes?"

"One of them is a cerdd. The computer identified him as a member of a dissident group that tries to stir up trouble in the city and on the plain."

"And?"

"He has a flute looped around his neck. Computer says that hideous noise accompanying each of the attacks was flute music."

"Interesting. Then you presume a connection between the forest savages and the dissidents."

"It would seem so. Two of the others were savages from the forest, a full grown male and a cub. The cub has a crudely made instrument imitating the flute. I suppose it's some kind of fetish."

"You said four."

"The last is the most curious. A redheaded woman. Not a native. The computer has no I.D. on her but she looks a little like a McNeis. Scota Company has been trying to tie into this sector for years. The McNeis himself has hair I'd call a close match to hers. If the McNeis has a new development in technology that lets them punch through a defense screen . . ." He shrugged.

"Unsupported speculation." The dry repressive voice cut through the engineer's too rapid flow of speech. He wiped beading moisture from his face and waited.

"Get your captives patched up if necessary. I will dispatch a technician with a psychprobe. Do you have the native settlements plotted?"

"Yes, Illustrious."

"Level them. You shouldn't need help for that. Do you?"

"No, Illustrious." The engineer scowled at the console, his fingers curling into claws.

"Good. Pick up what you can about the dissidents from the cerdd. If the redheaded woman's a spy, she'll be filled to her eyebrows with anababble. If she's not, she's even less of a problem."

"Yes, Illustrious."

"Get what you can from the woman."

"Yes, Illustrious."

Without further words the speaker's voice was replaced by a carrier hum. The engineer swung around in the swivel chair, cursing softly, long fingers shaking. He stepped across the room with short, nervous steps and thrust a toe into Tipylexne's side, noting his flaccid lack of response. "Hah." He took a step to the side and stood looking down at Aleytys. With his foot he pushed her broken leg aside, staring thoughtfully at the bloody mess with its jagged end of protruding bone. Then he left the room.

While she waited to see what would happen, Aleytys explored the bodies of her friends and found them hurt-free. Prodding her reluctant brain into lumbering activity she finally decided that this was logical since they were on the ground when the stunner hit. She still felt no connection with her body; her mind was a free-floating point with eyeless vision.

The engineer walked in again with another man. He touched Tipylexne with his foot. "This one first. Check him out."

The doctor dropped to his knees beside the cludair and ran a gently buzzing machine over his body, moving it in wide sweeping arcs. He grunted and moved to stoop over Gwynnor, then Ghastay. "Nothing wrong with them."

"Good. What about the woman?"

The doctor moved to hover over Aleytys. As he moved the buzzing instrument over her body, he frowned. "Funny," he muttered.

"What?"

"Two compound fractures in the right leg. Simple fracture of the right arm. And no other injuries. None!"

"So? What does it matter? Patch her up so she's fit to be questioned."

The doctor's round, meaty face grew a sudden sheen of sweat. He swallowed, his prominent eyes bulging even further as he shifted his gaze nervously from the woman to the engineer. "Questioned?" His voice was hoarse with an odd tremolo that plucked at Aleytys' already taut nerves. There was a subtle wrongness about the man, like a false image laid over the true, an evil shadow on a basically decent man. She looked further and saw a metal socket set into the bone behind his ear and felt sick. Phorx addict. The part-vegetable, part-animal thing that indulged its hosts with bouts of exquisite happiness. And ate away at his brain.

"The Director is sending a psychprobe, if that's any of your business. Have her ready." He turned to go.

The doctor's jowls shook. His hand groped helplessly in the unresponsive air, then he staggered to his feet and plucked at the engineer's sleeve. "Isn't that illegal? The Singh-Catal-Manachay Convention . . ."

The director jerked his arm free. His nostrils flared with anger and contempt. "You should know the Wei-Chu-Hsien triad were not signatories to that bit of nonsense, or you'd be in Rehab long since. Instead, we support that little pet of yours."

The doctor winced, his brows drawn down in a painful grimace. "A psychprobe destroys the mind as it works. They'll be vegetables." Oily sweat flooded his face; he was trembling so badly he could barely stand.

"You think the Director plans to let them live? You'd better go on with your work, doctor, while you're still capable. Isn't the phorx due for feeding soon? Would you like it to go hungry?"

The doctor shuddered. Without another word he knelt beside Aleytys and opened his case.

Chapter XIII

Chu Manhanu smoothed his thumb over the ratrail moustaches that marked careful parentheses around the narrow line of his mouth. Lips pursed in fastidious distaste, he examined the cludair briefly, glanced at Gwynnor, then moved to stand over Aleytys. His flat black eyes slid over the casts that weighed her leg and arm flat to the floor. "You're the only one injured."

Unable to lift her hands because of the tangleweb's clinging resistance, Aleytys shrugged. "I fell out of a tree."

"You know who I am?"

"No." She let the cool tone of her voice tell him how little she cared.

"I am Company Director, woman. What happens to you depends on me."

"My, how terrified I am."

"That's the point, isn't it? Why aren't you afraid?"

"Of you?" She laughed and he winced.

"Your hair is very red."

"A birth gift from my mother."

"McNeis or Mctany?"

"I haven't the vaguest notion what you're talking about?"

He dusted the palms of his hands together lightly. "No matter, the probe will answer for you." He moved on and settled into the revolving chair by the console. "Doctor."

The bulky man stepped through the door uncertainly, sweat still gushing from his pores. There was a blank, glazed look to his eyes. "Yes, Illustrious?" His voice was thick and halting.

"I expected to see the engineer in this room."

"I . . . I don't believe he was expecting you, Illustrious."

"No doubt. Where is he?"

Lips moving shapelessly, the doctor worried over the question, then mumbled, "He went out to burn the villages as you told him, Illustrious."

"Hmm. Is the woman in shape for questioning?"

"She fell twenty meters on knotted roots."

"I think you exaggerate."

"At least five times her height," the doctor amended hastily.

"You still haven't answered my question, doctor." Chu Manhanu's voice was gentle, almost apologetic, but sweat again gushed from the doctor's coarse pores and ran in lazy runnels down his jerking cheeks.

"The only injuries she has are breaks in her arm and leg."

"How delightful. Very good. A terse, exact answer, doctor. Perhaps you will continue to answer as succinctly. Which is the leader of that group?"

The doctor hesitated briefly, then pointed at Tipylexne.

"I wonder why you changed your mind." The Director ran his thumbnail over the soft oiled hairs of his moustache.

"Changed my mind?" The doctor sputtered under the chill impact of the Director's gaze. "What man would take orders from a woman?"

"Who are you trying to convince?"

The doctor shrank in on himself. "It has to be the forest male," he muttered. "The others are cubs, though the woman might be dangerous. I don't know."

"Your sexual preference blinds you to the obvious. Who was in the tree?"

"The woman."

"Who, then, was the prime mover?"

"You want me to say the woman. But wouldn't the leader be on the ground directing the efforts of the others?"

"You'd be on the ground, I'm sure. Power, doctor. Information, doctor. Direct and immediate." He rested a hand precisely on his knee, then positioned the other over it. "Have the natives given trouble before?"

"Why ask me?" the doctor burst out, forgetting caution. "You know the answer."

"Petulance, doctor?" With calm precision he moved his hands, placing the bottom hand on top this time. For a moment he contemplated the new arrangement, moving his fingers fractionally to achieve the most graceful pose. "Was the tree searched?"

The doctor stared blankly.

"Was the tree the woman fell out of searched for the instrumentation she used to cause the damage?" Manhanu said with terrible patience.

"I . . . I think so. Engineer Han . . ."

"Is not here. Does the woman have any internal injuries?"

"None."

"And you don't find that odd?"

Stubby fingers caressing his throat, the doctor muttered, "Odd things happen."

Chu Manhanu held up his hands and examined the backs with satisfaction. "Remove the casts."

"What?"

"Remove her casts." Manhanu said patiently. His voice sank to a whisper but the doctor quivered while the muscles in his face twitched out of control.

Sinking heavily beside Aleytys, he rummaged in the case he had left against the wall and pulled out his vibrosnips. Setting the blade at one centimeter, he dug runnels in the stiff plastic. Then he took a small hammer and beat it sharply against the casts along the lines of cleavage. The casts fell off neatly.

"Remove those." A finger moved gracefully at the bandages underneath the cast.

The doctor stared with disbelief as the bindings fell away, revealing pinkish skin with swiftly fading marks where the torn skin had been. He probed the flesh with shaking hands, not caring if he hurt her. Then he dug his thumb into her arm. "Gone!" he shrilled. He jumped to his feet, shaking all over. "She was injured, I swear it."

The Director's nostrils twitched with distaste. "Calm down, doctor. Of course she was injured. Here." He flipped a small black box to the goggling man. "Put this on her."

"Psi freak," the doctor mumbled as he fumbled the box open. "A damn psi freak." Inside the box he found a chain-mail collar with a massive, clumsy locklatch and a flat black disc with the Company sigil incised on the front. "What's this?"

"Put it on her. Around her neck."

The doctor stared at the Director's smiling mask and

crawled hastily toward Aleytys' head. Ignoring her angry glare, he shoved her chin up, swearing as the metal collar slid through clumsy fingers. Finally he fumbled the end through the lock slot and pulled it taut.

Aleytys gasped and began to choke.

"Not so tight, fool. She has to talk."

Breath shrilling through his teeth, the doctor adjusted the collar. He started to clamber to his feet.

"Not yet. Stay there. Here." The director tossed a small hexagonal rod to the kneeling man. "Touch the red end to the lock. Good. Now touch it to the character on the disc. Ah! Now, bring the rod to me." The doctor staggered to his feet and shuffled to Manhanu, holding the small rod in a shaking hand. Manhanu shoved it up one of his wide sleeves. "Now. Stand over by the door and keep your mouth shut." He lifted one of his long slim hands in a graceful gesture, pointing at the wall beside the door.

The doctor glanced longingly at the door. Then his shoulders slumped and he shambled across the room to stand, leaning heavily against the metal wall.

Chu Manhanu replaced his hand and smiled with quiet mockery at Aleytys. "The good doctor called you a psi freak, madam. While I deplore his choice of words, I fear he is right about you. I'm quite certain there were no esoteric in-instruments in or around that tree. We had the harvester shielded, as I'm sure you know, yet you had no trouble breaching the shield. Remarkable."

Aleytys frowned. She felt too much at a disadvantage lying on her back so far below his eye level. Ignoring him, she flexed her body and contorted herself into a sitting position. Then she inched back until she was sitting with her back braced against the wall. "You knew before you came."

"Intelligent, also. Madam, the collar you wear contains an inhibitor that will prevent your making use of your talents."

Having felt the too familiar disorientation from the inhibitor, Aleytys didn't bother answering him. She lowered her chin and felt along the smooth line of the mail and realized there was no way she could break it.

Chu Manhanu watched with infuriating superiority, the corners of his mouth curving into a chill smile. He took the rod from his sleeve and began smoothing his thumb over its hexagonal surface. "A small thing." He fitted it between thumb and forefinger, holding it up so she could see it. "The only hope you have left. You may have noticed that the clasp is clumsy and out of proportion. Aesthetically revolting but necessary, madam. If anyone tampers with the lock, your lovely head will be blown off your shoulders." His mouth curled farther as he savored the consternation he read in her face. Then he turned away. "Enough chatting. Doctor."

The sudden, sharp demand jerked the doughy body away from the wall and brought the doctor shambling into the center of the room, a nervous tic distorting the shape of his mouth. "Illustrious?" he muttered.

"Bring the technician and the probe."

The doctor stood without moving, eyes fixed on the Director's face as the smile gradually soured. Then he stumbled with stiff reluctance from the room.

Aleytys closed her eyes. "Harskari?"

There was a faint amber glow and a feeling of effort, of thrusting struggle. A feeling of wait, wait, wait . . . sighing, she opened her eyes. "What do you want?"

"As soon as that dolt of a doctor returns, we psychprobe you to find out who and what you are."

Aleytys swallowed, fear bitter in her throat. She sucked in a deep breath and tried to calm herself. "The doctor said a psychprobe destroys the mind."

"A sad loss." His eyes ran over her body and rested on her hair. "Han had some interesting speculations about you."

"I heard. Stupidity. McNeis? Scota Company? I've never run across either."

"You want to tell me who you are?"

"No. It's none of your business." She closed her eyes, turned her head away. "Harskari," she whispered. "Hurry. Please. All of you. Please." The tangleweb held her body passive or she would have been thrashing about, dropping into a total panic. As it was, she wanted the reassurance of the mother figure Harskari, like a child terrified by a nightmare made real.

A faint yellow glow and a feeling of struggle. A tinge of purple, outlined in black. They were fighting . . .

The director leaned back watching her tense her muscles against the restraint of the web, a slight smile of enjoyment on his face.

Gwynnor tugged at his hands, hot anger alternating with the chill of despair. He had grown accustomed to seeing

Aleytys dealing calmly with all sorts of problems. The peithwyr and the machine, even his own hurt and anger. There was an assurance about her that had annoyed and comforted him. Now . . . now he watched her whisper and moan. He felt ashamed for her.

A low rumble drew his eyes to the door. A silent, composed man in the green tunic of a technician pushed a humming machine in on a small dolly. At a gesture from the Director, he wheeled the machine to Aleytys and knelt beside her. Ignoring her struggles, she clipped electrodes onto her head and neck, then slipped a helmet down and snapped restraining straps in place. Then he stood again and moved behind the machine, looking down on its reading face. Gwynnor shivered, sensing a heavy danger. He hadn't understood anything that had passed between Aleytys and the Director, but he knew Aleytys was terrified and the Director was evil.

Fury beat hotter in him. Hatred for the starman who had stolen her dignity. Without thought for his own danger he called out sharply, "Aleytys!"

She responded instantly, eyes snapping open, head jerking up. He saw intelligence return to her face. After a brief smile, she turned away, closing her eyes again, her face ugly under the tight pull of her intense concentration. He didn't know what she was trying but watched expectantly, ignoring the lazy triumph on the face of Manhanu.

A light chime sounded through the thick silence. For an instant she thought it was the diadem and began to relax.

The technician spoke. "The probe's ready, Illustrious."

Aleytys felt a sick helplessness. Her mind worked stiffly without its usual gathering of haloed concepts, kept rigidly to one line of thinking by the straitjacket of the machine humming above her. "Harskari," she shrieked, not caring this time who heard her. "Shadith! Swardheld! Help me . . ."

Ignoring the noise the Director said, "Ask her who she is."

The words punched into her brain and her mind went totally rigid. Pain . . . oh god . . . pain . . . "Aleytys!" she screamed. "My name is Aleytys."

"More."

"Raqsidani. . . . . . of. . . . of. . . . Jaydugar. . . ."

"That's no use. What is her ancestry? Her father? Her mother? Is she related to the McNeis?"

"No . . . oh . . . oh . . . oh . . . Mardha . . . Raqsidani . . . Azdar, father . . . Madar . . . mother . . . mother . . . no . . . mother . . . Vryhh . . ."

"What!" Dimly through the searing, burning pain she saw him leaning forward, eyes glittering. "Mother!"

"Sh . . . shareem . . . a . . . a Tennathan . . . of Vrithian . . . Shareem . . . Shareem . . . Shar . . ."

"Enough. Where is Vrithian?"

"No . . . no . . . I . . . I . . . don't . . . know . . . I don't know . . ."

He turned to the technician. "More force."

The technician protested. "I don't advise it, Illustrious."

"Nonsense! That bitch can take it. Do what I tell you."

Shrugging, he twisted the rheostat, sending an additional surge of power through the electrodes.

A light chime sounded through the humming of the machine. On Aleytys' head threads of light flickered in and out of visibility, then partially solidified into a circlet of delicate blossoms curving around the dull metal of the helmet.

The diadem chimed again, the sounds matching the on-off flickering of the jeweled centers belonging to the thread flowers.

Aleytys felt/heard a roaring in her ears. Though she found it hard to think, she gathered her anger and threw it into the fight, feeling a building pressure of rage looking for an outlet.

Things like slimy translucent worms wound in multiple turns around her arms and legs. The rage in her came out in bloody flames that licked along her flesh and seared the worms into black dust. She moved her legs and felt a little better. Shaking her body to throw off the dust she stood up and glared at the staring Director. Behind her, the straining probe made small crackling noises and stopped its machine hum. Small threads of blue stinking smoke began creeping out of the polished carapace.

The diadem chimed again and everything froze. But memory came flooding back to Aleytys. The killing rage flowed away as the realization of her escape filtered through the noise and pain in her head. She jerked off the helmet and electrodes and threw them at the floor. The diadem settled into the red gold strands of her hair, having passed like a ghost crown through the metal and wiring of the helmet.

She felt her three friends driving with her own will to fight the influence of the inhibitor, and with that feeling, a warning that she'd better hurry, a warning rendered doubly urgent by the shaking in her knees.

Wading with difficulty against the gelatinous thickness of the air, she swam toward the Director, watching his eyes open   open   open   open until whiteness ringed the staring black pupils and dark-brown iris. Watching his mouth open   open   open in a soundless cry. Watching his hands slowly   slowly   rise   helplessly, rise   futilely rise   to fend her off. She forced her hand into his sleeve.

The fabric was stiff, resisting the probing of her fingers. She was getting dangerously weak. Ignoring the increasing pressure of Manhanu's clinging hand, she forced her fingers into the sleeve pocket and closed them around the hexagonal rod.

It felt impossibly massive. Sweat trickled down her straining face as she brought her other hand into the sleeve, caught the rod between her palms and tore it free. She pushed herself back from the Director, stumbling haphazardly, recklessly backward until she crashed into the wall.

She brought her hands up slowly, fighting the massive inertia of the metal rod.

The diadem chimed, the sound breaking uncertainly then rippling through the five separate notes of the heart stones. As the stiffness melted from the air, Aleytys' breathing grew shallow while her heart boomed in her chest and the blood roared in her ears. With a last tremendous effort, she touched the white end of the rod to the disk on the collar.

She crashed to her knees, her hands flying outward as the immediate pressure inside her head exploded in a great expanding roar.

Gwynnor goggled open-mouthed, then slumped to the floor, his eyes glazed over.

Tipylexne and Ghastay twisted briefly on the floor then lay still.

The Director opened his mouth wide in a silent scream, then fell, boneless as a rag doll, back against the console, eyes like prunes staring blankly at the far corner of the room.

A guard form slumped across the open doorway.

Aleytys rubbed her hand across her eyes, trying to gather her whirling thoughts.

"Aleytys." Harskari's contralto voice was more shaken than Aleytys had ever heard it.

Flattening her back against the wall, Aleytys let her legs fold slowly, sliding to the floor with a solid sound. "What?"

"Replenish your energy. Quickly." Harskari didn't bother to add that the engineer could not be away much longer, or that at any moment Aleytys' precarious control of the situation could slip.

"In a minute." She looked around searching for the rod that had flown from her hand.

"Aleytys!"

"All right. All right." The black water was life pouring into empty veins. She was a flaccid old wineskin and the new black wine filled her taut. She brushed the hair from her face and snatched up the rod. When the collar was off her neck, she stared at it, fury rising in her again at the abrupt return to slavery. She closed her hand over the collar and turned angrily to the Director, who was shakily fumbling at his face.

"Aleytys." Harskari's face formed, stern and reproachful. "Leave him alone. What's done is done. You have responsibilities. Gwynnor. The cludair."

"The cludair," Aleytys said thoughtfully, then she grinned. "Swardheld, friend, we've got ourselves a hostage."

The black eyes opened and he grinned back at her.

Chapter XIV

"Come in. Carefully. And alone."

The engineer ran cool eyes over her. She sat, legs crossed, leaning back in the swivel chair, her hands resting lightly in her lap. He watched her, his mouth twitching, the corners of the thin lips tucking in and down. Then he stepped through the doorway and stood relaxed but alert, facing her. "You turned them loose."

"Do I need to answer that?" She sniffed. Looking past him at the shadowed form of his companion, she said brusquely, "Send your friend for the doctor. He's locked away in the dormitory." A quick lift and fall of her hand. "He can tell you things you need to know."

The engineer looked back over his shoulder. "You heard?" The dark figure moved slightly. "Good. Bring him." As the heavy form stalked off, he turned back slowly, his black eyes boring into hers. "Why are you still here?"

"You had a visitor."

His eyes narrowed briefly before he could stop the reaction. "The technician with the probe?"

"He came. Someone else, also."

His narrow black brows pressed down while he thought. "The Director?"

"Very quick." She tapped the fingers of one hand on the back of the other. "The cludair now have an illustrious guest."

His thin nostrils pinched together, then flared wide, and his long thin mouth curled up in a mocking grimace that didn't quite qualify as a smile. "That won't get you anywhere."

She chuckled, the sound pure amusement in the cold metallic chamber. His eyes narrowed again. "The cludair had a long chat with a pair of guards you sent into the forest awhile back." She rubbed her thumb beside her nose. "A son of Chu drags a bit more weight than most. The guards had quite a bit to say about the strength of family ties."

The smile on the engineer's face crawled farther up his cheeks. "Hostage?"

"Oh, never. Guest with full honors." Once again she chuckled. "No suicide, Company men. Being warned, the cludair will prevent that." She spread out her hands in a wide gesture. "Why should an honored guest be so unmannerly?"

His mouth straightened. "The guards. What guards?"

"The cludair brought them back here. Not the first pair. The second."

"Ah. Those." He dropped his eyes to his hands, straightening the fingers and bending his flexible thumbs back and forth. "There were no marks on them."

"The cludair have a very effective green magic."

"Magic? Pah!"

"Don't deny what you can't understand. Green magic it is, coupled with a comprehensive knowledge of the effects of local herbs."

Behind the blankness in his expressive face, Aleytys sensed the busy working of his subtle mind. "Herbs. Maranhedd?"

"No."

"Still . . ." A sly flicker of the almond-shaped black eyes underlined the sudden flare of greed that brought amusement fluttering through Aleytys' diaphragm. "Drugs that can break conditioning . . . would they trade?"

"Good." She grinned at him. "You give us another bargaining chip."

"So?"

"Do you really want to stay in this perambulating bug?"

He didn't answer but she caught his sudden flare of interest.

The doctor shambled into the room. He looked a mess, hair lank and greasy, the straggling ends poking out around a soiled face with olive shadows staining his temples, painting his quivering jowls and discoloring the sagging purses under his eyes. Those eyes slid uneasily, turning, turning, refusing to look at the others.

"Doctor!" The word brought the fragment of a man cringing around to face the engineer's slim arrogant figure. He straightened his back slowly, his swimming eyes fixed on Han's collar latching. "What happened here?" Han said sharply. The contempt in his master's voice passed unheeded over the doctor's numbed brain.

Fumbling in his sleeve, the doctor said slowly, "The Director came. He wanted you. I told him where you were. He ordered the cast broken off the woman. He brought the technician in and told him to link her to the probe. He questioned her about who she was. He got excited about something . . . I forget what. He ordered the technician to increase power. She did something . . ." The dragging voice slowed further until it degenerated into an uncouth mumbling. Eyes glazed and unseeing, he fumbled in the sleeve again and finally drew forth a sweat-stained paper, folded and sealed. He held it out.

Mouth tight with disgust, the engineer took the letter with the tips of his fingers. After dropping it onto the console, he plucked a handkerchief from his sleeve and rubbed vigorously at the battered paper. Then he dropped the handkerchief on the floor and examined the seal. "Chu Manhanu."

"Right." Aleytys let her foot swing a little. She was getting tired of maintaining a casual pose while tension knotted her stomach. Too many things could go wrong even now.

"I presume you know what's in here."

"Read it." She slid off the swivel chair and moved past him to stand in the doorway. "Let's take a walk. This place makes me feel uncomfortable."

Flicking a fold in the paper against his thumb, he smiled. His sudden flush of triumph warned her that he planned something, but she waited quietly for him to join her. Absently, he thrust the still unopened letter into his sleeve, drawing his hand out as he came up to her. Then that hand flicked out and she felt a hard pressure against her side. "Your cludair friends might be willing to make a trade. After we ask you some questions."

She shrugged. "I used an energy gun on the probe. It's a lump of slag."

"Too bad. Move."

The diadem chimed softly, flickering into substance around her head. Calmly she stepped away from the sleeve gun. "Thanks, Harskari," The yellow eyes looked amused but impatient. Hastily Aleytys pried the tube from the engineer's stiff fingers. "Okay, my friend. I have it."

"Happy to serve, young Aleytys." The amber eyes twinkled. "You do keep us busy."

"Sorry." Holding the reluctantly moving tube, she backed off a few paces. The diadem chimed a second time and melted away.

The engineer stumbled as the flesh he had been braced against was suddenly removed. He stared at Aleytys who stood a full meter from him, the sleeve gun held casually in her hand. "How . . ."

"Show blue to a man born blind." She jerked her head toward the outer door. "Walk with me to the edge of the forest."

The engineer took a step backwards, black eyes narrowing.

Aleytys sighed. "Don't be an idiot. I don't know your name."

"Han Lushan," he said absently, black eyes darting about as he looked for a way to escape.

"Don't be an idiot, Lushan. I don't have to lure you anywhere. If I want to spend the energy, you'll go where I want v   ant."

"You think so?" Anger stiffened the muscles of his face. He straightened and glared at her.

"You want it that way?" She leaned slightly toward him, blue-green eyes glittering. Her insides quivered sickly as she waited to see if her bluff would work.

After a stiff minute, he shrugged. "Relax, woman. What happens now?"

She backed against the wall. "Move outside."

He brushed past her and thrust the heavy door open, metal knocking against metal with a dull clang.

She moved out quickly before he could slam it shut in her face. The heat and humidity hit her like a blow. She sighed and brushed a hand over her forehead, wiping away the sudden beads of sweat.

He smiled grimly, black eyes hard. "I'm interested in seeing how you handle the trap your cludair friends are in. You've got nothing to bargain with. Try to hold Chu Manhanu hostage and you invite massive retaliation. The house of Chu will assume he has suicided whether or not he has the will to do it. Or the opportunity. They'll burn the forest to an inch thick layer of sludge."

"You underestimate the cludair." She moved to his side and together they began strolling toward the edge of the clearing. "To say nothing of me."

"Stupid savages." He looked at the forest frowning. "Spears to fight rifles."

"Don't you wish you had even a spear." She stopped and leaned back against a massive trunk. Flipping a hand at the ruined harvester, she asked, "Talking of stupid, why's a man with your ability stuck on that thing?"

"Ability is not always admired, witch. Especially when combined with a hasty temper." He reached back and undid the clasp that held his thick straight hair clubbed at the nape of his neck. "House of Chu," he said as he cupped the clasp in a hand. He pointed at the insignia on the side of the harvester. "Chu. I'll be lucky to keep my head on my shoulders."

"Why?"

"That son of Chu. You think he'll leave witnesses around if by some chance he comes out of this?"

"I hadn't thought of that." She let her head fall back against the rough fragrant bark and stared at the shreds of cloud blowing across the sky. "How many villages did you burn out?"

He snorted. "I bombed hell out of a bunch of trees. Lifescopes couldn't find a sniff of a single concentration of hot bodies. Anyone killed we got by accident."

Aleytys looked at him, startled by the sudden change in his personality. "Huh. You've peeled off a mask or two. Why the change?"

"Why not. No reason to keep on playing the loyal Company man." He stretched and yawned, the heavy, humid breeze blowing his coarse black hair around his face. "It's a relief. To be myself a short while."

"But you'll put the face back on again when you're back inside." She nodded at the harvester.

"Of course. One must survive." He ran his eyes over her, moving from the top of her head to her feet then back to her face. "Who are you?"

"Nobody. Nothing. A woman."

"McNeis?"

"Back to that? No." She wrinkled her nose. "My being here is accident. A hesitation in my wandering, engineer of the house of Chu."

"Not Chu." She frowned as she heard the anger in his voice. "Not Chu," he repeated. "Look" He held out the hair clasp and traced the design with a forefinger. "House of Han." He bent the clasp back and forth until it broke into two roughly equal pieces. He handed her one and stuck the other into his sleeve. "My house is Han." His mouth curled into a tight sardonic smile. "I said I had a hasty temper. A mistake to flaunt that sigil."

"Why?"

"Han's in disgrace. But we're not erased from the Book yet." He pointed at the piece of clasp she was swinging between her thumb and forefinger. "You owe me, witch. You owe house of Han a favor for my life."

"Nonsense." She dropped the clasp as if it was hot.

He picked it up and thrust it at her again. "I don't say I won't get out of this. Keep that, witch. Show it and you'll be welcome in my father's house."

"Hunh! An odd sort of blackmail. I don't owe you anything."

"Blame me for trying?"

"Certainly not. All right." She closed her fingers over the bit of soft metal. "Walk your tightrope, engineer. I hope you don't fall off."

"I won't. I suppose I should wish you luck." He sighed and

the relaxed, smiling man who had been chatting with her slid into the cold, amoral Company servant. "The Company wants you, woman. Take care."

Chapter XV

Aleytys turned her back on the charred gap in the forest green. "So no cludair were caught."

Tipylexne's pointed ears twitched. His lips curled back to expose outsize canines. "Our Xalpsalp dreamed the warning to the widow of each circle and the people dispersed, as you said. The houses were destroyed but life goes on. There are other circles waiting for the people."

For several minutes they walked in silence in the bright gloom under the trees. Ahead, the muted sound of construction and the shriller sounds of cludair voices floated back to them.

"You were lucky to find a circle so close to home."

Tipylexne chuckled. "The seed was planted in my father's time. The Khaghliclighmay clan was growing strongly so Father of Men prepared for the time of splitting. When the mother tree had grown a seed, he planted it." They walked into the clearing. "Here." He swung a hand around indicating the circle of home trees. "These all share a common root system. Underground . . ." He stamped on the barren earth. "The roots grow together making a web that kills other growth and clears the ground for us." He pointed upward. "The trees grow independently until one branch touches another then these grow together so that after a number of years we have many strong pathways on different levels circling the clearing." His shoulders lifted in sad resignation. "It takes many years to grow a hometree circle until it can support a settlement. And the seeds themselves take thirty years to mature. When our clan splits next year, those who leave won't be able to stay close. I don't know where they can go.

It will be difficult, so many clans without homes because of the starmen."

A girl planting wirebush in the notch where a limb grew out of a trunk saw them and called out a greeting. "Hey-aa, Father of Men, fire sister."

"Hey-aa, little cricket. How goes the planting?"

"Wirebush is being stubborn. He grows angry because he is moved from his seed rooting and he threatens to die for sheer spite." She laughed and returned to her coaxing, crooning the stubborn weed into acceptance of its new location.

"She seems very skilled at what she is doing."

Tipylexne nodded. "If Inkatay reaches the fullness of age, she will be Xalpsalp, as Qilasc is now. She has the gift."

Aleytys saw abruptly how little she knew of the day-to-day life of the cludair and felt a brief depression at this reminder that she was an outsider and didn't belong here. She shrugged off the momentary gloom as Qilasc came into the clearing.

Behind her, several males marched in single file, bent over under the weight of huge curving sheets of bark. Behind them came others loaded down with sticky coils of vine. They placed their burdens in the center of the clearing next to bark and vine already piled high. As they turned to retrace their steps, Chu Manhanu came stalking into the busy clearing, a scowl twisting his narrow face. Behind him, his adolescent honor guard strutted with obvious pride in their task.

The two processions met. Qilasc stepped back, moved her sinewy body in a complicated obeisance, rule beads clacking loud in the sudden silence. As she straightened, Manhanu swept past with a brief nod, the amenities having been observed, giving him back some of the honor snatched so precipitously from him at his capture.

Aleytys moved back so that Tipylexne stood between her and the dark, angry eyes of the Director. Although the cludair's head barely topped her and his body was lean and wiry rather than bulky, she felt better with less of herself showing to exacerbate the tension in the situation. As the prancing boys followed their charge into the forest on the far side of the clearing, she said quietly, "He seems to be accepting his detention better than I expected."

His canines flashing briefly as the corners of his mouth curled up, Tipylexne looked after the Director. "He's been very careful to avoid any situation where we'd have to make clear the difference between guest and prisoner."

"Oh. I suppose that's a good sign."

"We'll know when the council meets and the bargaining begins."

"Have you decided what you want from him?"

"Yes. Nothing." His eyes went back to her. After a moment's grave consideration, he went on. "His absence and the right to live our own lives in our own way."

A group of children ran chattering past them. The tip of his mobile nose twitching, Tipylexne watched them while they circled in noisy excitement around Ghastay as he strutted along practicing trills on his flute.

"Changes." Aleytys touched his arm. "We've interferred, Gwynnor and me."

"If silence has value, it will return to balance when balance returns to our life."

"When I'm gone." She saw the mob greet Gwynnor and the whole flock disappear along the path toward the burnt-out clearing. "When we're both gone."

Tipylexne nodded.

The long day chugged along with agonizing tedium. Restless and irritable, Aleytys wandered about watching the women rebuild the houses and put the new settlement in order. Qilasc and Tipylexne were too busy to talk to her for more than a few minutes and she felt guilty when they left off their work to answer her aimless questions. She fidgeted about the circle until a cludair apologized courteously the third time for stumbling over her. Then she ran her fingers through her hair and stalked off into the forest, heading for the stream.

Gwynnor had his apprentices practicing their fingering and running over and over and over a simple progression of notes. He looked up and smiled briefly at her then went back to work, correcting and praising. Aleytys leaned against the bole of a smooth-barked giant, but the deadly dullness of the exercises soon drove her off down the stream.

When distance and intervening trees muted the practice session to a distant thread of sound that blended happily with the brush-brush of water song, she dropped onto a thick patch of grass padding the bank and watched the water slip past her toes. After a while, she curled up and went to sleep, a heavy daze filled with bad dreams and too many memories.

"Aleytys." A hand shook her lightly.

She came slowly from the sodden depths of her stupor and

blinked up into Tipylexne's shadowed face. Grunting with effort, she pushed her stiff body up to sit with her hands
pressed against her aching head. "Madar," she groaned, "this
was a mistake."

"Mistake."

"Sleeping." Her body felt heavy, unwieldy, her mind sluggish. "What time is it?"

"First fire. My woman asks that you share our evening
meal before the council gathers."

"How goes the building?"

"Completed."

"Already?"

He looked amused. "Yes, fire sister. The forest is generous
to those who ask properly." He dropped beside her with a
loose, easy fall, sitting on his heels, knees spread so that he
could bend close to her, nostrils flaring as his cat eyes
scanned her face. "You are without peace."

His closeness set her nerves on edge. Quietly, because she
liked and respected him, she touched his cheek, then shifted
her body, tactfully pretending to search for a more comfortable position. As she moved, she brushed against his leg. The
touch of the soft silky fur over the hardness of muscle
brought her a sudden intense awareness of his maleness.

At the blatant outpouring of sexuality, with its accompanying intensification of her female odor, Tipylexne drew back,
surging erect with swift fluid ease, waves of helpless embarrassment churning out from him to jar against her sensitized
nerves.

She stared down at her knees, rubbing the thinly buried
bone with her thumbs. "It's hard to know what to say."
Fighting against her own embarrassment, she looked up.
"May I speak of woman things to a hunter?"

He stepped into deeper shadow, repugnance, curiosity, and
a hesitant friendliness pouring out from him in waves that
washed over Aleytys until she barely managed to string two
thoughts together. Breathing hard, she raised her barriers,
feeling absurdly hurt by the need to cut herself off from him.

Taking his silence for consent, she said slowly, "My
bleeding time is close, Tipylexne. It makes me . . . um . . .
what do I say . . . it makes me react strongly to a male
presence." She gave a short bark of laughter. "Is that
expressed delicately enough?" Spreading her hands in a

helpless gesture, she went on. "And I find you very much a man."

The fur over his chest muscles stirred, ruffling up in little waves. When he spoke, his voice was harsh, as if his throat was constricted. "You shouldn't talk to me of these things. Qilasc . . ."

"Is not here." Impatiently she jumped to her feet and confronted him. "Since I'm so repulsive, I'll take myself off."

"It's not that I refuse," he burst out. "I cannot. Fire sister, I . . . the . . . you . . . you smell wrong." At the look on her face, he spread his hands helplessly. "Not bad. Wrong. The . . . the reflex in me is triggered by the . . . the scent of my woman when she is with desire and then we dance the two-backed dance. Your flesh is smooth, the texture is wrong, I smelled your desire, but the smell is wrong. Do you understand?"

She sighed. "Yes." Running her hands through her hair, she shook off some of the lingering dullness from her too heavy sleep. "I'm starting to get hungry."

Tiplyexne stepped from the shadow onto the brighter gloom of the path, relief flooding from him. Together they began walking back toward the settlement.

"How's the Director doing?"

"He stalks about the camp like a bull wcywuks, demanding honor over and over." Tipylexne snorted, mouth pulled into a contemptuous grimace. "An empty man. Two fingerlings mocked him until Tatto, my brother, cuffed them to obedience. He pretended not to notice."

"He's no fool."

"A man without honor."

"And so all the more dangerous."

She felt his shoulders move as his almost soundless laugh whispered past her ear. "You know the weheyq?"

"The strangler vine that grows as you watch? I nearly fell in a patch of it a few days ago but your son warned me in time."

She could feel Tipylexne's sudden burst of pride and smiled to herself as he went on.

"Inkatay sang a loop around his guest house and Tatto fed it some squirrels pretending loudly to pay great honor to our guest. I don't think he'll go walking about in the dark."

She laughed but shook her head, forgetting that the

blackness under the trees combined with the cludair's less effi-
cient eyes to make the gesture invisible.

"The armlings who guard him have very respectfully . . ."
Amusement rippled into his voice. "Very respectfully ex-
hibited a number of interesting trophies, boasting their delight
in their skill as hunters. There was a tree cat's teeth and
claws—Old Grandaddy, that my father's father and his three
brothers netted late on one hard winter. And the fire snake's
skin with fangs intact that you saw hung as spirit guard to
the rafters of the longhouse."

Aleytys chuckled. "Gave me nightmares for a week."

"They might have exaggerated the dangers out under the
trees a trifle." Once again she heard his breathy laughter. "A
common trait of newly blooded males."

"Good. But that's not what I meant."

He reached out and touched her cheek, striving to read
what he couldn't see. "What is it?"

"How far do you think you can trust that snake once he's
out of the forest?"

Tipylexne was silent a moment. She could feel him trying
to puzzle out exactly what she was saying. "You think he
won't keep his word?" He sounded and felt increasingly unhappy.

"Only if it's to his advantage. You said it yourself. He's an
empty man. A promise he makes is good only as long as you
can force him to honor it."

"I'll have to think about that."

Ahead, the center fire cast feeble red gleams into the dark.

"The council meets tomorrow?"

"Yes. Fire sister . . ."

"It wouldn't be a good idea for me to be there."

"Qilasc was to talk with you about this, but . . ." His
shoulders moved past hers as he shrugged, the silky hair tickling her skin and rewakening a pale echo of her need. She
moved a little to one side so he didn't touch her. "It would be
a kindness if you would not be there," he said quickly.

"With my long nose out of cludair business."

He made an apologetic choking sound in his throat. "We
are . . . we are very grateful for your help, fire sister."

"But I smell wrong and I disturb your peace."

"Would you have me lie?"

"No." She sighed, then patted his arm lightly. "Don't disturb yourself, my friend. I'm not offended."

They walked slowly into the clearing, talking quietly as they moved toward Tipylexne's family tree, a comfortable space separating the two bodies, conflict and embarrassment sunk under a quiet friendliness.

Chapter XVI

Aleytys moaned in her sleep and rolled onto her stomach, snakes hissing and coiling around her with mottled scales glistening damply, great red triangular heads darting at her, retreating, darting again. She shuddered, her body hot and tight in the grip of the nightmare.

A tree cat howled somewhere in the distance. The noise jerked her free from the disturbing images. She elbowed over onto her back and lay panting and shaking on the rush matting.

She scrubbed her hands across her face, then sat up, gasping as her head throbbed with a dull heavy pain. Her skin was sticky-slick with sweat, the tunic clinging to her body, twisted around her tight enough to waken a rush of claustrophobia. She sucked in a lungful of the stale, sodden air then breathed it out again as the walls seemed to close in on her, increasing the claustrophobic pressure. She dabbed at the sweat trickling between her breasts, then crawled cautiously out of the guest house.

The wirebush stung her ankles as she stepped carelessly onto the top loop of the laddervine, shocking her into momentary alertness. As she swung down over the cinnamon-scented bark, she muttered irritably at the stupidity of putting such a plant into a such a place until she remembered that the itch was a small price to pay for freedom from snuggling tree snakes.

She clung to the trunk and struggled to clear the wisps of sleep from her head. The forest had been benign so far but barely so. Her ignorance of the ways of life here had landed her in danger several times; only luck and a persistent young cludair had saved her skin for her. To walk into the forest with a head full of clouds was idiotic.

When she stepped onto the ground she heard, faintly, the sound of Gwynnor's flute drifting back from the direction of the stream. She hesitated, uncertain whether company was unendurable or necessary. Overhead, the moon thrust a pale grey-green edge into the ragged circle of open sky. The night was barely begun, less than two hours into sleeping time. Rubbing her arms she stumbled down the newly pounded path to the stream, following the sound of the flute.

Gwynnor sat, back curved into the curve of the tree trunk, drawing absent-minded, shapeless doodling from the flute.

Oh god, she thought, if that was Vajd and I was back . . . back home . . . if that was Vajd . . . oh god. She stumbled against the tree and surrendered to a pain of loss that time seemed unable to diminish. She turned her face against the crumbly, spicy bark, struggling to rip away at the invading memories and force them back into the closet where she could ignore them and get on with living.

"Aleytys?" Gwynnor touched her shoulder. There was worry in his voice. And uncertainty. "What's wrong?"

She pressed her face harder against the bark. "Memories." Her voice was hoarse and muffled against the tree. The bark tasted sharp and musky.

His hands moved over her shoulders, stroking her hair aside so he could massage the tense muscles of her neck. At the touch of his fingers she shuddered, and shuddered again as her body response overwhelmed the ache of memory. She broke away from him and walked blindly, rapidly onto the the grass beside the stream. She dropped heavily onto her knees and stared up at the pitted face of the moon, rubbing unhappily at her aching breasts.

Gwynnor lowered himself quietly beside her and watched her out of cat eyes whose slit pupils were open wide until they approximated circles. The narrow segments of iris glowed with a faint phosphorescence. Absently, without taking his eyes from her, he groped for the flute and held it loosely in his fingers.

Aleytys sighed, her stiff body loosening. She let herself lean back until she was sitting instead of kneeling. She hugged her arms over her breasts, fingers wrapping around her upper arms. She dug at the grass with her toes, crossed over her legs right over left, then left over right. Then right over left.

Yawned. Twisted from side to side. There was no comfortable way to sit but moving brought no relief either. Her body ached with restless energy that gnawed at her, twitched like army ants crawling up her arms, her back, her legs. Watching her struggle, Gwynnor lifted his flute to his lips and coaxed a soothing dreamy melody from it, attempting to calm her nervousness. Aleytys looked at him, then away, chewing on her lip. For the first time, the water magic failed to work and the song of the flute brought no ease to her aching spirit. Too many memories. Too much pain. Too much her body's betrayal.

Gwynnor let his music trail off. The starwoman was crouched beside him, sitting with her knees pulled tight against her breasts with her chin resting on her crossed arms. Even the tiny hairs on her arms quivered with the disturbance that flowed beneath her skin. He watched her suffering, helplessly. Her sexual readiness was a club, smashing repeatedly against his senses. He put the flute aside once more as his body responded to the spicy disturbing odor that steamed from her.

"It's almost finished here," she said suddenly.

"Are you sorry?" He struggled to keep his voice even and drew his legs up his growing stiffness.

The bright hair jerked as she shook her head. He wanted to touch it, to hold the smooth curve of her hair against the matching curve of his hand.

She rubbed her hand over her face, looking harried. "I like them."

"I know." He looked away, unhappy at his sudden jealousy of Tipylexne.

"What about you? Still coming with me to the city?"

"Yes." His fingers slid briefly up and down the silken smooth length of the flute lying on the ground beside him.

The starwoman moved restlessly, straightening her legs out and leaning back against the tree. The moonlight was strong enough for him to see her teeth set on her lower lip, her brows coming together in a brooding frown. "You told me one of the others in the Dylaw's band was your lover."

"Yes." He squirmed uncomfortably, wishing she'd pick something else to talk about. "I've grown past him now."

"That sounds cold."

"You don't understand."

"Probably not." Her voice was muffled. He looked around to see her knees pulled up again, her face hidden by her crossed arms. The thong that held her hair in a long tail had come loose and the silky mass was falling in a tangled waterfall over her arms. He slid a hand along the ground and stroked a strand with trembling fingers. "I suppose you don't have the same ways where you grew up."

She turned her head. He saw her bright, troubled eyes fix on his face, "I've met men who loved men on my travels. I don't know if I can understand it. Why. . . ."

"Affection. Loneliness. The need to touch and care."

"Oh." The sound was curiously forlorn.

"Men are lovers. For a time. But women are wives. For life." Surreptitiously, he touched himself, felt the hardness under his hand and sighed. "The one is a brief thing," he murmured. "A storm in spring. The other is a lifetime long, ebbing and flowing with the seasons. Children come, grow, leave home in a pattern as old as dark and light. Man and wife grow old in a sharing that is strong and warm and good." He felt drained and unhappy, wanting her now to go away and let him deal with his problem.

She jumped to her feet, throwing the hair back over her shoulder with a quick twist of her head. "Don't the wives want some of that springtime storm?"

"The babies keep getting made." He looked up at her. "Go to bed, Aleytys. You're making me nervous."

"You!" She swung her arms over her head and arched her back. "My god, Gwynnor, this damn conversation is all I needed."

"You started it." He swallowed. "Go away, woman."

"Gwynnor?" There was sudden comprehension in her face as she plucked her mind from her own troubles and really looked at him. She dropped to her knees. "I'm a fool. You said you'd grown beyond your friend. I don't smell wrong to you?"

"Holy Maeve!" His body was as hot and taut as a burning rope. Before he could lose his nerve, he blurted, "Would you share my storm time, Aleytys?"

Chapter XVII

Moving carefully so she wouldn't wake Gwynnor, Aleytys stood up. The cerdd lay on his stomach, sprawled loose-limbed across the patch of grass, his mouth open, snoring just a little, looking totally and pleasantly depleted. She smiled down at him, feeling a warm affection for him that, at present, had little sexuality in it.

Humming softly, she waded into the stream and sat down so the water flowed around her, coming up her ribs almost to her breasts. With handfuls of bottom sand she scrubbed the sweat and stains from her body until she felt comfortably clean. She stretched, yawned, then waded out and sat down on the grass to let the breeze flow over her and fan her dry, leaving her skin feeling sweetly cooled.

A tree cat padded from the shadow across the stream and stood watching her. Aleytys leaned back against the tree trunk, lacing her fingers behind her head, watching the cat with a grave curiosity of her own. She probed gently at the predator, exploring its feral psyche, then let it drink and sent it away, sighing with the memory of her magnificently terrifying companion so long ago, the black tars, Daimon. Idly, she wondered whether the big catlike animal was still alive, roaming the mountains of Jaydugar where even man was little threat to his well-being. But she was too content just now to dwell on the past. She stretched again and yawned hopefully.

Something clattered beside her. She looked down. Gwynnor's flute. She picked it up and looked it over worriedly, exploring the smooth, polished surface of the instrument for possible injury. No nicks or cracks. Good. She chuckled as the shape of the flute and the way she was handling it reminded her of her activities not so long before. Still holding the flute, she settled back against the tree.

A purple glow expanded then contracted in her head. Then hovered there, pulsating with a vaguely apologetic air.

"Shadith?"

Purple eyes opened hesitantly. "Lee . . ."

"What's wrong?" Aleytys sat up and looked around alertly.

"Nothing. I . . . I just wanted to talk to you."

"You never hesitated before."

"That was different."

"How?"

"You needed us."

Aleytys relaxed against the tree, sniffing appreciatively as her back pressed perfumed oil from the bark, a wryly amused smile turning up a corner of her mouth. "So?"

Shadith seemed embarrassed. She kept fading out. "It's *your* body."

"Sometimes I wonder about that."

"Lee!"

"Just joking. Stop dithering, Shadith. What do you want?"

"Music!" The word was packed with an almost desperate longing. "I'm a singer, Lee, and a maker of songs. How long since . . ."

"You want me to wake Gwynnor?"

"NO!" Shadith's violet eyes blazed. "No, Lee. I want . . . I want your body. For just a little."

"Why bother to ask?" Aleytys frowned. "You never did before."

"If I tried it without your consent, Harskari would peel me raw. She's got a bad case of ethics, that lady."

"I suppose she's listening now."

"My god, I hope not. She and Swardheld have gone off . . ." Shadith's face contracted into a thoughtful scowl. "It's hard to explain."

"What are you really, all of you?" Aleytys moved her hands slowly over the crumpled grass beside her thighs. "I've got a sort of interest in knowing," she said dryly.

Shadith giggled. "Point to you, Lee." The thin brows shot up into the exuberantly curling hair. "How the hell should I know?" She shook her curls until they danced about wildly. "All I really know is that I'm aware. I feel that I'm the same person I was before the diadem trapped me. I think. I feel— at least I do when the diadem's on a living body. I remember. I learn. What am I? God knows. I sure don't. Maybe Harskari does, but she's not talking."

Aleytys frowned. "But you're the one who knows about complicated technology."

Shadith shook her head. "You've got an exalted idea of my learning, Lee. So I can deal with machines a trifle more sophisticated than a hammer. Ha!" She turned thoughtful. "I suppose, since you come from an agrarian-pastoral context, you would find a machine-city culture difficult to understand, making me look smarter than I am."

"Funny."

"What?"

"This is the first time I've really just talked with one of you. We share a body and we're still strangers."

"Which brings me back to the beginning. I starve for music, Lee. It's been forever since I've been able to do more than listen to snatches of sound. Please?"

Aleytys felt a painful reluctance to let another intelligence displace her, but she shook off the brief distaste. "Go ahead, Shadith." With an uneasy laugh she flowed her hands down along her body. "Such as it is, it's all yours."

Briefly disoriented by the transition, Aleytys scratched around inside her head until she felt comfortable, then she relaxed and lay back to enjoy Shadith's enjoyment of her skill.

Shadith lifted the flute and examined it, touching the polished wood with gentle reverence. She lifted the flute to her lips and blew, exploring the possibilities of the instrument as she got to know more about the possibilities of the body she wore.

Slowly, quietly, the tentative notes smoothed out and began blending into a complex, exciting music, something far beyond anything Aleytys had ever experienced. The music grew stronger and louder, penetrating to the bones of her body, going far far beyond the simply pleasant and tuneful. Demanding music. Disturbing. Demanding. Irritating. Demanding. Beautiful. Terrible. All at once and all in turn.

Gwynnor woke. He sat up, became conscious of his nakedness. Half-dazed by the music pouring around him, he fished for his tunic and slid it over his head, smoothing out the wrinkles as he turned to face the starwoman sitting beside him, legs crossed and back straight to give her lungs maximum expansion. She had his flute and was playing . . . extraordinary . . . he could make no judgment of the sound, but the skill . . . extraordinary. It shamed him. He grew angry and jumped to his feet.

She ignored him.

Fiercely, he snatched the flute from her hands. "Why didn't you tell me? You let me boast my skill when you . . ."

"Gwynnor!"

The word struck through his anger, stopping the rush of words instantly. It was not Aleytys' voice, not the voice he had begun to know as well as his own. Timber, accent, sound, all different. One of the demons had her. He swallowed and took a step backward. "You . . . you aren't . . ."

"I am called Shadith."

He moved his head, looking anxiously and hopelessly around. "Let her go. Where is she?"

"Here." Shadith laughed, the sound, a silver trilling wholly unlike Aleytys' contralto chuckle. "Come back and sit down, Gwynnor. Aleytys gave me her body for a little time."

He shook his head trying futilely to drive out the fog of confusion roiling around inside. "I don't understand."

Her mouth curled into an impish smile while the blue-green eyes danced with mischief. "Gwynnor, shame. You guessed about us long ago."

"Demon!"

"Don't be silly. Ask Lee when she's back. More like guardian angels, although I can't claim to be very angelic." She sobered. "I'm sorry, seeing this bothers you so much. Damn. Harskari will peel me for sure. It's just I was so very hungry to make music."

"Aleytys is here?" He stared at her. "How?"

Shadith sighed. She looked wistfully at the flute held loosely in his fingers. "All right. Walk a way into the forest, please. When you return Aleytys will be here."

Some minutes later he came slowly out of the shadow. He came over to her and bent down to stare into her face.

"It's me, Gwynnor. Shadith is gone."

His fingers trembled on her cheek, then his hand cupped around the curve of her face. "How could it happen?"

"I can't explain, Gwynnor."

"Cannot? No. Will not."

"Yes. That's true." She moved her head away from his hand and groped about her for her tunic. "It's a private thing."

"How can you . . ." He dropped to his knees and touched her face, her hair. "How can you suffer such violation?"

She shook her head and moved away again, drawing the crumpled tunic over her head and smoothing away the creases. "I can allow a man within my body without it being violation. You should know that."

"It isn't the same."

"It is. What is given freely and with affection can never be stolen. They are my friends and my companions."

Overhead, the moon had almost left the clear space. Aleytys got up and walked over to stand beside the stream, letting the soft brush brush of the waterflow come into her and work the timeless water magic, the elemental song that nearly always brought peace and healing for a time, at least, to her troubled spirit.

On his knees, Gwynnor watched her move away from him. He felt like running to her and holding her tightly, not letting her go, never letting her go. Holy Maeve . . . He pressed his hands over his eyes. We're too different, he thought. I have a life. She has a life. He jumped to his feet and left her standing beside the stream, so absorbed in thought she didn't even notice when he went.

Chapter XVIII

Ghastay grinned at Aleytys. "Same old tree."

She looked up into the heavy foliage. "Same tree. You go back and let Tipylexne know we're in place, keeping an eye on what's happening."

He nodded briskly and raced away. Aleytys turned to Gwynnor. "We'd better go up now."

He nodded and went down on one knee so she could use the other as a step up. She looked at him and sighed.

"Gwynnor . . ."

He looked up, his face grim. "You made it quite clear, Aleytys. This morning. Your life and mine are separate."

"Damn. We were friends."

"I thought so. Before."

"You knew all along I wasn't going to stay. Did I ever lie to you about that?"

"Not with words." He got onto his feet and stood, glaring angrily into her face.

"Nor any other way," she insisted. She put her hand to touch his arm. He jerked away. "All right, I shouldn't have slept with you." She shrugged. "I don't claim to be perfect."

"You act like you think you are."

"Ay-mi, we sound like quarreling children. Come on, relax." She chewed on her lip. "You seem to think I'm some kind of . . . I don't know. I'm a fallible human and so are you, but can't we approximate maturity?"

He took a deep breath and let his petulance slide away. "You expect a lot." He knelt again and grunted as her weight rested briefly on his knee as she sprang for the limb. When she was settled she lowered the rope and he climbed up beside her.

The Director came striding from the forest accompanied by Qilasc, Tipylexne, and several stony-faced guards with a double line of immature females beating a slow ponderous rhythm on large nut shells, the whole presenting a face of immense dignity. Watching from her perch, high up in the tree at the edge of the clearing, Aleytys smiled, momentarily delighted by the absurdity of the whole scene.

The door on the harvester opened. First came two armored guards, then the engineer. Han scanned the trees around the clearing with wary eyes, then turned to face the procession.

Chu Manhanu held up his hand, halting the parade. He waited solemnly for the engineer to approach.

Lushan bowed deeply, schooling his face to the proper respect. Even from her tree, Aleytys could feel his startled appreciation and knew it was for her, not Chu Manhanu. He'd wondered how she'd pull it off. Again she smiled. Now he'd see.

Manhanu nodded, grudgingly acknowledging the engineer's profound obeisance. "Han Lushan," he said brusquely, "you wasted time and lives. More important, this operation has been unprofitable."

Han Lushan waited, a growing bitterness behind his obsequious mask. Aleytys frowned, remembering his prediction of trouble after Manhanu got back. Apparently he was to be appointed goat for this operation. She chewed her lower lip, hating the idea.

Gwynnor touched her arm. "You can't mother the world," he whispered.

She wrinkled her nose. "I know," she whispered back.

In the clearing the Director was explaining how he had, by his consummate diplomacy, talked the forest people into providing tribute semiyearly, wood and wood products at no cost whatsoever to the Company. Hence there would be no need for the harvester; it was to be transported to the city and transferred from there to Hagen's world where, hopefully—this was said with heavy sarcasm—the next man in charge of it could avoid getting it wrecked beneath him.

Aleytys felt the amusement and deepening appreciation concealed by Lushan's Company face. She lay along the limb resting her chin on her crossed hands, watching the play unfold beneath her. Judging by his words, the Director was convinced that the agreement made him look good. He'd have a strong incentive to maintain it. Each time she probed him, though, she felt vaguely uncomfortable. To reassure herself, she tried again.

Anger . . . satisfaction . . . an eerie double aura . . . as if Manhanu himself had two minds . . . like the doctor in a way . . . a weak, innocuous dying-away glimmer and a cold savage overlay . . . she could feel but get no hold on him . . . if there was a second life in him it was hidden beyond her ability to discern.

For a moment the Director looked up, his face turned toward her. As if he could see her. As if he knew she was there. Watching. She shivered. He smiled and looked away.

Qilasc bowed deeply to Manhanu. She gestured to the young females who began the slow, steady beat once more. Once, twice, Qilasc bowed again. Then, with a silent Tipylexne beside her, she turned and marched slowly from the clearing, stepping in time with the hollow beat of the nutshells. As they vanished under the trees the Director stalked into the harvester, the engineer trailing behind.

Gwynnor stirred. "What happens now?"

"We wait and see what he does."

"Will he keep his word?"

"I don't know." She scanned the clearing with eyes and

mind. "He's not trying to start the harvester. At least, there's that."

"He looked at you."

"Um. There's something really peculiar about that man. Let's wait here until he takes the machine away. If he does that . . ."

"How long will that take?"

"If he means business, I expect he'll move it before the day's out. It's still early and with these long days . . ."

The steamy heat worsened as the sun rose higher. Nothing much happened in the clearing. A guard came out one time—no armor—walked around the harvester, came to the forest and relieved himself against a tree, then went back inside.

A little later, a skimmer came from the south and settled beside the machine. The Director came out accompanied by the engineer, talking in low tones. Although Aleytys strained to hear, she could catch none of the words. Then Lushan went back inside and Manhanu climbed into the skimmer. A minute later it rose, hovered a moment just above treetop level, then darted away.

More waiting.

"I'm getting sleepy." Gwynnor slid back along his limb until he was braced against the bole. "Much more and I will go to sleep, and fall out of this damn tree."

Holding onto a secondary branch, Aleytys swung around to face him. "I've got to stay here until I make sure the harvester's gone. Why don't you go back to the village and see if you can arrange supplies and a boat to take us down river and around the cape to the city."

He nodded. "You take care."

She lay down again, eyes fixed on the clearing. "I will."

Chapter XIX

A fresh breeze slid along the water, stirring through her hair and making the furled sail slap against the boom. Aleytys wrenched her eyes from the silent, watching cludair and examined the river. It was several meters wide here, larger than any river she'd seen before . . . except maybe the one Captain Arel landed by, six worlds back. What was that one called . . . she shook her head . . . so many worlds, so many strange names . . . she could hear a waterfall somewhere to the west. Walking closer to the water, she leaned out and found she could see the edge of the plateau, visible as a level shape against the paler blue of the sky. She thought she could see a vague vertical cutting the blue. The waterfall? It was further away than the sound seemed to suggest. She shook her head.

Silent as green ghosts in the gloom under the trees, Qilasc and Tipylexne waited for her to step into the boat.

Gwynnor sat in the sailboat's stern, holding it against the bank, a paddle thrust behind the root of a tree that was gradually leaning farther and farther out into the water. One day soon it would fall and go floating off to the sea. Like us, she thought.

"Aleytys, you going to stand there another hour? My arm's about to break off."

She looked unhappily at the small bobbing craft. "I'm supposed to get into that thing?"

"Unless you want to walk." Gwynnor grinned at her. "Just move slow and careful. Jump around and you'll have both of us in the water. The boat's a bit tender in its handling."

"I won't put a foot through the bottom?"

"No, Aleytys, that's not what I mean. Come on before my arm really does fall off."

Aleytys glanced at the forest for the last time, saying a silent farewell to the forest people. Then she gritted her teeth and swung one foot into the boat. It shifted under her weight and she grabbed wildly at the mast, knocking her hip against the boom, sending it swinging around, nearly decapitating Gwynnor. The boat rocked back and she slammed her head painfully into the mast.

Gwynnor ducked as the boom came around at him, pulling the oar free so that the boat drifted out and began moving faster as the main current caught it and pulled it along. He grabbed the tiller and steadied the boat's wild swings, edging it into the center of the river where it began moving swiftly and smoothly through water, glassy green and deep.

Aleytys clutched at the mast, gradually regaining her nerve. A narrow ledge ran along the curved sides of the boat. Without thinking, she started to lower herself onto this seat.

The boat began rocking ominously as her weight shift destroyed its trim. Gwynnor threw his body to the opposite side as Aleytys froze in mid crouch. "Aleytys."

"Wh . . . what?"

"Dammit, when you move remember, you balance the weight on one side of the center with the weight on the other. Or we capsize."

She nodded, a small tight dip of her head, being too scared to venture on any larger movement. Holding onto the mast so hard her fingers ached, she lowered herself until she was sitting in the exact middle of the boat on the floorboards. Carefully, she unlocked her fingers and flexed them slowly, then folded them on her lap.

"You all right?"

She looked up. "Yes." Her eyes moved beyond him. The tongue of the forest touching the river had already vanished, hidden around a curve. The banks on both sides changed to gradually rising rose-red cliffs. A vast desolation hollowed her. Tears gathered in her eyes. Angrily, she brushed them away. Crying. What the hell for? The desolation spread. Chilled her. She pulled her knees up, ignoring the slewing of the boat, surrendering to the violent emotional storm that threatened to tear her apart. In a last concession to her pride, she dropped her head onto her knees, hiding her face behind crossed arms.

Gwynnor relaxed as the river slid the boat down the channel, swift, smooth, and steady. No need to raise sail. Going fast enough. He looked back over his shoulder. Farewells are always difficult, he thought. He straightened again, blinking as the low morning sun shone right into his eyes. He frowned.

Aleytys was bent over, head on knees, her body shaking with hard, hoarse sobs. "Aleytys!"

She didn't seem to hear. The great wrenching sobs that shook her body, even shook the boat, went on and on endlessly.

He clutched at the tiller, scowling at feathers of white water breaking the jade not far ahead of the bow. Miserable in his turn, he sat helpless, tied to the tiller bar, unable to touch her, comfort her, as he wanted. Able only to wait for her storm to subside. To wonder why? What had brought it on? To be reminded, painfully reminded, that this was an alien being, another species whose thoughts and emotions were sometimes incomprehensible.

Aleytys lifted her head, the turmoil within her worn to a dull, aching misery. She looked around, took in Gwynnor's worried face, took in the jade-green sweep of the water, the high red sandstone cliffs, the pale sky interrupted by thready clouds. Sighing, she slid around so she was lying curled up on the floorboards. In minutes she sank into a heavy sleep.

When she woke the sun hung low in the sky, turning Gwynnor's head and shoulders into a black bust against the glowing crimson. She levered her stiff body up, moving with exaggerated care.

Feeling the boat move, Gwynnor nodded briefly to acknowledge her return to consciousness, then went back to scanning both sides of the river.

"Gwynnor?"

"What is it?" he said impatiently.

"You think you could move the waterskin where I can reach it?"

He lifted the skin by its shoulder strap, swung it back then forward, releasing it at the end of the forward swing so that it plopped to the floorboards in front of her feet.

"Thanks." She took a mouthful of the warmish water, sloshed it around, then let it trickle down her dry throat. Then she drank again, taking a few small sips until the sick, cottony feel was gone from her mouth. She replaced the stopper and settled the skin by her feet.

She looked around. The red cliffs were gone and the river had spread until it was twice the width she remembered. On either side, trees stood in water that crept on and on under their spreading branches. She could see no end to it. The trees had a ragged, pallid look as if dipping their feet continually in the black water had leeched some of the life from them. Even the air flowing past the boat had a stale decayed smell. More and more patches of reeds grew up around dead trees that were bone-white skeletons reaching up from the thickening reedy fringe.

Gwynnor was frowning anxiously as he continued to swing his head from side to side, examining the dead trees with particular care.

"Is there something dangerous in that mess?"

"Not to us out here."

"Why work for a sore neck?"

"Night. Moonless night. I don't plan to sink us on hidden snags or wander off the main channel. There's supposed to be a lay-by somewhere around here."

"Spend the night in that?" Aleytys shuddered.

He shook his head, a sharp impatient jerk. "No. Of course not. Siglen-du has a bad name. The lay-by's a platform in one of those dead trees. We'll stay there for the night."

She wrinkled her nose at the still, black water under the trees. "What lives in there?"

"According to trader tales, nothing we'd like to meet."

"Have you ever come this way before?"

"No."

"Oh, great!"

"Don't worry. I've listened to trader's talk about the river and the Siglen-du. Besides, I asked Tipylexne." He frowned. "As long as we keep to the main channel, we'll be fine. But, dammit, if we miss the lay-by we'll be in the delta in thick dark."

"I haven't the slightest idea what you're talking about." She looked over her shoulder at the wide ribbon of river unreeling from the line of the horizon. She jerked a thumb at the muddy greenish-brown liquid sliding past the boat. "That doesn't even look like water."

Curiosity widened his cat eyes.

"Trees, I know. Rocks. Grasslands and even deserts. But I've never seen an ocean. Except from up there." She flipped a hand at the sky. "What's a delta?"

"Where . . . huh! there it is." He dug the paddle into the water and began angling the boat inshore.

"Can I help?"

Grunting with effort, he fought the current. "Just sit still," he managed, spitting out each word at the end of a stroke.

The current let go reluctantly but he gradually edged the boat to the right. As soon as he was out of the main channel, the water slowed and he was able to angle more sharply toward the dead giant, thrusting bone-white limbs far out of the thicket of reeds. Then they were in the reeds, poling the boat through the bundled pithy stalks, stirring up foul-smelling mud. Something lay dead not far away. Dead and rotting, the sweet putrefaction hanging in the air like some over-ripe perfume. The stench became unbearable.

Aleytys held her hand over her nose and breathed as shallowly as possible, unwilling to protest because to speak she would have to open her mouth and she deeply didn't want to do that. For the first time since she woke she was glad to have nothing in her stomach.

As Gwynnor shoved the boat through the reeds he stirred up another nuisance, clouds of insects that added a whole new dimension to their discomfort. Landing on every square inch of exposed skin, biting, crawling, the bugs swarmed over them.

Several birds went flapping wildly into the air, their harsh croaks protesting this intrusion into their home place. Aleytys caught fleeting glimpses of water serpents curving silently off into the noisome fluid, and other things she couldn't name but instinctively recognized as something to avoid.

Eventually, Gwynnor brought the boat alongside the bleached white trunk of the dead giant. A laddervine, yellowing with age, climbed up to a large platform a good twenty meters above them.

Batting fretfully at the bugs, Aleytys frowned. "Do we have to stay here?"

"The air'll be cleaner on the platform. Maybe even cooler. Get the packs while I tie up."

"Yes, master."

He looked up quickly, saw her grin, and went back to working the mooring rope through a hole bored in one of the knobby roots.

Aleytys pulled the packs from the nose of the boat and left them sitting on the floorboards by the mast. "I'm afraid to move."

"Want to spend the night down here? With the snakes and the other things?" He grunted with satisfaction as he tested the knot with a quick jerk on the line. "Don't forget the waterskin."

He took two steps and stopped at the mast. "On your feet, Aleytys." He picked up his pack and slid his arms through the loops. As he adjusted the tump strap on his forehead, he went on, "A matter of keeping the ship trimmed. Sudden moves are stupid. Getting out, catch hold of the vine and let it take a lot of your weight before you move. Understand?"

"Easier said." She stood up, cautiously, freezing as the boat rocked under her, starting to breathe again when the swaying damped out. A little more calmly, she slid her feet along the floorboards until she was beside him, her hand just below his on the mast. "What now?"

"Hand me the waterskin. Don't pick up your pack till I'm out of the boat."

"Right." As she moved her pack into position with her foot, he slipped his arm through the shoulder strap of the waterskin. "At least I've acquired a good, empirical notion of what tender means when applied to boats."

"Nothing like experience." He leaned out and caught hold of the laddervine. "Give me your pack as soon as I'm a little way up. You'll have an easier time without it overbalancing you."

"Thanks." She closed her eyes as the boat rocked wildly when he swung onto the vine. She heard little scrabbling sounds as he began climbing.

"Aleytys!"

She pried her eyes open. He was half a meter up the trunk, leaning out, reaching for the pack. Swallowing hastily, one hand locked around the mast, she scooped the pack up and managed to extend it far enough for him to catch hold of the strap.

Agilely as a treecat he swarmed up the vine, disappearing in seconds over the edge of the platform. Almost immediately he came down and stretched out a hand. "Take it slow. Don't try jumping or you'll end up to your waist in the muck."

Aleytys shuddered. Moving with exaggerated care, she pried loose her fingers from the mast and leaned over to catch hold of his hand. She got out of the boat and onto the laddervine with an ease that surprised her. "Hey, you think I'm getting used to this?"

"Come on. The air's a lot better up there."

The platform was about ten meters square, with a bark hut sitting modestly in the center. The packs and the waterskin were piled in a heap beside the reed mat that shielded the doorway. Aleytys took a deep breath for the first time in the last several minutes. A relatively cool, clean breeze swept across the platform, stirring the debris that lay haphazardly all over the sunbleached reed matting. Pieces of bone. Tattered leaves. Bird droppings. Other fragments too small to be identified. She kicked fretfully at the mess, then stretched and sighed.

Gwynnor came backing out of the hut, a battered twig broom in one hand. Brushing the dust and cobwebs off his short fur, he pointed at the platform, then the hut. "You want to clean that or that?"

"I was never that great with heights." She looked at the hut, then up at the sky where dark clouds were beginning to gather. "How watertight do you think the hut is?"

"It's old. About time for the traders to build a new one."

"In other words, we better look forward to a damp night."

The sun was still up when they finished clearing the lay-by. As Gwynnor relieved himself over the edge of the platform, his urine arching wide, Aleytys rummaged in his pack and pulled out the firebowl and its grill. He came back as she was piling small twigs in the hollow and making sure the rounded bottom didn't make contact with the highly combustible reeds.

"Feel better?"

He grinned. "It gives a man a proud feeling."

"Lord of all you survey." She scraped a match over the metal and set the fire burning. "After you wash, maybe you can dig out the waybread and the smoked meat." Gradually, she fed more and more of the twigs until she had a little crackling blaze. Then she fitted the grill in place over the bowl and set the waterpot on it.

Gwynnor came quietly up behind her. He reached over her shoulder with the bread and meat.

"Thanks." She took the food then looked up at the lowering sky. "How long before it rains?"

He knelt beside her, the flames setting, sliding crimson gleams in his short silvery fur and the abundant grey curls clustering over his head. "It comes when it comes."

"You're a big help."

"What difference does it make?" He tore a mouthful from

the loaf and began chewing at the dense, tough, flavor-filled bread.

Aleytys yawned, feeling comfortably tired even after her long sleep. "You're right. Why worry about what I can't change."

As the small fire played warmth over their faces, they chewed placidly in a companionable silence until they finished the bread and meat. The water boiled and Aleytys tipped in the cha leaves, swirled them around vigorously, then poured the steaming liquid into the two mugs.

Sipping at the cha, they moved to the western edge of the platform and sat crosslegged, watching the sun dip slowly behind the treetops. The sunset was spectacular, the dark rain clouds flushing gold, then crimson, then purple, then slowly darkening as the last tip of the rusty sun vanished.

"Aleytys."

"Mmmh?"

"This morning. What was wrong?"

She swirled the dregs of the cha, watching the leaf fragments circle the bottom of the cup. "A mourning time," she said slowly. "The cludair were so relieved when I left. I couldn't help remembering that I had no home. No place where I really belong. I liked them, you know."

"I know."

"I thought they liked me."

He touched her arm. "They did, Aleytys. Tipylexne, Qilasc, all of them, they felt you were a friend."

"Still . . . they were happy when we left. That hurt." She fell silent again, eyes fixed blindly on the mug, now held still between her palms.

When she spoke again, her words came slowly, the syllables dragging under the heavy weight of her desolation. "I haven't cried like that for two years. I cried a little in nightmares but was dry-eyed in the day. I think I was mourning for my lost innocence, for the friends of my childhood I'll never see again, for the three men I have loved and used to their destruction." She set the mug beside her and began rubbing her palms up and down over her thighs. "Vajd . . . father of my baby, my first lover, my teacher and my conscience. Any goodness I have in me I owe to him. He had his eyes torn from his head because of me. I went from him to Miks Stavver, my starthief. A loner and a clever man. I used him. I forced him on pain of insanity to go searching for my stolen baby. He didn't want to do that. I wonder where he is now, if he found my Sharl, my baby. From him I went to my gentle nayid Burash. He . . . I . . . I saw him burned to ash half a meter from me when he ran to warn me of danger. My god, he ran out and the guard burned him. Two steps from me. Two damn steps." She looked down at Gwynnor's hand resting on her arm. "You see what happens to men who try to help me." Shaking off his touch, she rubbed her hands across her face. "Well, that's it. All the terrors and needs and wretchednesses that add up to my being in this place at this time. And it all landed on me this morning."

He nodded. "I know a little about losing friends. And lovers."

"Your teacher."

"Yes." He held her hand between his, his higher body temperature making a pool of comforting warmth around her fingers. "You're going on?"

"What else can I do? I have to find my baby."

"How long are you going to be in the city?"

"Depends on how soon I can get on a ship. A day. A week. A month." She shrugged. "It's hard to make plans without data. What about you?"

"I have to make peace with my family, see what's happening around home. Do a little thinking." A few large drops struck against his back. "Rain's here."

She laughed unsteadily. "It announces itself."

Together they drowned the last embers of the fire, and pushed everything else into the hut, leaving only the water pot and the mugs out to catch as much water as they could.

Book II:

THE CITY

Chapter I

Gwynnor swung the tiller, aiming the boat across the current toward the blunt wharf. As the boat slid neatly beside the landing, Aleytys stepped out and snubbed the bow rope about the mooring post. Gwynnor watched her straighten and toss her head back, letting the brisk sea breeze blow through her bright hair. He smiled at the unconscious ease with which she coped with the problems of moving in a touchy boat. Two weeks sailing had done that for her. He bent forward and swung her pack onto the heavy planking.

"End of the line." Her voice was hoarse. She looked at him sadly.

"You remember what I told you?" He felt a sudden reluctance to let her go.

She nodded. "Up the stairs." Turning away, she swung a hand toward the wooden stairway crawling up the cliffside in repeated uneven zigzags. "Then past the market and past cerddtown. To the monorail. The road splits there, going one way to the port and the other to Star Street. And the rest of the city is dangerous for me. I should keep away from it."

He looked down, his fingers playing with the tiller bar and plucking at the rope. Then he lifted his head. "Cast off the rope, Aleytys." As the boat swung away from the wharf, he called, "Good faring."

Letting the boat drift slowly toward midchannel, he watched her climbing up the cliff, moving from landing to landing, looking back continually, her body getting smaller and smaller until the last detail he could make out was the shining red-gold of her hair. She halted momentarily as she reached the top, waved a last time, then disappeared.

Gwynnor rubbed his hands over his face, then got briskly to work, letting the boom swing out to take maximum advantage of the brisk following wind.

It was very early, the sun a fingernail clipping on the horizon behind him. The morning sea breeze was fresh and steady, coming in off the ocean, blowing west where he wanted to go. He wound the sheets around a cleat and settled at the tiller, keeping watch for snags and sandbars though the Company kept this part of the river dredged free. They liked their vegetables and meat fresh and plentiful.

He chuckled. Less than a month before he'd have found only evil in this dredging. A destruction of things as they always had been. He felt immensely older, even wiser, though that made him smile a little at himself. But he had changed and he felt the change was an improvement.

The morning passed pleasantly and quickly. A little before noon he reached the landing of Derwyn grawh, his home village. He tied up in the shadow of a pair of ancient wrinkled oaks, two of the many that gave the village its name. After making sure the boat was neatly tucked away close to the bank, he slung the pack over his shoulder and strolled slowly along the pale tan sand of the rutted roadway.

The road curved out around the planting of cyforedd trees set in a gentle arc between river and village to protect the people from the caprices of wandering water demons. The dry, tart smell of their fluttering clusters of long, thin, green-grey needles, their papery many-pieced bark, brought intense and painful memories tumbling back.

He stopped by the tree nearest the road and touched the trunk for luck. His back turned to the village, he lingered there, stripping loose small fragments of brittle bark, sniffing with a painful pleasure at the sharp, biting scent of the needles. Too many hard words were said at the time he left, words difficult to unsay now.

But time was passing. He shrugged the pack a little higher on his shoulder, took a deep breath, then stepped back into the middle of the road.

He turned the first bend. Rhisiart's house. Gwynnor frowned. The iorweg vine climbing over the rustic stone wall was torn and turning brown. In one place the wall itself was broken, the tumbled stones lying haphazardly about, some even sitting out in the road with a two-week film of green lichen spreading over them.

The gate was broken, with only the bottom hinge to hold the shattered, charred timbers in place. And there were weeds growing between the flags that led past the house to the smithy. Weeds? In Rhisiart's yard? Modlen would never . . .

Modlen? Feeling a chill congealing in his middle, he moved on, walking more quickly, almost running.

He glanced along the roadway before he turned into Blodeuyn's lane, intending to see his father before he went on into the village for news. The village square was empty. Shaking his head, he jogged down the lane toward the family farm.

Gwilym's farm. He let out the breath he hadn't realized he was holding. The wall was intact, the iorweg green and abundant, tumbling over the stone in exuberantly healthy growth. But the gate was shut. In the middle of the day? And there was an unaccustomed silence behind the walls.

The stillness shook his fragile calm until he was almost afraid of breaking it, but he pulled the bell rope, shivering as he heard the harsh clang-clank of the cowbell.

A deep male voice demanded his identity.

"Treforis?" Gwynnor's knees shook and there was a slight tremble in the name.

"Who. . . ."

"Gwynnor."

"Alone?"

"Yes. What's wrong? Where's father?" He heard scraping sounds, then the gate swung open. Treforis stepped out, swung his head hurriedly from side to side, scanning as much of the lane as was visible. Gwynnor frowned. "I told you I was alone."

Treforis glanced hurriedly at the sky, then grinned at his younger brother. "Come in, then. Don't stand around, lad." He caught hold of Gwynnor's arm, dragging him through the gate. "Hold still a minute." He swung the gate to and slammed double bars into their heavy cast-iron hooks.

Moving at a trot, responding to the intense sense of urgency in the bigger man, they circled the lone cyforredd planted as house guardian before the door, then stepped through the formal maze and walked more slowly into the silent dim interior of the old house.

Treforis stopped just inside and shouted, "Esyllt. Bring wine. My brother is home." He touched Gwynnor's shoulder with a big shaking hand as if, in touching his brother, he reassured himself. The woman's startled face appeared in a doorway then disappeared as she went back into the woman's hold to fetch the wine.

"Forgive, Gwyn?" Treforis shook his massive head. "Not

much of a homecoming for you. But we can sit by the fire and trade lies a little." Abruptly, he caught Gwynnor in a warm hug then thrust him back, running measuring eyes over him. "You're looking older. And bigger. Maybe you'll reach mansize yet, little brother. Come." Like a gusty wind he blew through the hallway and into the familiar manroom. He pushed Gwynnor into one of the big wing chairs and pulled the other around so he was facing him, a small fire crackling on the hearth between them.

Esyllt came in with a wine jug and two glasses on a tray. "Welcome home, brother." She smiled, her pleasant face beaming with her delight in seeing him again. She set the tray on a small table beside her man and left them to their talking.

Gwynnor sipped at the golden wine, finding as much pleasure in the memories it evoked as he did in its mellow taste. "I expected a colder welcome."

Treforis sighed. "The father always held you dearest to his heart, little one, so it hurt him most to see you renounce him."

"I'm not a child," Gwynnor said sharply. "Stop treating me like one."

"All right. All right." Treforis gulped at the wine then set the glass down. "Still . . ."

Relaxing, his feet stretched out before him, Gwynnor frowned down at the glass he held between his two palms. "I can't see that, Tref, the way he kept carping at me." For the moment he pushed aside the implications of his father's absence.

"It was his way." Treforis' deep, slow voice came down heavy on the second word, forcing Gwynnor to face what he didn't want to know.

"Was?"

"Two months ago. Company man raided the shrine for maranhedd. Father was there like he always was after a good day of selling in the market. You know him. Too stubborn to let a bunch of bastards destroy a holy place." Treforis tapped his large fingers on the chair arms, his amiable face turned sad and brooding. "They burned him to ash. Like they did all the others there."

Gwynnor closed his eyes, the loss hurting more than he cared to acknowledge even to himself. Treforis left him in peace to deal with the shock in his own way, showing a sensitivity that he usually kept well-hidden behind a brusque, blunt exterior.

"How many raids since then?"

"We don't keep count. At first they were after the maranhedd. They kept hitting traders' pack trains. Like the time they nearly got you. So the traders stopped coming. Then they broke the shrine. After that they began going into the houses looking for it."

"Breudwedda?"

"Killed her with the shrine. Burned the place to the ground. No telling who was what. Killed them all. Even little Eveh, the youngest dysqwera. She used to run after you and athro Micangl. You remember."

"I remember. Holy Maeve, Treforis."

The big man shrugged. "After there was no more maranhedd on the maes and no Breudwedda to dream with it in any village, we started to lift our heads a little, thinking there would be no more raids. Some of the lads went on kaffan to the other villages. That's how we knew. Then we thought the Company men were finished with us."

"Thought?"

"Ay. We were wrong. We had one month free, just enough to start cleaning up the mess. Then they came back."

"For what?" He leaned forward, feeling intense curiosity.

"People. Young healthy lads and lasses. Taken alive."

"Why?"

"Who knows? We can't ask Breudwydda. She's ash. I thought maybe you might know more than I, having been with Dylaw and seeing more than us of the starmen."

Gwynnor frowned, swirling the golden wine around the bowl of his glass. "I don't know . . ." He tilted his head and stared blindly at the ceiling. "If she's right . . . damn . . . she said something . . . there was something . . . a wrongness . . . about the Director . . . the starmen have changed in the past year . . . she said . . ."

"She?" Treforis grinned. "I thought you'd taken up with that Amersit. So you're on the woman track now."

Gwynnor lowered his head and grinned back. "I had a stormtime you never saw the like of, Tref. She was a starwitch with hair the color of fire. She'd frizzle your ears, brother."

"Starwitch?" He scowled. "Starwitch!"

"Forget it. That's over. What about Catlin?"

"Our sister took up with Meurig Rhisiartson. They're trying to get the smithy going again, working at night, doing a little bit at a time."

"What happened there?"

"One of the first snatch raids. Company men tried for Rhisiart's daughter. You remember Sioned?"

Gwynnor nodded, remembering the small, eager face of the girl who refused to accept women's roles and got her way through the intensity of her perseverance. Rhisiart had even begun to teach her metalworking. "They got her?"

"No. You know what a bull old Rhisiart was. He came roaring at them, held them long enough for her to get to the fields. They made the mistake of crowding around him, and by the time they managed a clear shot at him, he'd kicked in a couple of heads and Sioned had gone to ground. Meurig was over here courting Catlin. We all heard the noise and came to do what we could, but by the time we got there, Rhisiart was burnt meat and Modlen dying after skewering the shooter with a kitchen knife. The Company men were gone, leaving their dead abandoned in the road."

"Sioned?"

"She hides out somewhere. We don't ask. Comes into town at night, sometimes, to have a jug of wine in Morgha's tavern and listen to the freemen talk. She gets food from one farm or another. The women keep her in clean clothes. Not a good life but, at least, the Company men can't get their damn hands on her. We all stay in the house in daylight. With ax and sword close to hand. Dartguns when we have them. It's been a week since they've tried to take anyone. More than a few of the bastards went home bloody last time. Ha!"

"They don't come at night?"

"Not so far." He shifted in his chair, drained his glass and slammed it down on the tray. "It's a poor homecoming, lad."

Gwynnor held out his glass. Treforis refilled it, then emptied the bottle in his own. The brothers raised their wine in a wordless toast then settled into a companionable silence, sipping at the fragrant liquid and watching the coals glow crimson and blue.

The wine warmed the tiredness and depression out of Gwynnor. He looked up. "What about the farm?"

"Growing weeds. Who's going to take a chance working out in the fields by day? And what the hell can you do at night?" He shook his head despondently.

Gwynnor ran his eyes over the solid figure in the chair across from him. The low flickering light emphasized the touch of russet in his brother's short silky fur and in the tight-wound curls between his pointed ears. A quick surge of affection warmed him. "What's the cut-off point?"

"Um. We can still salvage something if we get at the land by the end of the month." He moved a hand impatiently. "After that . . . well, it won't be an easy winter."

"Breudwydda's out but what about the village council?"

"Dithering." Treforis snorted. "Boundary disputes and market spaces. Birth lists. Death records. Kaffon pedigrees. That's all they're good for. They sit around with mouths moving but nothing comes out." He drained the glass and set it on the table. "Worthless."

"Anyone at all trying to do something about the raids?"

"Yeah. I told you. Defending the holds."

"Anything else?"

Treforis rested his hands on his massive thighs. He shook his head. "Like I said, a bunch of freemen without the responsibilities of farm and family meet at Morgha's tavern to trade lies about the great things they'd do, given the chance. I don't get to the village that often, don't like to leave Esyllt and the kids alone." He chuckled at Gwynnor's inquiring eyebrow. "Five of them now and another come spring." He slapped his large hands on his thighs. "Dammit, Gwyn, if I don't work the fields, how many of them will be alive come spring?"

Gwynnor set the glass beside the chair, too sick at heart to relish the wine any longer. "And no one's doing anything but talk."

Treforis moved his shoulders impatiently. "No one knows a damn thing anyone can do. Enough of this nonsense. How's your life gone since last we spoke?"

Chapter II

Aleytys watched the sail bloom as the small boat began moving upstream. She waved one last time, then stepped away from the railing, ducking her head to slip off the tump strap, a nuisance now she was walking on a level.

A brisk breeze stirred the thin layer of grit on the stone and sent the pulleys hanging out over the precipice on the ends of massive towers creaking with irritating irregularity. As she walked past the empty tables and deserted booths of the silent market, Aleytys frowned and looked to her right where the sculpted hill rose brilliant green and white against the pale blue of the sky. Hedges. Trees. Patches of lawn. Rings of houses, sterile and silent. Silent. Empty.

She trudged up the road, sand creaking loudly under her boots, the whine of the wind shrill and petulant in her ears.

Behind a row of trees with clusters of dusty green leaves thin as needles planted in a shallow curve, she saw a double row of small sandstone houses, their orderly gardens drying up for lack of tending hands, doors kicked in, gaping windows. A desolation where a neat pleasant village had been. As she stared at the houses, a pale cerdd face appeared briefly in one of the broken windows but the old male jerked out of sight when he saw her watching. She got the impression of hate and madness and threw up her shields.

Growing more troubled as she walked on, Aleytys moved back to the main road and trudged around the edge of the steeply sloping hill. The grassy slant beside her climbéd several meters, then leveled out at the first terrace. White plasticrete boxes crowded one against the other, with meager walks and an occasional window box with greenery or native flowers adding a timid patch of color against the white. On the next terrace small, individual houses sat in thin green strips of lawn. Painfully neat, painfully regimented, each one almost like every other one with only minor differences, like

120

those slight variations the friction of living imposes on identical twins. Regimented people living regimented lives in regimented houses. So Arel had said. She shivered, thinking about it. For a moment she wondered how the smuggler captain was doing. For a moment she wished with a gentle nostalgia that she was back with the three of them, hopping from world to world, using ingenuity, guess, and luck to pick up cargoes worth enough to pay ship costs and give the crew some pleasant nights ashore.

The third terrace was where the technicians lived, the engineers and doctors and minor administrators who kept the city alive and moving smoothly through its endless repetition of days. And accountants and chemists and courtesans and entertainers who dreamed they were freer than the servants, looking down on the white boxes of the lower levels with delicate scorn. Their houses were, on the surface, more individual, but they shared a subtle sameness that indicated their owners' acceptance of an insidiously imposed servitude. That level made Aleytys feel uneasy. She shifted her eyes further up.

On the fourth terrace, the landscaping was extensive and pushed to a heteromorphism so extravagant that it merged, at times, with the grotesque—an extravagance that, by its deliberate protest, affirmed the attitude of mind existing on the lower levels. She caught glimpses of ivory towers with convoluted complications visible even at this distance; the dream palaces where those with sufficient pedigree and sufficient credit could enjoy the unique dream sensations of maranhedd.

And at the very top of the edge of the eastern cliffs, looking out over the sea, the Director's citadel, with a glass-walled turret rising high and massive over the veil of greenery. And to one side, the twin towers of the monorail.

The monorail. It slashed up the hill twenty meters above the soil and rock. As she walked the road she could see the towers and the silver, gleaming streak of the rail. A three-car train flashed overhead, stopping briefly at the tech level before finally ending its journey at the palazzos. As she watched, three figures diminished by distance stepped from the forward car and moved quickly out of sight.

Aleytys turned her back on them and looked thoughtfully along the rail. Eyes searching for the far end, she moved into shadow then came out the other side. In the distance, lower and to her left, she could see distance-blued buildings and the sun-shimmered noses of several starships.

Excitement rising in her, she closed her eyes and murmured, "Hey, everyone. There's where we have to get. Think we can make it?"

Three sets of eyes blinked open. Three faces came out of darkness at the back of her head.

"Just how much do you want us to massage your ego, young Aleytys?" Harskari sniffed, her amber eyes narrowed. "Don't talk. Do. Then we can admire."

"Hey, isn't that a little rough?" Shadith frowned in her turn. "So she needs a little reassurance. Don't we all?"

Swardheld chuckled. "Ignore them, freyka. They're sour because Harskari's been reaming our singer about talking too much to the cerdd."

"Still?" Aleytys rubbed her nose. "At least they were quiet about it. Madar! If the three of you started brangling aloud, my poor head would shatter." She sighed. "Anyway, Star Street, here we come. I wonder if that poor innocent enclave is ready for the likes of us."

As she came around the continuous curve she saw a red sandstone wall joined solidly to the suddenly sheer cliff as if a part of the mountain had been sliced away to make room for the enclave. Ahead, the road vanished through a pointed arch semiobscured by the flickering film of a force field. When she reached the arch, Aleytys poked a finger at the screen, the rubbery invisibility resisting the intrusion, then letting the finger through. "One-way iris. Once in, I'm stuck." She glanced over her shoulder at the carefully landscaped mountain and the slope on the other side bluing into the distant plain. Gwynnor's loved Maes. She could see the thin line of the river winding in long curves toward the rising sun. Gwynnor. He'd be on that river somewhere . . . and out there . . . on the plain . . . a simple life tied to the earth and the seasons . . . a good life . . . for a moment she was tempted to turn around, to let the complicated threads of her life fall loose. The sea breeze sneaked around the mountain, blowing wisps of hair across her face, carrying the sea's pungent salt smells and the crisp green odor from the trees and the fresh-mowed lawns. The sand under her boots crackled as she shifted her feet. The russet sun just clearing the dim eastern horizon shone with increasing warmth on her skin. A good life . . .

Then the monorail car squealed past, sliding down the rail

toward the distant starport, kicking up a swirl of sand that stung her out of her dream. And it was only a dream. There was no place for her here. She squared her shoulders and stepped through the membrane.

The red sandstone walls rose high and solid around the enclave. On her left, the cliff hung precariously over the mountain side of the street, its shadow lying deep and frigid on the pavement. There was a fringe of green at the top, the only living green visible on Star Street. On her right, an equally massive wall rose high and daunting over squalid buildings.

She looked around as she moved with hesitant, slow steps down the street toward the center of the enclave. On the cliffside ugly, blocky buildings backed onto the rock, plasticrete-blown on a prefab form, painted garish colors. Heavy steel shutters rolled down over the lower floor windows. Doors closed, locked up in this place that began coming alive only about sundown. The sea breeze swooping down over the walls blew fragments of paper down the narrow plasticrete street. Sludgy water in the gutters. Thick. Black. With greenish scum around the edges and a faintly sour smell. On the wallside, narrow alleys crept back into stinking shadow, little more than shoulder-wide cracks between the structures fronting the street, leading to the other crazy buildings growing like starlings' nests glued to the outer wall.

She stepped over the outflung hand of a drunk snoring on the sidewalk. Further down the street a man came from a building, yawned, rubbed his stomach, then ambled across the street, disappearing down one of the alleys. She felt a faint relief and the eeriness of the empty morning clicked suddenly into solid mundanity.

Garish flashing signs were cold gray on buildings that had managed to accumulate a thick patina of grime, especially at the shoulder level where thousands of groping hands had pawed in search of a precarious equilibrium before tacking off down street to one of the dingy hostels.

She shivered, depressed by the tawdry, dingy street too visibly revealed by the clear morning light. She walked on, sand grains from the road outside still clinging to her soles, crunching loudly against the roughened surface of the plasticrete sidewalk.

A man slammed folding bars aside and came yawning into the street, pulling a hose behind him. Still yawning, he thumbed the catch on the nozzle and sprayed a stream of water on the sidewalk in front of his shop, hosing the gutter there clear of its accumulated filth. Aleytys grimaced and stepped back as drops of turgid water splashed on her boots. They were dusty and caked with mud but that was clean dirt. She shuddered to think that liquids and muck mingled in the gutter puddles.

"Watch where you're pointing that thing." She glared at the pudgy man.

He turned to stare at her. He had furry, gray eyebrows and a bald head. The brows wiggled up, pushing the smooth freckled skin on his head into corrugated wrinkles. Aleytys realized, abruptly, that she'd forgotten to switch languages and had been talking in cathl maes.

She shrugged. "Forget it," she said in interlingue.

He shut off the flow of water until she was past him, then went back to spraying the front of his shop.

Along this stretch of Star Street, shopkeepers were coming out one by one to look up and down the street and yell insults to each other. Though the bars remained tightly shuttered and dark, the other shopkeepers were slowly getting their places ready for business, though obviously in no hurry about it. The silence of the street began filling up with voices. Small groups accumulating and breaking up, some sleepy grousing, and a few appreciative noises as Aleytys moved past them.

She glanced casually in windows as she went by. Junk of all kinds, bright and cheap to catch the transient visitor's eyes. Carved wood and embroidery from the villages in the plains. Bits of lace. Bright ribbons. Drugs. Depilatories. Packaged food. Thread and needles. Repair kits. Knives. Tools. Guns. Pornography. Books. Jewelry. A herbalist's shop, its sign, a case of acupuncture needles in self-glo plastic hanging above the dusty door, with ginseng roots preserved in an anonymous amber fluid sitting on shelves in the window along with snakeskins and other less identifiable leaves and powders. She hovered in front of the barred window, peering into the dim, dusty interior, fascinated by the strange images on fly-specked charts.

Then the breeze brought the smell of cooking food. She was suddenly ravenous. Following the drifting scent, feet moving faster and faster, she hurried along the street, passing other shops, other beings—human and otherwise—ignoring both in the growing urgency of her hunger.

A sign glowed feebly, its bright colors turned sickly in competition with sunlight. Bran's. A name? The steel shutter was rolled into a compact rod above an entranceway masked with dripping lines of polished seeds. The bead curtain clattered loudly as she pushed the strings aside and stepped into the warm, odorous interior.

"A minute, dearie. Let old Bran get her pies sizzling."

Aleytys moved to the wide counter and slid onto a high, backless stool. The counter was a solid piece of wood, a hand's breadth thick, with a hinged section to let Bran into the small, square room where several tables sat upon a new-waxed floor, their wooden tops shining with the same care and effort expended on the counter.

Bran was a massive female, big rather than fat, her skin stretched smoothly taut over the heavy muscle beneath. She stood with her back to the shop, dropping folds of pastry into bubbling hot oil, pies that looked small in her large, shapely hands. Her hair was silvery white, thick and straight, woven into two braids that were pinned into neat coils over each long-lobed ear. Long, elaborate earrings dangled beside her heavy neck, swaying with a delicacy that contrasted absurdly with the aura of formidable strength that clung to the old woman.

As the last pie dropped neatly into place, the water can on the stove began to whistle wetly. Bran snatched up a rag in one hand and a cha pot in the other. She tilted the boiling water over the crips curled leaves, adding the brisk astringent scent of brewing cha to the other tantalizing odors filling the shop.

For two weeks, Aleytys had swallowed journey bread that had grown staler and staler. Had washed smoked meat down with stale, lukewarm water. She laughed. "If I don't eat soon, despina, I'll be jumping you."

The old woman chuckled. "I'm too tough for tender teeth like yours, dearie. What will you be having?"

Aleytys pulled a handful of coins from her tunic pocket. "Depends on your prices," she murmured, poking at her meager supply of money with a forefinger. "A cup of cha to start."

Bran fished a mug from under the counter and filled it with the steaming amber-brown fluid. "Half drach."

"Ah, and those rolls?" She pointed to a pyramid of nut rolls heaped high on a platter that stood on a shelf beside the stove. Rolls glistening with brown-gold glaze, crusted with nuts, exuding the tantalizing yeasty smell of fresh-baked bread.

"Half drach the three."

"I'll have three." She sniffed appreciatively at the meat pies crisping in the oil. "And those?"

"A drach apiece."

"I'll have two of those when they're done." She counted out the coins and put the remainder back in her pocket.

Bran set the rolls in front of her and turned back to her bumping pies, flipping them over deftly with a quick flip of her spatula. Then she poured a mug of cha for herself and leaned against the counter, sipping at it and watching complacently as Aleytys tore into the hot, light bread. "Good?"

Aleytys swallowed and cleared her mouth with a gulp of cha. "Very. You made them?"

"Always had a good hand with pastry and bread," she sniffed. "Pies ready in a minute." Leaving her mug on the counter, she took up a woven wire scoop and skimmed the pies from the oil, sliding them neatly onto a draining rack. "You're new here. Crewin' a ship or workin' the street?"

"Neither at the moment."

Bran left the pies to drain and picked up her mug. With the sharper demands of her hunger appeased, Aleytys took time to examine her hostess. The huge old woman's eyes slanted obliquely, almond-shaped, black as coal, and brilliant with the lively spirit encased in her flesh. Her face was broad, the features large but still attractive. The only real sign of her age were the tiny wrinkles, less than a millimeter deep, tracking across her dark ocher skin into olive shadows at temples and jaw, sinking slightly deeper at the corner of her eyes and around her smile.

The black eyes measured Aleytys. "You'll never make a street girl, hon. Not flashy enough and too intelligent looking. Though you'd polish well, make a helluva asset to a high-class house. Not that you'd find one of those on Star Street. Going uphill?" She jerked her head backwards toward the cliff looming over her shop.

"No!"

"All right, glad to hear it. Ain't many starships come here with women crew."

Aleytys shrugged.

"Jumped ship, huh? Well, you picked a bad world for that,

hon. The Company don't hire women except as laybacks. I suppose you did what you had to, though." She sighed. "Let me give you a bit of advice, dearie. You stay on Star Street. I don't care what any of those bastards on the hill promise you, don't believe 'em. I know. Here, you might be poor, but you're free. Livin' inside these walls might look like we was in prison—well, these walls don't shut free air out, they shut it in. Go up hill 'f you don't believe me."

"Oh, I believe you, despina."

"Bran, hon. Too old for that fancy stuff." Her eyes went dreamy. "Was a time I had men bidding for me. Huh!" She glowered at the cha. "I had to go and listen to a smooth-talking snake. You watch out for them snakes when they come crawling down from their fancy houses for a bit of unregulated fun, you hear me, girl?"

Aleytys chuckled. "Thanks." She hesitated. The old woman radiated a curiously intense good will for her and she decided to trust it. "It's not a thing I want broadcasted, but if you hear of a way offworld . . ."

Bran sipped at the cha, then grinned at her. "Any place special?"

"In toward center. That's all."

"I'll keep an ear open. How many pies you said?"

"Two."

The pies went quickly. Feeling replete and deeply contented, Aleytys let Bran refill the mug and sat leaning on the counter, sipping at the strong, revivifying liquid.

"I need a place to stay while I'm here." She sighed and set down the mug. "Someplace reasonably clean and not too expensive."

"And a good lock on the door." Bran sniffed at the startled look on Aleytys' face. "You should know that. Some of those crumbs over there'd sell you for the chance to lick a Company man's arse."

Aleytys chuckled. "I can protect myself, though I'd rather not have to."

"A little thing like you?" Bran snorted, measuring Aleytys' wrist between thumb and forefinger. "I could break you in two without half tryin'."

"You might be surprised."

"Mmph. A room. Let me see. Blue's full up just now and she don't like women much anyway. Daywel? Laziest bastard I ever saw. Take you a year to shovel the filth out of his place. Kathet? He's got rooms and they're cheap. Except he got a lot of drunks and scrot smokers. They go funny, sometimes. Me, I wouldn't go in his place after dark if you paid me. Now Firetop runs a tight house. He'd give you a room if I asked. Lose yourself in the crowd, keep the Company spies from wonderin' about you." She pursed her lips and opened her hands, scanning the palms. "And there's Tintin."

"What's wrong with him?"

"Nothing much. Prices are a sin and a shame, but he don't hold with folks messin' around in his place. Mostly he gets the top techs on the starships. Lot of Captains stay there when they're not on their ships or up the hill. Some travelers, too. Trouble is, Company spies check it out all the time. You don't want them nosin' at you."

"That's twice you've said something about Company spies."

"Yeah, and twice too much. They sneak around listenin' to folks talk and keepin' an eye on money goin' in and out. We pay taxes for the privilege of squattin' here and those bastards are lookin' to squeeze the last drach out of us."

"How can you be sure I'm not one of them?"

Bran burst out laughing, holding her thick body and rocking back and forth on her heels. When she sputtered back to sobriety she said, "No females in that bunch. You think they'd trust a woman?"

"Their loss." She tapped fingers on the countertop. "Tintin's place. The ship captains really go there?"

Bran nodded. "You be careful, hon. Pick the wrong one to talk to and you'll end uphill, after all."

Aleytys nodded. She turned so she could look out the windows at the front of the shop. "I might need some kind of work if I have to stay a while."

A man walked past the shop, stumbling, swaying, his face drawn into a mindless scowl. Bran slapped the counter open and strode across the room, indignation snapping through her forceful movements. She thrust the bead strings aside and looked down the street after the shambling man. Then she strode back muttering, wiggled through the counter, slammed the leaf shut, and leaned on the slab, red-faced with anger.

Aleytys rubbed her thumb beside her nose. "What's wrong with him?"

"Never seen a scrot smoker before? Huh! K'Ruffin should have his butt kicked letting Henner on the street in that condition. What you saw was a murder on its way to happenin'.

Or a suicide, if Henner runs into someone tougher." She slammed her fist down on the counter, making the wood boom with the force of the blow. "That's the third time he's slipped up." More composedly, she explained. "He runs a smokeshop back by the wall. Supposed to lock the creeps in when they're on the stuff. Dammit, he must of got hooked on his own crud." She sighed and calmed down. "If he did, he won't last long. Lovax has been itchin' for a spot. Too bad. That young fruff's a slimy slug, the kind makes you want to pop it with your foot and then sorry you had to touch the thing. Reminds me. Keep away from him; he likes to play with knives."

Aleytys shuddered and turned so she was sitting with her side to the counter. There was a little lukewarm cha left in the mug. She sipped at it, then set the mug down, retreating into a calm contentment, absurd in the situation, but warm and comfortable. The hard, driving rush was over. She had plenty of time, the whole day ahead of her and a space of time after that for resting while she schemed her way offworld. She dropped a half drach on the counter and accepted another cup of cha. "What's your fruff look like?"

"Dark hair, dark eyes. Tall. Thin. Makes a good first impression. For about five minutes, maybe."

Aleytys chuckled, sniffed at the cha and swallowed a mouthful. "Happens. I met a woman once. Small, pretty, a porcelain doll. She had the personality of a pit viper. How do I find Tintin's place?"

Bran tapped the counter with her long, beautiful fingers. "Go that way," she nodded her head to the right, "till you reach the center square where the road to the starport takes off. On the east side is Dryknolte's Tavern. Tintin's place sits on the other corner. Minik, the jeweler, is next to him. It's got a name, um . . . Starman's Rest . . . no one ever calls it that. Just Tintin's place."

"What about a job?"

"What can you . . ."

The bead curtain exploded inward. Henner leaped through, landing in a crouch in the middle of the room, mouth working over incoherent obscenities, clutching a bloody knife in each hand. He turned glaring red eyes from Bran to Aleytys and back again. His mumbling grew louder.

Cautiously, Bran began inching a hand back toward the edge of counter, her broad face impassive.

With a sudden wild shriek, Henner straightened, threw the knife in his right hand, crouched again, muttering and rocking from side to side on his toes, eyes flicking around the room, stopping on invisible menaces. He snarled and threatened these with the remaining knife.

Bran clutched at her upper right arm, hand splayed out around the bobbing knife hilt, blood oozing from between her fingers. Inside, she was seething with fury, but cool caution kept a lid on it. Aleytys shivered as the soup of emotion in the small room threatened to overload her senses. Hastily, she pulled up her shields and sucked in a quavering breath.

Henner heard the sound, wheeled to face her, lunged at her, knife thrust point out, shrieking hate.

The diadem chimed. She felt the air stiffen while Swardheld snatched control of her body. He slid off the stool, catching Henner's arm, turning the knife. The diadem chimed again and Henner's interrupted leap drove his body forward onto the knife, thrusting the blade into his throat.

"Hai, you're quick." Bran stared at the girl, astonishment sagging her heavy jowls.

Swardheld turned, nodded, then climbed back on the stool and loosed his hold on Aleytys' body. "I wish you hadn't done that," she whispered, and heard an unconvinced grunt rumbling against her skull. She sighed, recognizing futility when she saw it.

Bran was leaning heavily against the counter. Aleytys touched her tentatively. "Is there a doctor I can . . ."

"Doctor? Phah! He's stretched out in k'Ruffin's den worse off than Henner here. Want to help . . . get that . . . that rag . . . there . . ." She waggled her head at a line of hooks where snowy white rags hung ready to wipe the counter or polish glasses and mugs. Her words were coming out in spurts. "Get . . . get the knife . . . out."

"No." Aleytys sighed. "I didn't want to . . . I'm a healer, Bran. Relax. You'll be whole in . . ." Voice trailing off in a whisper, she slid off the stool and braced her arms on the counter. She jerked out the knife and let it fall unheeded as she clamped her hands over the spurting wound. She reached out and the waters of the power river splashed down over them, pouring into the gaping wound, driving the cells to furious growth, dropping to a melodic humming as it played with blood cells, making them double and redouble until the blood loss was replaced. Then, flicking a last time through

Aleytys, cleansing the fatigue from her body, the image faded and she stood, blinking slowly, blood-stained hands holding tight to the old woman's arm.

Sighing again, Aleytys unclamped her fingers and settled back on the stool poking distastefully at the sticky blood on her hands and wrists.

Bran inspected her arm. The pierce wound was a faint line of pink that, even as she watched, seemed paling to her usual matte ocher. "That's a useful trick, dearie." She dipped the end of a clean rag in a water can and mopped the blood off her arm, shaking her head and clucking like an old hen. Then she turned to Aleytys. "Hold out your hands." With gentle, meticulous care she washed the blood away and dried the hands that looked baby small next to hers.

Aleytys flexed her fingers. "I'd rather you didn't tell anyone what happened."

"Why not? You'd make a fortune."

"As a psi-freak?"

Bran dropped the cloth in the laundry bin, frowning. "I see. Lots of fools around even on Star Street."

"What about him?" Aleytys jerked a thumb at Henner's body. "I don't want trouble."

"Ha. Wait here, hon." Bran grinned. "I figure you could take care of any bastard starting trouble in here." She slapped the counter open and edged through. "K'Ruffin made this mess and he can damn well clean it up." She charged out of the shop.

Aleytys poured another cup of cha and waited.

Ten minutes later, Bran swept back through the swaying beads, a small, greenish, insectoid being trailing after her, chittering querulously, hunched over under the barrage of Bran's verbal attack. Behind him a tall blue humanoid ducked his bullet head under the lintel and stepped inside to stand blank-faced beside k'Ruffin, flexing immense muscles until they rippled like ocean waves under his thick blue hide. He was totally hairless, not even eyebrows. His pointed ears twitched and moved about restlessly, his eyes were round and yellow, narrowed in the morning light since he was more nocturnal in habit than the others in the room. His mouth was very tiny for his size and, lacking lips, it pursed together like a sphincter. Aleytys shivered as she scanned him. He exuded a total indifference to the other life forms around him, was merely impatient at the fuss, wanting to get back to something he had been doing; Aleytys refused to imagine what that might be.

"You keep better watch on your creeps, k'Ruff'n. That berserker could have killed me! And Lovax is on your tail. He's hungry, you idiot. You ain't much but you're a wide place better than him. Now, clear this mess out of my place. I don't want no Company spies walking in on a corpse."

K'Ruffin shuddered. His stubby antennas drooped dejectedly. With short, simple words, he directed the other being to pick Henner's body up and follow him. Then the oddly assorted pair stumped out of the cookshop.

Bran nudged at the bloodstain with her toe. "That sets and it'll be a pain in the ass getting out of the wood." She shrugged and went back behind the counter.

"What was that?"

"K'Ruffin? I told you about him."

"No. The other."

"The big one. A Hasheen. He's other, all right."

"He made my skin crawl."

"You got taste. A junker ship kicked him off here and anything too bad for a junker . . ." She shook her head. "K'Ruffin took him on because the little bug's greedy as hell but scared of his own shadow. No one who had sense enough to put two thoughts together would mess with him when the Hasheen was around. They're treacherous, though." She tilted the cha pot. "Low. You want a refill on me? It's strong enough to float a starship."

Aleytys shoved her mug across the counter. For several minutes there was a comfortable silence in the shop as they sipped companionably at the warm, bitter liquid.

The beads clacked behind her. Aleytys turned slowly.

A small, gray man walked cat-footed to the other end of the shop and hoisted himself neatly onto a stool. He looked at the two women and tapped impatiently on the counter with the coin he held between his first and middle fingers.

Bran's face went blank. Aleytys could sense anger building in her, focused on the innocuous-seeming little man. Seeming . . . she touched him with the fingers of her mind . . . she could feel a cynical amusement expanding outward from him, a cruel cat nature under his colorless exterior. And . . . she struggled to conceal her astonishment . . . a lively interest in her.

"Kavass." His voice was high-pitched like an adolescent's

and rather comical coming from the withered little face, but neither woman felt any desire to laugh. Silently, Bran levered open the bottle of kavass and set it in front of him. From under the bar she took a glass and several chunks of ice and set them beside the bottle. He slid the coin across the counter, smiling meanly as the old woman seemed reluctant to touch it. "Keep the change, despina."

She swept the coin into a money box and began fussing with the stove. She set a fresh can of water on the burner, emptied the leaves from the cha pot into the garbage hole, scrubbed the pot clean and dried it with care. By the time she had finished all her busy work, the little man had drained his glass and fixed his eyes on Aleytys for a minute. He slid neatly off the stool and prowled out.

Bran picked up his glass, touching it with fingertips only, and dropped it in the garbage hole.

Aleytys stared at her. "That's a good glass."

"Go see if he's really gone."

Aleytys walked to the curtain and stepped outside. She saw the small, gray figure walking through the growing crowd of sleepy, noisy people. No matter how crowded the street was, he had a constant emptiness around him. No one got closer than half a meter without sheering off. She shook her head and went back inside. "He's going off down street. Walking slow but not stopping."

"Good." She was scrubbing vigorously at the counter where the little man had put his hands.

Aleytys picked up her pack and rested it on the stool. "Who's he?"

"Company louse. Spy." She dropped the rag and turned the fire down under the bubbling water. As she shoveled new leaves into the pot she said slowly, "You better get on over to Tintin's; tell him I sent you. Drop back around sundown. Should have some idea by then what work's available."

"Thanks. See you later." Aleytys slung the pack over her shoulder and went out.

Chapter III

Gwynnor pushed the door open and stepped into the smoky lantern-lit interior. Several young cerdd were sitting around the fireplace arguing vehemently, individual voices lost in the noise of the common babble. As his eyes adjusted to the light, he recognized Siarl standing with his back against the bricks with Tue, Huw, Iwan, Ofydd, and Twm seated on the cushioned benches arranged in a circle around the fire.

He hesitated a minute, then walked over to join them.

Siarl saw him first. "Gwynnor?"

"Himself. Annerch, Siarl."

"Annerch, old friend." As the others stared, the young cerdd sidled past the benches and chairs to clasp hands with the newcomer. Siarl pulled Gwynnor into the circle. "Eh, now we'll have some real news."

Gwynnor shook his head. "I've been out of touch for awhile. What news I have, I got from Treforis."

Ofydd leaned forward, his long face drawn into a sneer. "You went with Dylaw."

Twm snorted. "Shut up, Ofydd. Let the man talk."

"Man? Huh!"

"When you come up with more than some dumb carping, someone might want to listen to you." Twm grunted. "What about Dylaw? What's he doing, Gwyn?"

Ofydd settled back, offended.

Gwynnor sat beside Twm. "Dylaw's bought darters from a smuggler. He plans to keep sniping at the city and raiding the starport."

Iwan plopped his hand on his thigh. "I told you. Didn't I tell you?" He glared around at the shadowed faces. "At least Dylaw's doing something, not just throwing words around."

Ofydd smiled bitterly. "That why you left him, Gwynnor?"

Siarl moved impatiently. "Shut up, Ofydd. You tell us,

Gwyn. Do you think Dylaw's really making any mark on them?"

Gwynnor shrugged. "Flea bites. If he ever made real trouble, they'd squash him like a bug. You thinking of trying something?"

Tue leaned forward eagerly. "I say we should get cerdd from all over the maes and hit that damn city hard before they wreck us so bad we'll all starve come winter."

Eyes moving sadly from face to eager face, Gwynnor shook his head. "That's a great idea, if you don't want to starve. You'd all be a layer of ash floating haphazard on the winter wind. You've seen their weapons. You must have when they raided."

"I still say . . ."

"We heard you, holy Maeve, haven't we heard you." The cool, sarcastic voice sliced through the fervid smoky air.

Heart beating with unexpected excitement, he stood. "Syfarch, Sioned."

"Annerch, Gwynnor." The girl stood in the middle of the room, hands on hips, scornful eyes on all of them. "Come to hear the brave ones fight the war of the words?"

"Treforis told me about Rhisiart. I'm sorry."

"Come have a beer with me and tell me what's happened to you." She ran appraising eyes over him. "You look older, cerdd."

Gwynnor caught Ofydd's jealous glare and smiled to himself as he left the cerdd to their arguing. "I feel older." He sat on the swiveling stool and took a foaming mug from silent Margha.

Sioned smiled at him. Her hair was a riot of black curls. She wore a dark, baggy tunic that failed to disguise the taut ripeness of her young body.

"You're looking well, Sioned."

"Good thing the light's dim in here." She sipped at the beer, licking away the foam with her pointed pink tongue. Gwynnor felt tension rising in him as he watched. Her nostrils dilated and the tip of her tongue traveled around her lips again. Then she shifted impatiently on the stool. "Well, Gwyn, what about you? What have you been doing?"

"Dylaw's an idiot. I was getting fed up with him when the smuggler landed. One of the starfolk from the smuggler ship cut loose from it and needed someone to take her to the city."

"You? I thought you couldn't stand them."

"Me, too." He dipped a finger into the drops of spilled beer and drew a circle. He put two dots at the top for eyes and drew a line for a mouth. "Like you said, I'm older."

"You said she. It was a woman?"

"Mm. We tangled with a peithwyr and got away alive because she had an energy gun. Then we got mixed up with the forest people, tangled with the Company men, and twisted their tails."

"The Company men?"

"Yeah." He touched his finger to another drop and drew long wavy lines on either side of his schematized face.

"Ah, Mannh! You beat them!"

"Not me." He brushed his hand over his face, erasing it. "The starwitch. She was . . . remarkable."

Sioned drummed her fingers on the bar. "Did you sleep with her?"

"Yes."

"And she left you."

He squeezed his fingers hard around the ceramic mug as he remembered too clearly the stormy ups and downs of his relationship with Aleytys. He thought about explaining, then said simply, "Yeah. She left me."

"Would she help us? If you asked her?"

"I don't know. She might be gone by now." He frowned at the warming beer. "By the way, Sioned, has anyone thought about going to the Synwedda for help?"

"How? No one goes on the river these days."

"What about at night? Treforis said they don't raid at night."

"Who wants to trust those bastards an inch? Beside, Synwedda might not want company. She hasn't asked for any."

"Still . . . someone ought to go."

She snorted. "Think you could get one of them that far from his hidey-hole?"

"I wasn't talking about them."

"You?" She drained her mug and set it down with a thump. "I'll go with you. I'd like to meet this starwitch of yours."

"Keep your fingers crossed she's still on Maeve. But . . ." He set his mug next to hers, pushing it until the two clicked together. "Synwedda first. Sioned . . ."

"What, Gwyn?"

He rested his fingers on the back of her hand. "Lie with me tonight."

"Me?" There was an odd shake in her voice. Surprised, he saw her lips tremble, then firm in a bitter line. "Just thinking of her gets you so excited you'd bed anybody, even me?"

He shook his head, feeling dazed by this sudden turn. "What makes you think . . ."

"Them." The bitterness was seared into her bones. He could feel it as a sad, sick agony in himself. He looked over his shoulder at the cerdd and saw them glancing surreptitiously at the pair of them.

"What is it?"

Her taut body relaxed suddenly. "They act like I'm some kind of freak, half-fascinated and half-repelled. Ofydd's the worst. He's crazy to have me and at the same time he hates me worse than . . ." She shook her head.

"Let's get out of here."

With Ofydd's eyes burning into his back, Gwynnor escorted Sioned through the swinging door.

Outside, clouds were building, blowing in tatters across the sky. The moon was just rising, casting long, fuzzy shadows around their feet. They walked slowly toward Blodeuyn's Lane.

"Ofydd seems to think you shouldn't leave with me."

"What Ofydd wants and what I want are two different things." She shrugged. Out in the moonlight, away from the other cerdd she seemed softer. "You really want me?"

"I really do." Fingers moving caressingly over the junction of her neck and shoulder, he looked back at the yellow glow from the tavern windows. "Has he tried to hurt you?"

"He's tried. I got a knee in where it hurts and got away."

"I'm glad."

"I know. He was a beast when you were lads. He's still a beast. I'm glad you came back, Gwyn."

He hugged her against him. "I didn't do so well before. He used to beat hell out of me."

"It'll be different this time and he knows it."

"You sound very sure of that."

"I am. And so was he. I don't think you realize the full difference these months have made in you, Gwyn."

"Apparently." He pulled her to a stop at the head of the

lane. "I don't want to go in yet. I want to talk to you. Come see my boat."

"Why not? It's early yet."

They strolled on in a companionable silence, feeling a warmth grow between them. Gwynnor found he liked this quiet pleasure better than the body-shaking firestorm Aleytys had awakened in him. They talked casually about unimportant things, memories of the time before the terror, his arm around her shoulders holding her close to him.

When they reached the landing, he pulled her down beside him to sit on the rough hewn, time-smoothed planks, the shadow of the old oak a dark secret pool over them.

"There it is. Cludair-built, with sails of Lliain woven here on the maes. It's a good boat. Tomorrow night we'll take off in it, if you still mean to come with me."

"I come. I want to see that witch." At his disgusted grunt, she chuckled. "How long will the trip take?"

"Coming up it took . . . what's that?"

"Maeve! The raiders." The deep hum of the skimmers floated to them on the wind, growing louder and louder. "Into the river," she snapped. "Quietly."

Gripping the edge of the landing, she slid into the river until only her head showed. Puzzled, Gwynnor followed and together they paddled along close to the bank until the steep-sided landing site gave way to the gentler muddy slopes where reeds grew in scattered clumps.

Sioned eased her way into a patch of reeds. Gwynnor followed.

"Help me," she hissed, "and be quiet." She began digging at the mud, pushing the reed bunches aside without tearing them so that she hollowed out a space for her body. She settled into the space and pulled the reeds back over her until she was almost invisible. Quickly, though more awkwardly, he followed her example and burrowed into the mud.

In minutes, the chill water had sucked the warmth from his body. Shivering and uncomfortable, he still managed a shaky laugh. In a hasty whisper, he said, "This isn't how I'd planned to be with you tonight."

"Fool." He could hear amusement quivering in her voice. A small, muddy hand snaked through the reeds and closed on his.

Behind them they could hear shouts and explosions in the village. Gwynnor moved restlessly.

"Don't," Sioned whispered. "You can't help."

"They're here for me."

"Holy Maeve, that's conceit." Her whisper mocked him but her hand tightened around his. "You can't know that."

"The very first night attack on the day I come home? After I helped screw Chu Manhanu?"

"It could be coincidence. Hush!"

The skimmers came flying low over the river, searchlights streaming in long liquid lines across and across and across the river and the banks.

"Get under water," Sioned breathed. "As long as you can. They've got some way to spot people but the water fools it."

Gwynnor sucked in a lungful of air then pulled his head under water. He lay there minute after minute until his lungs labored, hummed, the blood pounded in his head, his ears rang, and the cold . . . the cold . . . Drifting up till his nose broke the surface he let the stale air trickle from his straining lungs and carefully drew in fresh. Brilliant light skittered across his face, broken in shards by the screen of reeds. Startled, he ducked back under water as a brilliance whooshed out and seared across the surface of the water, clearing his face by less than a centimeter and burning the reeds to ash. The water hissed with the sudden application of heat, nearly parboiling him. Once again the lights flickered across the troubled surface of the water, then slid away. Gwynnor stirred feebly, but before he could surface for the air his straining lungs demanded, Sioned's hand pressed down on his shoulder.

And the light came back, hovered, then was gone again.

The pressure on his shoulder went away and he pushed his head out of the water, gulping the air in throat-tearing sobs. Sioned sputtered beside him. When the ache was gone from his chest he started to stand.

"No." She snatched at his arm. "Not yet."

"This is how you live?" He felt her shoulder move up and down against him as she shrugged. The whites of her eyes glistened in the fitful moonlight.

"Yes," she said quietly. "Though usually they don't bother us at night. Like I said."

In the dim light he could see her face crumple together. Then she shuddered, the water shaking with the movement. Uncertain what to do, he chewed at his lip and rubbed absently at the clinging mud on his arm fur.

After a minute she lifted her head, her face restored to its usual calm. "We can go back now."

He glanced to the west where clouds obscured the horizon line. "Will they come back?

"Who knows?" She moved past him and paddled back to the landing. Swimming close behind, Gwynnor found the movement warming his blood. Still, he felt oddly weak as he hauled his body onto the landing beside Sioned.

Scraping the water from his fur, he turned to her. "We need a hot bath and a warm bed."

"You do."

"If you think I'm going to let you go shiver somewhere on the maes, you've got water on your brain, love."

"Getting ahead of yourself, aren't you?"

"No." He tucked his forefinger under her chin, lifting her face so that the moon shone into her eyes. "What do you think?"

Her teeth flashed white as she grinned. "No."

"Come, lass." He pulled her against him. Arm in arm they walked around the cyforedd trees. "We'll get Treforis out of bed and scare up some hot water."

"You'll have to scrub my back."

He rubbed his hand up and down her spine, liking the feel of the supple muscle under the soggy fabric. "Mmm," he murmured. "My pleasure."

Chapter IV

The cook shop was filled with cheerful noise, Bran yelling long distance quips at her usuals. A constant stream of transients going in and coming out with plastic cups of cha and steaming meat pies clutched in fists, trailed off down the street to the noisy bars, gobbling at the pies and gulping the cha.

The street was alive with human, humanoid, and others.

Alive with color. Alive with noise. Noise, a deep pervading hum of voices interspersed with raucous music battling out from the bars. Slummers from up the hill in tight packs escorted inconspicuously by Company police. Traders and ship crews. A few star-hoppers stopping over till the traders they traveled with finished their business and were ready to move on.

Aleytys edged inside, flattening against the wall to avoid being trampled by a pair of ursinoids whose hair-trigger tempers and awesome size bought them a lot of tolerance.

Three street urchins ran back and forth between the counter and the tables, ducking thumps from Bran with wide grins, collecting money, dropping off orders, exchanging cheerful insults with the men and women seated at the tables.

Wriggling cautiously through the crowded room, Aleytys worked her body to the counter and wedged herself into a small space next to the wall.

Bran's brilliant black gaze flicked across her. She brought a mug of cha and waved away the half-drach piece Aleytys held out to her. "Hang on a minute, hon." She thumped a hand on the brawny arm of a sleepy-faced, gray-haired man dreaming over the dregs in his cup. "Hey, Blink," she bellowed, "shift your butt off that stool and let the despina sit."

He looked up slowly, blinked several times, then moved off silently, working his way with dreamy unconcern out of the shop.

Shaking her head, Aleytys eased onto the stool and sipped at the hot liquid. Bran stumped off and refilled the cha pots. Then she scooped sizzling pies from the oil, dropping new ones in their places as soon as all the brown ones were in the draining rack. Then she wiped her hands on a rag and looked around, black eyes darting purposefully over the crowd. "Rabbit!" she yelled.

One of the boys came running.

"Take over here a minute. I need breathin' time. Mind you, keep your hands off the rolls and don't burn yourself on the cha pots."

"Sure, Ma."

"Don't you 'ma' me, imp."

"Gramma?"

"Ha!" She aimed a swipe at his head but missed by a half meter. "Keep a respectful tongue in your head or I'll warm respect into another part of your skinny body, Rabbit."

He grinned at her and began filling the disposable cups with fresh cha. Shaking her head, Bran came down the counter. "No respect at all these days. When I was young . . ."

"You were probably twice as nimble-tongued."

Bran chuckled. "Right you are, hon." She settled her bulk onto a stool place near the wall behind the counter. "Well, girl, I've had a word or two with this one and that on the Street. Wouldn't mind taking you on myself, but . . ." She looked uncomfortable. "The work keeps those imps off the street and away from some bad habits they might be picking up. You understand."

"Yes." Aleytys sipped at her cha. "They're lucky."

"Brats." She radiated a fierce pride. "Every one of 'em. But they got a brain and a half between them. That's not what you're here for. Ummmm. Ulrick, the jeweler, could use a clerk. He's a tightfisted old miser. Well, he didn't have no openings till I described you, so I figure part of your job'd be warming his bed. So, unless you're really low, forget that one."

"How honest is he?" She thought a minute. "As a jeweler, I mean."

"Buyin', he'd squeeze an obol till it yelped, but he'd give a reasonably honest appraisal if you stood fast." Bran's black eyes darted about warily, then she leaned closer, her voice almost inaudible as she spoke. "If you've got stuff to sell, he'd keep it quiet and give a honest price. But don't tell me. Don't tell anybody. These things get out. You could end up on Lovax's list."

"I'll remember. Anything else?"

Bran straightened her back, grunting with effort. "Blue don't like women much, but she might give you a go as a bouncer to put the arm on drunks and busted gamblers. She runs games on her second floor, rents rooms on the third, and lives on top of it all. It can get rough. You'd earn your pay."

"Can't say that sounds very appealing."

"I saved the best for last. Dryknolte. You must have seen his place. Biggest and best on Star Street. He needs a hostess." She pressed her back against the wall and stared blankly over the noisy room. "His last girl ran across some creep and ended up in a back alley with her throat cut. He hasn't replaced her yet and his business is hurtin'."

Aleytys twisted the mug back and forth on the counter.

"There are plenty of women on Star Street. What's his problem?"

"He don't want whores. Needs a kinda special woman. He likes to think his place is refined. You'd have to make his customers feel good, listen to their problems, smile at them, make them feel like they're fascinatin'. All you have to do is listen and smile a lot. You sit at the tables with them. They buy you drinks. Dance with you, maybe, if they have compatible forms. You don't have to go on your back 'less you want to. If you do, the house gets its percentage. Don't forget that."

"I'm not much on drinking." She scowled at the mug, clicked her thumbnail against the side with a small clinking sound. "It doesn't sound like much of a job. What's the pay like?"

"You work that out with Dryknolte." Bran grinned at her. "Dearie, don't worry about the drinkin'. What you get is cold cha or colored water. What they pay for, that's something else. Don't fuss," she said as Aleytys scowled, "what they're really buyin' is your time. As to it bein' not much of a job, you come tomorrow and tell me how easy it was. Hunh!"

Aleytys sipped at the cha. "Maybe he won't hire me."

"Never know till you try. He's expectin' you."

Aleytys jerked her head up, staring at Bran. "You took a lot for granted."

The old woman examined her hands. "It's the best job. What the hell."

"Thanks. I appreciate the help."

Bran's broad face creased into a delighted grin. Don't forget. Come by tomorrow and tell me what a snap your job is."

"Sure." Aleytys pushed the mug to the far side of the counter and slipped off the stool. She pushed through the noisy crowd and exited through the dancing bead strings.

Dryknolte's Tavern was a big wooden-faced building with a carefully austere image. Even the sign manifested a conscious restraint. One word. Dryknolte's. Chastely carved in wood. Illuminated by a hidden light. Aleytys looked down at her worn tunic, smoothed the plain gray fabric over her body with nervous hands. Leaning against the building, supported by her right hand, she wiped her boots against the back of her trousers. Pushing stray tendrils of hair off her face, she squared her shoulders and pushed back the door.

She came through the narrow right-angled foyer into a

shadowed high-ceiled room. Dim, secret booths lined the walls and scattered tables dotted the floor. A few groups sat, talking quietly at the tables. She hesitated a minute. Behind the bar, a big rock of a man, an image in carameled charcoal, looked up, noticed her, and beckoned.

As she walked across the room she studied him, her nervousness increasing. His face was a strong inverted triangle, wide at the temples, narrowing over high cheekbones to a too-small chin. His nose was a second triangle jutting from the first, a narrow bony projection with pinched but mobile nostrils. A knife scar slashed past one eye and down across the hollow cheek to catch the end of his upper lip, pulling his mouth into a perpetual sneer. His light eyes assessed her while he polished a glass held daintily in his large hand, set it down with gentle precision and picked up another, watching her from tawny yellow eyes with a feral gleam that stiffened her spine and woke a turbulent contrariness in her. She climbed on the stool and waited for him to speak.

"You the girl Bran told me about?"

"Yes."

"She tell you what the job is?"

"Yes." She brushed her hair back from her face. "What do you think? Will I do?"

His eyes ran over her, inspecting her with cool insolence. "You got the looks. She said you know how to defend yourself."

"If I have to."

His thin lips split suddenly into a broad grin. "Don't make a habit of killing my customers. Bad for business."

"Hunh! I got the job?"

"You'll do." He nodded toward a door behind the bar. "Come round the end and go through there." His mobile nostrils quivered as he looked over her clothing. "You can't work in that. Erd, the Flash, will find you something to wear. Soon as you're dressed, come back here and I'll run through what I expect you to do."

"One thing. Bran said I don't have to go on my back for you."

He shrugged. "Up to you. It's not part of the job but any extra you make that way, the house gets a percentage."

"Bran told me."

Fifteen minutes later she came back, hair brushed to a red-gold curtain, wearing a translucent blue-green dress that matched her eye-color. It floated mistily about her body, concealing just enough of her to send a man's imagination steaming. Dryknolte's yellow eyes gleamed.

Aleytys lifted herself onto the stool, suppressing the instinctive antagonism that he stirred in her. "I feel peculiar."

"You look fine."

She rubbed her hands together nervously. "Erd's work. He did my hair, too, But I don't think he likes me."

"Doesn't like any women. But he knows his business."

"I don't worry about other ways of being, unless they mess up my life." She smoothed her hands nervously over her hair. "I need a glass of wine. Take it out of my pay."

"On the house." He poured the wine and watched as she sipped at it.

"Talking about pay, how much?"

"Twenty oboloi the week."

She sighed and pushed the glass away from her. "I'm not hurting that bad. Sorry to take up your time."

As she stretched a foot toward the floor, he held up a long-fingered hand. "How much you want?"

"More like twenty oboloi the night, payable each night."

"Three."

"Fifteen."

"Five." His mouth closed in a firm line, the scar-lifted lip looking more like a snarl than ever.

"Ten and I don't work after midnight."

"Five and you don't work after midnight."

"Five. I don't work after midnight. And I get an hour to myself halfway through the evening plus a place where I can sit by myself."

He looked at her thoughtfully, the feral light flickering in his eyes. She stared back, a challenge in her own gaze. Green-blue and gold eyes crossing like swords. After a minute he nodded. "Done."

She relaxed and reached for the wine. "Nice place."

"I like it."

Part of the wall behind the bar was a huge mirror, reflecting the quiet room behind. As far as Aleytys could tell, she was the only female in the place. "Do your customers bring their women here?"

His face chilled to a savage mask. "No."

"What about female crews?"

"No mixing in my place."

"What's that?" Aleytys pointed to a small minstrel's harp hanging beside the mirror, almost lost amid the clutter of kick-shaws and trifles from worlds scattered across the cosmos.

He twisted his head around, following the pointing finger. "That harp? A blackgang timbersmith off a timbership left it one drunk night a couple of years ago. He ran out of money and traded the harp for a couple jugs of sheesh-water."

Aleytys sipped at her wine and closed her eyes. "Shadith," she whispered.

The purple eyes snapped open, glowing brilliantly. "Can I play it? I damn well can! Thanks, Lee."

Aleytys set the glass down gently and looked up at Dryknolte. "May I see it?"

He reached up and set the harp in front of her.

She drew her finger through the thick dust on the sounding board. "Got a rag?"

Carefully, dreamily, she drew the rag over the wood and strings, removing the dust accumulation of two years while Dryknolte stood watching her, a dark scowl turning his mahogany face into a horror mask. When she finished, he lifted the dirty rag between two fingers and dropped it behind the bar, then polished angrily at the smear of dust it left behind.

Holding the harp on her lap, Aleytys finished the wine in her glass. "Well. Tell me what I'm supposed to do."

"You going to play that thing?"

"Maybe. Go on."

"You work from noon to midnight." At her challenging stare, he added smoothly, "With your hour off, of course."

She nodded and waited expectantly.

"You move around. Table to table. Don't spend too much time with anyone. You're not getting paid to chat. You listen. You smile. You keep them feeling good. Keep them drinking but don't be obvious about that. Each table has to buy at least one drink for you. That keeps you with them for about fifteen minutes. After that they either buy you another drink or you move on. Two drinks a table. No more. Got it?"

She nodded.

"You understand that what they pay for won't match what you're drinking."

"Bran told me. It's just as well. I'm not much of a drinker."

He grunted, looking pleased, which surprised her somewhat. "Like I said, laugh at their jokes and listen to their sad stories. Don't get pushed if the talk gets rough. Just let them know you're not amused. Act high class. You can handle that. What's your name?"

She stared thoughtfully at her image in the mirror. "I don't want to use my name here. You make up one for me."

He drew a long finger over her forearm. "Amber," he said abruptly. "We'll call you Amber." He took up her hand and cradled it between his large, molasses-colored palms. "For your skin."

"Good enough." Quietly, she freed herself. "Now. Something else. Listen to me a minute. If you like what you hear, we'll see about adding another obol to my pay. For my singing."

He looked at the harp sitting in her lap. "So. Show me."

She closed her eyes. "Shadith, your turn." She felt the singer expand through her body and withdrew her control, settling back contentedly, waiting to see what Shadith chose to do.

The Singer ran her hands over the harp. "It's well-made," she murmured.

Dryknolte straightened, his eyes boring into her as he noted the change in stance and inflection. Then he backed up until he was leaning against the shelves behind the bar, watching her intently all the while.

Shadith settled the harp. With quick competence she tuned the strings, touching them gently with exploring fingers, testing them to see if the years of dusty idleness had affected their strength. When she was satisfied, she looked up, smiled at the faces turned her way, staring at her image in the mirror.

Quietly, she began singing, working her way through one of her own songs, singing the lines first in the original language then translating them into interlingue. Her voice fell on the new silence like drops of mountain water, clear, pure, cool.

When the Singer finished, Aleytys whispered to her, "Lovely, friend. You make me shiver with delight. Sing more."

Shadith laughed. She sang a bubbling, lilting song about a spaceman clumsy as a bear, but blessed with incredible luck so that each disaster he tumbled into turned gold in his hands. Then she laid the harp on the bar and retreated.

Dryknolte was staring at Aleytys. "What the hell are you doing on Star Street?"

"So I get the extra obol."

He brushed that aside. "Yes, of course. Who are you, woman?"

"Nobody." Aleytys touched the harp with exploring fingertips, taking pleasure in the silky feel of the polished wood. "Bran is right, you know. There's more freedom on Star Street than the hill will ever know. I hate being circumscribed."

"You got any idea what kind of money you could make?"

"More than I need or want." She shrugged. "I do what I have to do. Without getting myself tied up in limitations. So. For one extra obol I sing for you once each night."

Dryknolte glanced at his customers. Several of the humanoids had pushed back their chairs and were coming toward the bar. Under the impact of his yellow glare they stopped and stood, shifting from foot to foot, eyes on the woman sitting quietly, harp resting near her fingers.

Dryknolte grunted. "Time you got to work, Amber. Actor!"

A big man with a long golden beard ambled calmly, unhurriedly over to them.

Dryknolte leaned on one hand and flipped the other in a quick supple gesture. "Amber, this lump of hair is the Actor. A better man than he looks." The beard split in a grin showing gleaming teeth. "He'll take your orders, bring your drinks, and break the heads of any grabbers. He knows the business well enough. Listen to his advice, but don't try to seduce him."

"A pleasure." Aleytys held out her hand. "Why not try to seduce him?"

"He's keeping too many women happy already. One more'd kill him."

Aleytys laughed. "Poor man."

The Actor bowed gracefully, his huge hand swallowing hers. "Don't believe him. He's just jealous."

Dryknolte grunted, suddenly not amused any longer. "Amber, pick out a table and get to work."

"Sure. Damn, my knees are shaking, and look at this." She held out trembling hands.

The Actor patted her shoulder. "Get moving, lass. You're on salary now and our esteemed employer has been known to dock pay for wasting time. What's worse, he'll go after my poor inadequate stipend." The beard split again in a tragic grimace and the big man's eyes took on the sadness of a deserted puppy's gaze.

Clutching at his arm, swallowing to overcome her nervousness, she slid off the stool and looked around. "Which one?"

The Actor nodded at a table where three men were sitting, older types with the harsh lines of authority in their faces. "Bunch of ship captains there. Three of them, so they won't be looking for action; besides, it's early yet. But expect to listen to a lot of windy tales. Each one'll try to outdo the others."

"That I can take. Come on."

Chapter V

Treforis laid his hand on Gwynnor's shoulder. "You can stay. You know that."

"I know. We went over that back and front." He touched his brother's hand then moved away and swung down into the boat beside Sioned. "Your children, the farm. I won't set them at risk, brother." He looked up, smiling into Treforis' troubled face. "Besides, someone has to go see what the Synwedda will do for us."

Treforis slipped the rope loose and tossed it to Sioned. "A smooth journey, brother."

Gwynnor waved, then leaned on the tiller, moving the boat into midstream. Crouching beside him, Sioned let the sheets run through her hand as the sail swung round to catch the night breeze that flowed over the plain toward the sea. Rope caught once around her hand, she leaned against his knees, looking apprehensively at the lowering sky. The cloud cover this night was heavy and black, casting a deep pall over the land. The wind blew fitfully, driving them along fiercely awhile, then dropping away until only the current pulled the boat along.

"It'll be raining soon."

Gwynnor touched her head with soothing fingers. "Another wet night."

"But safer."

"Probably."

Sioned sighed and rubbed her head against his hand. The little boat jerked down the river in explosive spurts as the wind rose and died. The darkness grew more intense, interrupted by occasional flashes of lightning. One struck so close they could smell it and hear the sizzle of the water. She huddled closer to Gwynnor. He stroked the springy coils on the top of her head, feeling her terror.

Then the rain came down, hard and heavy, driven by whirling winds so there was no way to shelter from the deluge. After fighting the tiller a short while, Gwynnor hauled Sioned onto the seat, pushed the tiller bar into her grasp and stumbled forward to take in the sail, sloshing through several inches of water. The cycling winds sent breaking waves over the sides and the clouds emptied themselves, rain falling so thick and hard it was a steady, befuddling pressure. He fought the sail into a compact bundle around the boom, binding it in place with clumsily tied reef knots. Then he sank to his knees and began scooping the water out with the bail.

Since the storm was too violent to cover much space, the wind blew them from under the center and the boat settled at last to a steady slide along the main channel. Gwynnor scraped the bail over the floorboards for the last time. There was still a thin film of water on the boards but it was seeping through the cracks into the space between the floor and the keel. In any case, it was too shallow now for profitable bailing. With sore and shaking fingers he worked the swollen knots loose and raised sail again. Then he settled at the tiller beside Sioned.

"You all right?" He took the bar from her and watched as she flexed cramped fingers.

"I'm alive." Sioned scraped the water from her face and shook her hands to flick the water off.

"You sound surprised."

"I am." She glanced back upstream, wincing as the lightning walked in jagged legs over the land. "I'd rather be under roof in storm time."

He chuckled. "And in bed, love."

"Ha. You laugh now. I didn't see you laughing back there."

She plucked in disgust at the soaked tunic and flicked at the beads of moisture weighing down the silky fur on her arms.

"Look. There." He pointed to a dark mass rearing up against the faint sprinkle of stars where the clouds thinned out.

Sioned dropped her hands onto her legs. "Caer Seramdun?"

He nodded. "Starman's hold."

"She's up there."

Gwynnor watched the dark bulk slide closer. "I don't know."

Sioned was silent, her brooding gaze fixed on the defining mass as the river pulled them closer. "I see the landing," she said suddenly. "Are you going to stop?"

"No. I told you that."

"I thought you might change your mind now that we're here."

He sighed. "You mean you thought I couldn't stay away from her. Sioned," he said wearily, "don't be a fool. There're more important things to think of than the state of my urges."

"Fool!" She flounced impatiently, sending the responsive craft into a complex series of yaws.

"You'll have us capsized if you don't hold steady," he snapped. "Sit still!"

Ahead, they heard the slow pound of the surf. Another few minutes and they were sliding past the sandstone cliffs. The boat began to jerk about as the estuary began to influence the current. Gwynnor caught Sioned's hand and closed her fingers around the bar. "Keep the nose straight. I'll get the sail down, then pilot us through."

With Gwynnor standing watch in the bow, the little boat rode the main channel into the bay. Sail up again, they headed for the island visible as a low black cloud on the horizon.

Chapter VI

Shadith laid the harp on the bar and retreated. Aleytys stretched, fitting herself back into her body. She leaned on her elbows, scanning the room. More of the tables were filled tonight. Dryknolte stood, arms folded across his massive chest, looking pleased. Aleytys felt pleased herself at this evidence of her success.

Then the pleasure chilled in her breast. The little gray man came from the foyer and moved to a narrow bench in a dark corner. He didn't bother to look at her. He didn't need to. Everywhere. He popped up everywhere. In the cookshop an hour ago when she was talking to Bran. Outside Tintin's place this morning. Chu Manhanu. It had to be. But why? She shivered. What did he want? And why was he waiting? It didn't make sense.

She pushed away from the bar, heading out at random, stopping at the first table she came to. A thinnish, dark-haired man with a clever, smiling face. Sitting alone. "Will you join me?" His voice was deep and pleasant.

She hesitated. He fitted too closely the description of Lovax. A few hours ago Bran had warned her again about the man, saying he was sniffing around trying to find out more about her. She glanced at Dryknolte. He was placidly polishing the bar and talking with a long, lean man with a shock of gray-white hair. Reassured, she sat down. "You must buy me a drink."

"I know the rules." He nodded to the Actor. "Bring the despina what she wants." As the big blond man moved off, he focused on Aleytys. "They call you Amber."

Aleytys nodded. "And you?"

"Grey." He lifted his glass and sipped at the wine as the Actor set her drink beside her and took the price from the pile of coins in the center of the table. When the big man

152

was back at the bar, Grey spoke again. "Your songs interest me."

"Oh?" There was a raging curiosity in the man that he was holding in precarious check. He lusted to know who and what she was.

"I have a sister. Some years older."

"A songsmith?"

"No. A scholar. Specialist in ancient languages."

"So?"

"What's that language you were singing in?"

"Why?"

"Answer a question with a question?"

"Why ask the first question? It's none of your business."

"Curiosity, Amber. About how you know that language and that particular song." He raised an eyebrow, his mouth stretching into a sardonic grin. "There's a cycle of poems from Before Time, recorded in an almost forgotten tongue. My sister came on them in the course of her work. Interesting. The products of a wandering poetess, a red-haired wench drifting from world to world, too restless to settle in any one place, her origins obscure."

"So?"

"The cycle is several thousand years old. Far as I know, my sister's the only one to hear and translate those poems."

"Interesting."

"That all you're going to say?"

"One song. Couldn't two song-makers have the same inspiration?"

"Same words? Same language? And it's not one song, it's all the songs you sing. Every one belongs to that cycle. The last time we met, Marishe made me sit and listen to her recordings. Every damn one of them. While she raved about them." He leaned back in his chair and lifted his glass in a mocking salute. "Same language, same sound, even same phrasing as on the recordings. Fascinating."

"And you'd like an explanation." With a low, amused laugh, she stood. "How dull your life would be if you understood everything." She moved off to a table where three humanoids greeted her with boisterous appreciation.

The evening passed calmly enough. At times, she looked up and met the gray man's bored gaze. And each time she turned away with a hollow feeling in her midsection, moving on to another table. Blue Halevan! Actor had to escort out two drunk ursinoids, two travelers of indeterminate sex who made her a proposition startling in its complexity. A captain of a privately owned space yacht. A catman from Sesshu . . .

She shook her head, smiling at the furry catman. Speaking in his own tongue, she murmured, "You honor me, Sslassa, but my honor does not permit. There are many others on the Street who can accommodate your needs." Still smiling, her face aching with the need to maintain the stretching of her lips, she stood and walked quietly away as his eyes reddened with rage. He half stood to go after her, but the Actor was there, a blond meat mountain half a meter taller than the small-boned felinoid, his square white teeth gleaming between mustache and beard in an amiable smile that didn't come close to reaching his chill brown eyes. Grumbling under his breath, the catman slammed out of the tavern.

Aleytys leaned on the bar, feeling a little weak in the knees. Actor came up beside her.

"Thanks."

"My job. The three over there by the door. Came in about fifteen minutes ago. Tipped me good to get you over. You want to go?"

She looked into the mirror, searching for the ones he meant. "My god, they're hideous, Actor. Like six-foot spiders . . ." Her voice died as a chilling suspicion danced across her brain. RMoahl?

Actor was at her shoulder looking into the mirror, also. "Might make a change from the itchy types you been getting the last hour. At least those oids won't be trying to get you in the sack with them."

Aleytys closed her hands into fists. "Ever seen their kind here before?"

"No. Anything wrong?" He touched her shoulder. "Want me to chase them?"

For a minute she was tempted, then she shook her head. "Dryknolte'd like that! He'd have your beard off hair by hair if you went around chasing off the paying customers. No. Go tell them I'll be over in a minute."

As Actor left, she glanced once more at the mirror. "RMoahl," she whispered. "The Hounds on my trail." She shifted her gaze and caught sight of the wizened face of the little gray man. "Damn. Everything piling up. . . ." She beckoned Dryknolte over. "I need a minute to myself."

"You had your hour."

"You want to see me come to pieces in the middle of the floor?"

He jerked his head at the door behind the bar. "My office."

"Thanks."

He followed her, stood in the doorway as she sank down into one of the chairs. "Something wrong?"

She felt the antagonism he awakened in her flare up, wondered if he felt it, too. "Nothing a little peace and quiet won't cure."

The yellow eyes glittered. "You're doing a good job, if that's what's bothering you."

"No." She rubbed her hands over her face. "I know that."

"That Company spy?"

"You saw him?"

"Don't be stupid."

"I'll deal with him when I have to." She looked down and found her hands clenched into fists. Carefully, she straightened her fingers. "I can't explain. Let me have a little peace, will you?"

Offended, he stepped back and shut the door with a controlled anger, just avoiding slamming it, which was twice as frightening in its implications of violence barely checked.

Aleytys sighed. She let her head fall back and closed her eyes. "Harskari."

The golden eyes opened and the thin, intelligent face formed around them. "You were right, Aleytys. They are RMoahl."

"Damn. Why didn't I sense them before?"

"When we lost them at Lamarchos, we forgot about them. Foolish."

Aleytys crossed her arms over her breasts. "That doesn't matter now. They're here. What do I do about them?"

Harskari was silent, eyes focused on distance.

"Well?"

"They want the diadem back."

"So? You know I can't take it off."

"I imagine they plan to take you with the diadem. Put you in that hole where we sat for four hundred interminable years."

"Can they do that?" She jumped to her feet and began pacing back and forth across the small room. "How'd they get the diadem in the first place?"

"They found it where Swardheld's bones had gone to dust."

"Mn. I don't want to sit around some damn museum waiting for my bones to rot."

Harskari nodded. A sudden smile lit her face. "According to your mother, that might be a long, long wait."

Aleytys threw herself into the chair. "There isn't much you don't know about me, is there?" She struck at her temples in sudden anger. "My god, everything!"

"More than we want to know, young Aleytys. That's the way things are and none of us can alter it."

"Ay-mi, Harskari, what am I going to do?"

"Consider. The RMoahl sit peacefully at their table. And they have made no hostile move toward you yet."

"You think I should go talk to them?"

"Yes. Information is always useful. We'll be watching."

With sharp, angry movements, Aleytys jerked herself from the chair and stalked to the door, muttering, "Watching. Always watching. Don't I know? I know . . ."

Dryknolte glanced briefly toward her, then turned away.

"First things first," she muttered. She walked over to him. He scowled down at her. "Well?"

"A man your size looks silly when he pouts." She smiled at him when he opened his mouth to protest. "Look. You offered. Thanks. But there was no way you could help. A woman's problem."

He relaxed, patted her shoulder. "You all right now?"

"Yeah." She saw the glow in his eyes and was abruptly glad she didn't plan to stay around long. With a mumbled apology she moved around him, hesitated at the end of the bar, then walked across the room to stand, smiling her professional smile at the three RMoahl.

"Will you join us, woman?"

She nodded at the Actor and sat in the chair he placed across the table from the largest of the RMoahl. "If you buy me a drink, despoites."

When the Actor had set the glass in front of her and retreated, she sipped at the cold cha and looked briefly at each of them. "Suppose we start by exchanging names. I am called Amber."

The sensory antenna growing from the orange pompons on both sides of the largest RMoahl's head twisted in gentle ripples as his wide mouth spread in an appreciative open-mouthed smile. "I am koeiyi Sensayii." He clicked a nipper claw at the RMoahl on his right. "The second is Mok'tekii. The other is Chiisayii. As to who and what we are, you know that. As to why we are here, you know that, also."

Aleytys suppressed a queasy fluttering in her stomach and kept an impassive face as she nodded. "You don't waste time."

"We want what is ours."

"You must know I can't give it to you. It has grown into me."

"We will take you with it."

"Sorry. I don't see it that way." She leaned back in the chair, sipping at the cha, smiling her meaningless, professional smile.

"Then we have to force you to come. We would prefer not."

"No doubt." She tapped her fingernails on the glass. "How do you plan to accomplish that? Point a weapon at me and order me to your ship?"

"That would be ineffective."

"You're damn right. How far would you get?" She flicked a hand at the room. "There's a few here might object." She glanced at the door. The gray man had acquired a companion, a tall, skinny type with dark hair and shiny dusky skin. He was dressed in a wrinkled matte black tunic and baggy tights and looked like a broom handle wrapped in a shroud. As she watched, Grey walked past her without a glance and went out. The skinny spy went out after him. She frowned.

"You'll make your life much easier if you come with us."

"What? Oh." She shook her head. "No."

"Our ship waits. Make up your mind to this, Amber. We will have you, one way or another."

"No. I've got things I need to do. And I don't plan to sit out the rest of my life in some dusty hole."

"The diadem is ours."

"Well, dammit, I didn't steal it. Why the hell should I suffer for your ineptitude!"

"You got in the way, so you take the consequences of your act. The diadem belongs to the RMoahl."

"It belongs to the wearer. Do you have any idea what it really is?"

Sensayii clicked his nipper claws impatiently. "What does it matter? We will never let slip away what is ours."

"You bare your ignorance. The diadem is not a thing . . ." She examined him over the rim of her glass. "No, I'm wrong. You know much more about it than you want to say."

Sensayii's feelers twisted and untwisted frantically, and the hairs of his orange pompons rippled like grass in a high wind. The other two were visibly agitated, jittering about on the padded benches Dryknolte had supplied to fit their nonhuman anatomy.

In the face of their continued silence, Aleytys went on. "As you know, the diadem is not a simple piece of jewelry. You imprisoned three souls in your damn treasure vault. How do you answer to them for four hundred years of utter boredom?"

"Three!"

Aleytys shrugged and drank from the glass. She glanced toward the door. The little man sat in the shadow, unnoticed and inconspicuous. She wrinkled her nose and brought her attention back to the RMoahl. "They are vehemently opposed to returning to that dullness. We fought you before and won."

"You had help."

"I'll always have help. I can summon help from the very stones beneath your feet. Remember Lamarchos?" Her smile faded. "I can't always control the summoning, RMoahl. Push me too far and men will die, no matter what I want."

"Then come."

"No." She stood up. "Have a good evening, despoites. Dryknolte hopes you have enjoyed your stay in this place."

She walked away, head high, shoulders squared, though her knees shook so she was afraid of stumbling. She slid onto the stool and flattened her hands on the bar. Dryknolte came over. "I need a glass of wine," she said quickly.

He poured the wine for her. "They bother you?"

"No."

"Your hands are shaking."

"I don't like spiders."

"You shouldn't have to look at ugly things." His voice was softened and he reached out to stroke the smooth skin on the back of her hand.

She shrugged and moved her arm. "I'll survive." She gulped down the last of the wine and beckoned to the Actor. "Who now?"

"The two over there. One's a ship's captain. The other, ship's doctor."

She chuckled. "I should make you split those tips, Actor." She swung off the stool. "Let's go."

The rest of the evening went without incident. The RMoahl sat without moving, watching her continually. The little gray man sat ignored, on the bench by the exit. Dryknolte's yellow eyes followed her about. By midnight, Aleytys felt giddy with the pressures thrusting in on her from all these factions. She was tempted to jump on a table and introduce them to each other before falling down in a shrieking fit.

When the clock hands met at the top of the face, she moved gratefully around the end of the bar and through the door, hiding a yawn behind a hand. She nodded at Erd, the Flash, and went to the dressing room, a narrow closet with a curtain sagging across the doorway. With a weary sigh, she ran a thumbnail over the closures and stepped out of the filmy costume. As she thrust a hanger under the shoulder straps she felt eyes on her. She wheeled. Dryknolte stood outside the curtain watching her over the top. Swishing the costume in front of her, she glared at him. "Get the hell out of here."

He stood looking at her for another full minute, then turned and left.

"My god." She fumbled the hanger onto the hook and hastily pulled her worn gray tunic over her head. "The world is full of crazies." She sat and pulled on her pants, then her boots. "All coming at me, dammit. How the hell am I going to get out of this mess?"

Ignoring Dryknolte, she hurried across the crowded room and stepped into the cool night. The sky was clouding over, threatening to rain, the air thick and humid. Star Street was still filled with revelers, though their shouts tended to boom hollowly in the tension that preceded the impending storm. She turned to her left and began cutting the exitway to Tintin's place.

A tall, slim shadow stepped out of the darkness and moved beside her. A hand fell on her arm. She felt an aura of evil and looked up into a gentle, pale face with large dreamy eyes. "Who are you?"

"Lovax."

"I've heard the name."

"Don't believe all you hear. We should talk."

"I don't think so."

The RMoahl came out of Dryknolte's, following her, three looming black shadows like huge devils. She could feel a frisson of terror shudder through Lovax.

He glanced back. "What are those?"

"RMoahl Hounds. They think they own me. I got more company. Look."

The small Company spy had crossed the street and stood watching her as she talked to Lovax.

Lovax nodded. "I know about him. They want you uphill. I could protect you."

"Hah! I'm not that big a fool, Lovax. You couldn't protect a pile of dung from Chu Manhanu."

His fingers nipped at her arm until she grunted with pain. "Dungpile, let's go." His voice was soft and without expression. He took his hand away and she felt the prick of a knife against her side. "Or I slit your talented throat right now and take my chances."

Aleytys shuddered. Swardheld's black eyes opened but he made no move to take her body. "Go with him," he rumbled. "Get away from the audience. Then we'll take care of him." She let herself tremble more and let Lovax guide her into the narrow alley running behind Dryknolte's tavern.

He pulled her along at a pace near a run, dodging in and out of the stinking, dark ways between the blocky buildings huddling next to the outer wall, finally darting into a doorway and up carpeted stairs until they were standing in a noisome, pitch-black hallway on the third floor of the anonymous structure. He slapped a key against the door and sidled quickly through the widening opening, pulling her with him.

Careless, now that he was in the safety of his lair, he dropped her arm and pointed at a low couch.

Aleytys shook her head. "No. I'm sorry about this, Lovax. Thing is, you're even worse than Bran said. I know that. Psifreak, Lovax. Empath. I know you now." She shook her head and spoke quietly, not bothering to whisper. "Swardheld, he makes me want to vomit. What do we do?"

Lovax frowned. "What kind of . . ." Knife in hand, he leaped at her.

Swardheld took over smoothly. He swayed to one side, the knife missing him by the width of a hair and, before Lovax could recover, smashed his elbow into the pale man's throat, crushing the larynx. Lovax crumpled in a boneless sprawl, shuddered once or twice, then went totally limp, mouth open as in a soundless scream, eyes wide, terrified, staring horribly at the ceiling.

Swardheld stood over him. "In a way it's not fair, Lee. Your looks always mislead them." He searched the pockets until he found the key, Aleytys was glad she had no control over her body now, since she felt horribly sick. Swardheld shook his head. "I hope you never get used to this, freyka." He moved away, keyed the door open and stepped into the stygian blackness in the hall. As he shut the door, he murmured, "But you have to admit we're cleaning up Star Street." He felt his way downstairs and out into the street. "I'll stay in possession till we get back to Tintin's. These alleys are treacherous."

He moved swiftly along, throwing the key into a pile of garbage after turning several corners. Aleytys felt uneasy. The winding alleys confused her. "You know how to go?" she whispered anxiously.

"Verdammt, freyka, think I'm blind? I watched the way as he brought us here."

She was relieved when he finally emerged on the side street leading to the starport. Swardheld leaned against the wall and relinquished control of the body. For the first time, Aleytys had some difficulty reestablishing herself. The body slumped to its knees, nearly fell on its face in a clutter of paper and scraps of food before she managed to fit back in place. Rubbing hands nervously over her forearms, she half ran across the street to the double doors of Tintin's place. She stopped a minute to arrange her face and catch her breath, then went inside.

Tintin looked up as she came in. "A man was asking about you a little while ago. You want to earn your living on your back, go find another place to stay. I don't hold with that."

Aleytys sniffed. "No need to ruffle your feathers. I don't peddle it." She turned her back on the sour face and started up the stairs. Behind her, the doors pushed open and the three RMoahl started to enter. With a gasp of outrage, Tintin jumped up and darted across the lobby, protesting volubly as he went. Aleytys giggled, grateful for the first time for the old man's prejudices.

Her room was on the third floor and Tintin didn't believe in spending money on lifts. She sighed with relief as she stepped up the last step and began walking down the hall. A hot bath for her aching body, then bed and sleep. A good, comfortable double bed with plenty of room to toss about if she felt like it. And all the world and all her problems shut outside the sturdy door for a little while.

The narrow hall was poorly lit. Tintin didn't believe in spending money on extra lighting, either. She wasn't paying much attention to where she put her feet so she stumbled and nearly fell over a soggily resistant something lying in the middle of the worn carpet.

A body. Oh god, what else! What else on this damn endless day. Gasping, she dropped to her knees and touched the man. She felt a faint flicker of life. She leaned closer. Blood was still moving sluggishly from great gaping wounds in his chest and stomach. No time to waste, though. She flexed her fingers, summoning her will, forcing her aching mind to concentrate on the roaring of her symbolic power river and, as the healing power gathered in her center and roared along her arms, she pressed her hands on the wounds, letting the black water flow into them, praying she wasn't too late.

The dim spark brightened, and all at once, blazed. The man, whoever he was, had a tremendous will to live. He should have been dead already, should have died from the shock of the terrible wounds, but . . .

The flow diminished to a trickle as the water tickled the blood cells into furious growth to replace the nearly total blood loss. And with a last flick of effort, washed through her body to cleanse out the poisons of fatigue.

The man opened his eyes. "Wha . . ."

"You're all right, now."

He sat up, looked at his torn clothing, at her bloody hands, traced the disappearing marks of his wounds. "A woman of many talents," he began.

"Hush." She heard footsteps on the stairs and a querulous muttering. "Quick. On your feet." She frowned as she realized belatedly who he was. "What are you . . . never mind . . . no time . . . I don't want Tintin finding us here. He's mad enough with me now." She jumped to her feet, staggered as her knees locked, then ran on her toes to her room, pressed the key against the lock and pushed the door open. "In here."

Grey slid past her into the room. Aleytys eased the door shut, dropped the key on her dressing table, stripped off her

tunic and boots, ignoring the man's startled exclamation,
kicked off her pants and slid her arms into a flimsy wrapper
snatched from a hook beside the door. Darting to a chest of
drawers, she fished out a clean towel and a sliver of soap,
then trotted back to the door. Her hand on the latch, she
turned. "Look, I'm going for my bath. Old Tintin's on his
way up to complain about something. I'll meet him in the
hall. You just keep your mouth shut and don't open the door
to anyone but me."

"Aren't you taking a dangerous chance? What do you know
about me?"

"You said you were curious. Well, I have my share of curiosity, a big share. Besides, I'm empath. You can't lie to me."

"Surprise, surprise. Here." He threw the key to her. "Better
have this. Then I don't need to guess who's at the door."

"Yeah. Right. Thanks." She dropped the key in her pocket
and went out.

Tintin came puffing up the hallway, meeting her just in
front of the huge, shapeless bloodstain. "You tell your bug
friends to keep outta my place, woman. I don't want 'em
here. Don't like 'em and never have."

"Talk to Dryknolte. I didn't invite them."

His bleary eyes narrowed in anger. "I don't need you.
Plenty of other places for you to stay."

"I like it here."

"Trouble, that's all you are." But he didn't quite dare order
her out of the house, not with Bran and Dryknolte sponsoring
her. "You keep 'em out of here, you hear me."

Aleytys shrugged. "I'm tired and I want my bath. You
through?"

"Women. Always trouble." The bent little figure shuffled
off toward the stairs muttering complaints to himself.

With a tired laugh, Aleytys went on to the bathroom at the
head of the stairs.

Chapter VII

The eastern horizon was showing streaks of red when Gwynnor brought the boat alongside the landing. Above them, the red sandstone sloped back steeply in a broken terraced surface. A wooden stair crawled in lazy zigzags up the slant. Sioned looked apprehensively at the sky. "Would the starmen follow us here?"

Gwynnor shook his head impatiently. "How could I know? Come on."

They started up the stairway. The risers were attached in some way so that they made each footstep a booming rumble that echoed from the reflective surface of the stone. Sioned reached out and took Gwynnor's hand as the silence and the echoes played on her nerves, amplifying the exacerbation from the sleepless night, her quarrel with Gwynnor over Aleytys, and the residue of terror from the storm. Gwynnor pulled her close, glad to have her beside him, not taking her irritation seriously.

They were breathing hard by the time they reached the top. Wind-sculpted cedars clung precariously on the brink of the precipitous slope. Behind these, a box hedge loomed, wild and untamed on the outside but neatly clipped on the inner surface. The red stone had been crumbled and replaced by a layer of soil covered by lush green turfs until a velvet lawn stretched in a horseshoe ring about the front of the graceful stone structure ahead of them. A crushed red gravel walk, raked neat as a swept floor, edges razor clean, broke the horseshoe of green in a straight line to the portico of the temple.

Sioned halted, pulling Gwynnor to a stop beside her. "I don't think we're supposed to walk on that."

"How else do we get to the temple? Come on. Don't be an idiot!"

Reluctantly, Sioned stepped onto the gravel, shivering at

the crunch crunch of her feet. She looked behind and winced at the disturbance their feet had made. Gwynnor tugged at her and she walked faster, still uneasy in the rigidly disciplined landscape that seemed antithetical to human presence. "It doesn't like us," she muttered.

Gwynnor shook his head, feeling none of her trepidation. "You're letting your imagination beat you, Sioned. You've lived hard the last couple of months and you're worn out." He plunged ahead, pulling the reluctant girl along with him.

At the end of the path, two heavy posts supported a lintel from which hung a verdigris-stained copper gong wider than Gwynnor was tall. A log with a padded end hung in front of the gong, suspended from paired supports.

Gwynnor looked at Sioned, one hand resting on the log.

"All right, if you have to." She backed away, raising her hands to cover her ears.

"We came to see Synwedda." He threw his weight against the log, forcing it back, then using the stored momentum to crash the padded end against the gong, sending a deep vibrant note thrumming over the mountaintop.

As the great demanding note died to a humming silence, he stepped to Sioned's side and stood waiting in front of the dark, silent arch opening into the building.

An eerie figure in a hooded white garment with long hand-concealing sleeves came silently from the darkness to stand like a formidable human question mark in the archway.

Gwynnor lifted his head and stepped forward, confronting the acolyte. "The cerdd live in terror on the maes. Breudwyddas are dead. Maranhedd has been taken from us, every grain. Now young cerdd are being stolen. We come to see what the Synwedda proposes to do about it."

After a moment's silence, a slim hand crept out of the sleeve and beckoned. Then the acolyte turned and paced swiftly, noiselessly, into the interior.

Sioned hung back. "I can wait out here."

"No. Come in with me. I need you."

She moved closer to him. "Thanks, Gwyn."

They followed the silent, gliding figure into the heart of the temple, a strange room, like a polished cylinder drilled vertically through the stone, opening onto the sky. The floor was tiled around the outside, with a circle of immaculately raked earth occupying the center. A tree grew from the earth, branches spiraling up the trunk, their fluted tips brushing against the walls of the cylinder. Clusters of grey-green flowers, withering into fruit, dropped a heavy, over-sweet perfume on the continually circling currents of air, a fragrance like rotten apricots, dazing the brain, slowing the metabolism. Gwynnor and Sioned stood uncertainly for some time, caught by the drugged air and low, burring chimes.

Until Sioned grew angry. She straightened, her eyes burning fiercely, furious at this manipulation of her mind and body. The whole of her life had been spent rebelling against her culture's demand for female submissiveness and she resented this attempt to put her back on her knees. She slapped Gwynnor, first on one cheek then on the other, shocking him out of his stupor.

His eyes swung past her.

The Synwedda stood in the arch across the cylinder, a narrow white figure with a cloud of silver-white hair springing from her narrow head, framed under a drooping limb of the strange tree. As Gwynnor watched, the figure grew more sharp-edged, the clarity of her power blurring the reality of everything around her. The numinous power sent thrill on thrill through him. He would have fallen on his knees except that Sioned, still deeply resentful, stood rigidly erect beside him and he felt a commitment to support her.

"Chimes," she hissed. "Silly perfumed drugs. Stupidity!" She planted herself in front of the Synwedda. "Is that what you do? Is that ALL you can do?"

The old woman looked startled, then her face flushed with anger and the numinous brightness about her diminished.

But Sioned didn't give her a chance to voice her disapproval. "Company men raided the pack trains and stole the maranhedd. What do you do to protect your gift? Nothing! They raided the villages. What do you do to protect your people? Nothing! The shrines in the villages are broken down. What do you do? Nothing! Breudwyddas, your sisters, are destroyed, ashed! What do you do? Explain it to me. How do you act? I see no flames on Caer Seramdun. I see no skimmers raining from the sky with lightning playing in their guts. I see no concentrations of storm over the starcity, emptying continuously on that sore on Maeve's breast until the pounding rain has washed the pestilence away. I see no earth opening beneath the city to swallow the evil. And now the skimmers come for the children of Maeve. My father is dead! My mother is dead! I am driven to living in the fields like a

llydogen fawr or they'd have me in their kennels." She waved
a hand at Gwynnor. "His father is dead and the City men
came hunting for him. How much more has to happen before
you act. That's what we came to ask. What have you done?
What will you do?"

The fierce anger drained from Sioned. She leaned back
against Gwynnor but her clear leaf-green eyes never wavered
from the Synwedda's face.

The Synwedda was silent. Eyes the color of aged amber
moved slowly from Sioned to Gwynnor. Gwynnor held
Sioned and refused to yield, refused to betray the integrity
and outrage of his companion. As he watched, the edges of
the figure in front of him once again took on that numinous
clarity. Sioned made a small, distressed sound.

Then the supernal clarity of the figure evanesced, leaving
behind only an old woman standing quietly before him. Still
not speaking, she beckoned, then turned and disappeared
down the corridor behind her. Gwynnor and Sioned looked at
one another then followed, both too tired to protest further.

Chapter VIII

Aleytys stepped into the room and tossed the key onto the
bed. She draped her damp towel over the inner doorknob as
she pushed the door shut. "Grey?"

"Here." He rose from behind the bed. "I wanted to be sure
who it was."

She moved to the window and swept the heavy curtain
aside. A dozen meters away the wall rose in a dark curtain
with stretches here and there of spattered red-orange where
windows painted their shapes on the rough sandstone. The
fragment of sky visible was velvet black with no stars visible.
A storm was rising out in the bay. "It'll be raining soon." She
dropped the curtain and crossed her arms across her breasts.
"You asked Tintin about me and sneaked up here."

"Men must have followed you before." He dropped onto

the bed, feet stretched out in front of him, back resting against the wall.

"Huh. You think you flatter me, but you don't." She moved to the dressing table and sat down to brush her hair. "I'm not stupid enough to fall for that." When he didn't answer she sat silent a minute, pulling the brush through her hair. Under, down, over, down, until the red-gold strands fell into a smooth, tangle-free mass. She dropped the brush onto the table top and swung around, running her hands a last time over her head, pushing a few stray hairs back off her face. "Was it because of the songs?"

He flipped a metal disk into the air, caught it, flipped it in a high, spiraling arc, caught it again. "Catch!" He flicked it hard at her face.

Instinctively, she put up a hand and caught it, feeling a sharp twinge as it struck her palm. She opened her fingers and stared at the disk, watching it turn from a clear turquoise to a brilliant gold. "What . . ."

"A test. Come here."

She jerked her hand back and started to tell him to . . . but the disk grew warm on her hand and she found herself walking to the bed. Furious, she wrenched her will free and cast the disk contemptuously away from her, not caring where it went. "I think you'd better get out of here."

He stared at her, shaken by her successful escape. "Give me a chance to explain."

Aleytys sat by his feet, watching him warily. "Well?"

His wide mouth curled into a rueful grin. "I don't know how much of this you'll believe."

"Don't bother about that," she said dryly. "You can't lie to me."

"Empath. I remember. You said that before."

"Yes."

He rubbed his hand beside his mouth. "I told you about my sister."

"So?"

"Back there where the stars begin to thin out, there's a world called University. Its business is knowledge. Anything and everything. My sister's a scholar there. She went with a search group to a system in the Veil. Some puzzling ruins had been discovered on a world that should have had a broad spectrum of life. Had had, I should have said. There were ruins. Some cities once intensely populated centers. Now, not even plant life. Looked as if a worldwide plague had struck, killing off all life more complex than an amoeba."

"How do you know that?"

Grey grinned. "Don't ask me. I'm no dirt-sifting grave robber. I'm telling you what my sister told me. Naturally, the people from University proceeded very cautiously, but as soon as they knew it was safe they settled to a series of excavations at major city sites." He pinched the tip of his nose. "Naturally University kept the location of the Veil world secret."

"So?"

"Several things happened the second year they were there." He yawned and stretched, watching her face as she seethed with impatience for him to get on with the story. She wrapped her fingers around his ankle and shook his foot. "Stop that," he said.

Aleytys laughed and pulled his boots off. "You shouldn't put your shoes on the bed. Now . . ." She threw the boots on the floor. "Get on with it or I'll twist these off." She tugged at a toe.

He jerked his foot away. "Right. In the second year they were on that world, a group of the diggers came across an encysted spore that showed faint traces of life. By the way, they found recordings of your songs in the same cache. And a ship from Wei-Chu-Hsien Company dropped in for a lookover."

"Oh. I begin to see."

"Right. When the ship departed, so did a good selection of saleable materials. The encysted spore disappeared at the same time, leading to an inevitable conclusion."

Aleytys stirred restlessly. "I don't see what all this has to do with your being here."

"I mentioned that the spore tested out dormant but alive."

"I remember. So?"

"Not long after the Company ship left, my sister's group came up with a tentative translation of a plaque cast in noncorroding metal—a record of what had happened on that world. The more they checked it out, the more frightened they became. It seems the world was invaded by a parasitic form of life, a true parasite that eventually destroyed the life it inhabited. It reproduced by sporing in the presence of other potential hosts, the sporing process killing the host inhabited by the adult. And the spores seemed to be identical replicas of the first adult, so its knowledge and intent was passed on to its descendants. In a few years, the parasite had spread over the world. Somehow, a few men kept themselves free and developed a powerful plague. They turned it loose on the world, dying themselves in the process. When the plague died out, there was nothing more complex than a few fungi living on the world."

Aleytys shivered. "Drastic."

Grey said heavily, "It was necessary. Besides they weren't killing people, just animal hosts for a blob of goo that abhorred variety and difference so that it suppressed individuality to the limits of its considerable powers. That's what is waiting for this world." There was no laughter in his face now. He flicked a hand at the ceiling. "There's a ship up there. From University. If I . . . we . . . can't find the parasite before it spores, that ship is going to burn the life off this world."

"No." Her fingers twitched. Twitched again. "No. I won't let you do it."

"Me! Don't be stupid. There's no way I get off this world until the spore is found. If this world burns I burn with it."

She smoothed her hands over her thighs. "Who are you, Grey? What are you?"

"Hunter." He watched her intently, frowning slightly as she made no response. "Hunter Grey of Hunters Associates, on Wolff. Because of the connection with my sister, University set us tracking down the WCH ship. I'm one of five working teams. Our team succeeded in locating the ship that touched down on that world and tracked it here. The others met us here. They're all up there with the University ship. Waiting."

"You're the only one on the surface?"

"No."

"I see. You won't talk about the others."

"No."

"But . . ."

"I don't have to worry about right or wrong, Amber." He linked his hands over his stomach. "What I have to do is find the parasite."

She shook her head. "I can't understand you."

"How would you like your mind and personality destroyed by an invading parasite? Who then would breed that body to produce hosts for its spores? Who would gradually possess the bodies of all your people?"

She pressed her hand across her mouth, closing her eyes to shut out the horrible vision.

He jerked upright, leaned forward and stared intently at her. "If that thing got hold of a mind like yours!"

She swung around. "No. I'm not hosting any monster."

"I know."

"That thing?" She looked around for the disk but couldn't see it.

"You test high psi, but untainted." He leaned back and laced his fingers across his flat stomach. "The disk works when it's in contact with the flesh of the subject."

"And you can destroy the parasite?"

"Who can be sure? If the host is ashed, we expect the parasite will be destroyed."

"Unless it spores, one might escape."

"So we have to catch it before then."

"How does the parasite choose . . ." She licked her lips and stared at fingers that were beginning to shake again. "How does it choose its new hosts? Anybody who happens to be around at the critical time?"

"Why?"

"Just tell me."

"Marishe told me that it searches out the healthiest and most intelligent specimens of the host species. Puts them on ice till needed."

"That explains . . ." She chewed on her lower lip and flattened her hands on her thighs.

"You know something."

"I think it's about ready to spore." She pushed herself onto her feet and began pacing about the room, then went to the window again. Pushing the curtain back, she stared blindly at the rain coming down in sheets. Behind her, she heard the bed creak. "Let me think a minute, Grey. Be patient. I have to consider . . ." She let the words trail off. The bed creaked again as he settled back.

"Shadith," she murmured. The purple eyes opened, the singer's pointed face materializing around them. "You heard? They found your songs there. Do you know anything about this?"

The halo of bright curls trembled wildly as Shadith shook her head. "My songs might be on a hundred worlds, Lee. I never heard about this monstrous thing. It's Chu Manhanu, isn't it."

"I think so."

"Mmm. That's a problem. He's up on the hill and he damn well won't come near you till it's time to spore."

Swardheld's face formed around black eyes. "Go get him. The more time you waste, the more time he has to build up his defenses."

Aleytys frowned. "How?"

"Storm and take. We can do it." Swardheld's deep voice quivered with impatience. "Who can stop us? You know damn well what Harskari can do. You and Shadith can handle locks and screens. And I can do the fighting. What more do you need?"

"Information." Harskari's cool voice cut through their rising excitement. Her thin face was angry. "Swardheld, you tend to bull through situations. That works sometimes when there are no surprises. In this case it would be a disaster!"

"Dammit, woman, how much time do you think we have? You want to spend a few more eons sitting in the ash of a burnt-over world? I don't!"

"It doesn't have to come to that. Aleytys, I have a feeling you can pry the Director out of his stronghold. He wants you and he's still sure of himself in spite of what happened in the forest."

"And he doesn't know that I know about the parasite." Aleytys felt bile surge into her throat at the thought of such an invasion. "All right. It needs a lot of working out. I'd better talk to Grey."

She turned and met his curious eyes. "Don't ask," she said quietly. Mouth firmed in a grim line, she moved back to the bed and sat beside him. "I'm reasonably sure I know the host."

"Who?"

"Chu Manhanu. Company Director for this world."

"Sure?"

"You saw the spy who follows me around. I couldn't understand why he'd bother. Manhanu, I mean. If he was annoyed with me, all he had to do was order me taken out. Having me followed just didn't make sense."

"That all you got?"

"No. He has a double aura, as if two minds inhabit the body. One weak and growing weaker, the other like a battering ram."

"Empath." He stretched out on the bed until he was lying flat, smiling up at her. "I never thought of that."

"Liar. You've been planning to use my talents since I left you for my bath."

He chuckled. "Empath. Point conceded."

"So Manhanu has that twerp following me around so he can keep track of this bit of choice meat." She slapped her hand down on her thigh.

"Very choice."

"Idiot." She shifted on the bed so she could glare down at him. "He knows why you're here. I don't know about the rest of your people. You, he knows. Tonight at Dryknolte's, a long skinny type stood talking to my spy. When you went out, he followed you."

"Bony, dressed in dirty, wrinkled black?"

"Yeah."

"He found me. In the hall out there." He ran his tongue over his teeth as he stared at the ceiling. Then he grinned. "But I'm dead now."

"Until someone gets a look at you."

"Damn." He flipped onto his stomach and rested his head on crossed arms.

Aleytys ran her hands over her hair, then fiddled with the flimsy material of the wrapper. "You have a ship here?"

He turned his head so he could see her face. "The University ship will send a lander if we take out the spore. Why?"

"Room on it for me?"

"Why?"

"I've got a problem. You saw the RMoahl?"

He looked intently at her face. "I saw them and was surprised. A Hound triad doesn't usually get this far from home."

"They're after me."

"Why?"

She yawned. "Madar! I'm tired. It's been a really hellish day." She leaned back against the wall, pulling the wrapper over her legs when she was comfortably settled. "None of your business."

"Interesting. A Hound triad after you."

"What I want to know is will you take me with you off Maeve?"

"And get the RMoahl on my tail?"

"They don't give a damn about you. Once you let me

off. . ." She swung her hand through a wide arc. "No more problem."

He caught the flying hand and pinned it to the bed. "Come with me to Wolff."

"Why?" She let her hand rest under his, beginning to feel a stirring in her loins.

"Recruiting. You'd make a good Hunter."

"I don't know. If it means burning off worlds, I'll tell you now, I couldn't do that."

Fingers stroking the back of her hand, he stared thoughtfully at the wall in front of his face. "It's University who's going to burn off, not the Hunters. I suppose we share the responsibility, having accepted the assignment. I can't promise you'll never run into problems like this. That something happens once increases its possibility of happening again. Hunters Associates. Associates, Amber. Not Company. You wouldn't be required to do anything that went directly against your ethics." He craned his head around to look up at her. "Get through training and you'll have a ship of your own. And a hell of an interesting life. Of course, you might get killed."

"Nothing's perfect." She felt a lightness inside, and an intense greed. A ship of her own . . . a ship . . . she pulled her hand free and stretched extravagantly. "To be free," she sang. "Not tied to any world. To be able to go wherever I wanted, whenever I wanted without . . ."

"Hey, not so fast, Amber. Associates. Remember them? You'd be working for them. Doing the jobs they gave you. You can't just get in that ship and take off. Little things like maintenance and fuel to be paid for, to say nothing of the cost of the ship. Once you're a hunter you'll be on your own a lot, but you still would have a responsibility to the governing board."

She let her arms fall beside her and sighed. "At least, that's better than what I have now. I'll go with you."

"Good." He yawned. "Got any ideas about getting to Chu Manhanu?"

"Mmm. I think so. Maybe."

With a low grunt, he wriggled onto his back and lay looking up at her. "What is it? More Hounds?"

"No." She leaned on her elbow so her face hung over his. "Do you have to go straight back to Wolff?"

"Why?"

"There's a place I'd like . . . I need to visit. For just a little while. A few hours." Her fingers closed into fists. "A world called Jaydugar."

"Never heard of it. Where is it?"

"I don't really know anymore. It has a double sun. Horli is large and red, takes up half the sky. Hesh is much smaller. A blue sun with vicious radiation. The red occludes the blue every twenty some days. I'd have to figure out how to convert Jaydugari days into Standard, I suppose. There's a hydrogen veil joining the two. Would that be enough to locate the system?"

"Have to run it through the computer and see. You don't know the coordinates?"

"I wasn't thinking about coordinates when I left. Matter of fact, I never intended to return. Well . . . maybe that's not true . . . but I didn't think I could go back." She sighed. "My people were going to burn me for an evil spirit."

"And you want to go back?"

"I have to. A little while ago, I bore a son. I want to see him." At the lift of his eyebrows, she sighed. "It's a long and complicated story. I was sold for a slave by a crazy woman who went off with my son. A man who had been my lover went after her." She smiled sadly. "He was to take my son to the boy's father, since there was little chance he could find me by the time he got the boy back. If he did."

"I suppose we could make a jog in the course. If that world of yours isn't too far offline. I'll talk to our Captain."

"Thanks."

"So. Back to the monster on the hill."

Aleytys rubbed her hands across her eyes. "I'm tired. Damn. If I could get to some kind of haven, he might come for me. If he wants my body and my talents badly enough. If he's as close as I think to sporing."

"All he has to do is send his people for you."

"That's why the haven. There's an island out in the bay. If I could get there . . ."

"What good would that do? Skimmers, my girl."

She chuckled. "Telekinesis, Grey. What happens to a skimmer motor if a few necessary parts suddenly go missing?" She thrust an arm up and zoomed her hand around like a skimmer. "Zap! In the drink." She dived her hand at the bed, hitting the coverlet so hard the hand bounced.

"Empath. Healer. Telekineticist. What else?"

"Linguist. Automatic translator in my head. Hurts like hell when it turns on."

"My god, woman."

"Psi-freak, you mean."

"No, dammit." He bounced up, bent over her, hands planted on either side of her head. "I might be a little jealous of your talents but that kind of thinking . . ." His mouth worked as if he tasted something foul, something he wanted to spit out. "I hate it. It makes me sick to my stomach." He sank down on one elbow and stroked her face, smiling at her. "I've been wanting to make love to you. If you don't like the idea . . ." He used his free hand to stroke the hair back from her face. Then his fingers stroked her cheek over and over until her breath shortened. "I was terrified of asking." His grin widened. "If you don't feel like it, don't reroute my nervous system. A simple no will do."

With a little sigh of happiness, Aleytys caught his hand and pulled it over her mouth, kissing the palm with trembling lips.

Chapter IX

The shadowy, curving corridor ended abruptly in brilliant light. For a minute, the gliding white figure of the Synwedda was framed in the arched end, then they could see a portion of what looked to be a brilliantly lit garden.

It was a large patio in the center of the temple. A sun-warmed patch of lawn. Grapevines covered by purpling fruit climbed in graceful loops up one wall. Espaliered peach trees were trained against one another. Wild flowers from the plain nodded in the slow circling air, in one corner, an oak with its limbs constrained to grow within narrow limits so it wouldn't shade the other growing things to extinction. It added to the patio its nose-clearing brisk odor and the stern dignity of its presence. A pair of plank benches sat beside the rugged trunk.

The Synwedda stood by the benches, waiting for them.

Gwynnor crossed the oval lawn, Sioned silent, and still a little angry, beside him. They sat.

The Synwedda settled on the other, arranging her robes carefully over her knees. "I know what you've come to tell me."

Sioned clutched at Gwynnor's arm, her fingernails cutting into his flesh. "Why . . ."

"There are limits to what we can do here, limits I must respect. The evil had not reached the ripeness to allow its plucking. That you are here . . ." She looked first at Gwynnor then at Sioned. "That you are here shows the ripeness is at hand." She focused her dull, brown-gold eyes on Gwynnor. "The coming of the starwitch started a train of events. Your journey together was necessary, as was the arrival of the Hunter." She shook her head. "Don't ask me about him now. You will learn who he is soon enough. Your coming is, as I said, the mark that the last days of the evil come quickly."

Gwynnor stirred restlessly. "I don't understand."

"Does that matter?" The Synwedda's acerbic voice stirred resentment in the young cerdd. She sighed and leaned back, looking tired. "Smooth your feathers, Gwynnor. I summoned your cludair friends, Quilasc and Tipylexne. They will be here by nightfall."

"That journey takes at least two weeks. Aleytys and I . . ."

"One week. They came a quicker way."

"You knew I'd come . . . we'd come?"

"I knew I'd summon you, if necessary."

"Ah." He rubbed his forefinger over his upper lip. "What about Aleytys?"

"Can I compel her? No. She has made peace with those who are the source of Synwedda's power. But she will come. I mean to ask her aid this night. You and this child will take your boat to the mainland and pick up the starwitch and her companion."

"Companion?"

"The Hunter."

Gwynnor rubbed his lip. Then he faced the Synwedda, frowning. "How do we cross that stretch of water?" He jerked a thumb to the west. "We got across last night because the storm kept the skimmers in. We might not be so lucky again."

The Synwedda snorted. "Luck!" She placed her hands precisely on her thighs. "The storm was a sending and there will be another tonight at the proper time." She stood, shaking out the folds of her robes. "You both have passed a tiring night and face another as difficult. Rooms and food are being prepared. Rest. You will be called when it's time to leave. If you wish to see more of the island, feel free to pass through any door that will open to you."

Chapter X

Dimly, she grew aware of a presence moving in the room. Still locked in the remnants of deep, deep sleep, she felt a surge of fear that went slow and powerful down her legs, bounced against her soles, rose again in a mighty tsunami of terror that blasted her out of her paralysis. She flung her body out of the bed, landing on the floor, hopelessly tangled in the blanket.

Grey laughed. Aleytys was angry at first, then she relaxed and laughed with him. "I should have known. Give me a hand."

"I didn't intend to wake you."

She yawned and stumbled back into bed. "I wish you hadn't."

He draped his shipsuit over the chair and slid into bed beside her, pulling her against him so that she lay curled up and warm, her head on his shoulder. "I got hold of the ship. And the other Hunters."

"Mmmm." Her eyes drooped closed as she drifted back asleep, his voice a droning in the background of her mind.

"They know about the Director . . . they'll wait . . . watch . . . hope . . ."

When she woke again, he was lying on his stomach beside her, breathing heavily through his mouth, his coarse black hair flopping into his eyes. Gently, she brushed the hair back, smiling tenderly as he muttered disjointedly in his sleep. Careful not to wake him, she maneuvered herself out of bed.

There weren't many customers in Bran's cookshop since it was the middle of the morning. Aleytys slid onto the stool and smothered a yawn. Bran poured a mug of cha and set it in front of her. "Hard night?"

"You don't know the half." She sipped at the cha, relishing the invigorating taste of the hot liquid. "I think I'll eat back in the room. Wrap up some pies for me . . . mmmmm . . . about five, I think. I feel hollow. And do you have a liter-sized container for some hot cha?"

"You serious?"

Aleytys nodded. "I'm a bit tired of people, don't want them around me for awhile."

Bran nodded. She kept glancing over her shoulder at Aleytys as she wrapped the pies deftly in plastic-coated paper. Silently, she set the package in front of Aleytys, then turned to fill the liter bucket with hot cha.

The little gray man dropped a coin on the counter and prowled out of the shop.

Aleytys scrubbed a hand over her face, then dug in her pocket for the money. As Bran swept the coins off the counter with her long, beautiful hands, Aleytys looked around. The spy walked past the window, strolling off down the street.

She relaxed. "Lovax won't bother you anymore."

"Why?"

"He got to me last night. Took me to his den. He's there now. Very dead." She laughed unsteadily. "A few more days and he'll start to stink. Then everyone will know."

"I see. Like Henner."

"Very like Henner." She took the food and slid off the stool. "A crazy night. I don't like killing." She moved across the room and stopped by the beaded curtain, looking sadly back at Bran. "I really don't like killing."

Grey was at the window, looking out when Aleytys opened the door and walked in. She held up her packages. "Come and sit down. I brought food for you, too."

"Dammit, Amber." He jerked his head at the window. "Who the hell are you supposed to be feeding?"

"Me." Aleytys set her burdens on the dressing table. "Bring the mug from beside the bed."

"All that?"

"I said I was hungry." Taking the mug, she filled it with

cha. "Here." She tore open the paper and handed him three of the pies and some paper napkins. "I had a busy night." She bit into a pie, savoring the rich, meaty flavor.

Grey sat on the end of the bed, sipping at the cha. The meat pies rested on the rumpled coverlet, folded in the paper napkins. His hand dropped until the warm bottom of the mug rested on his thigh. "You advertised that?"

She swallowed and took a sip of cha from the plastic cup. "Too much conceit, Grey. You aren't the center of my world. Seems I had to . . . to kill a prominent figure on Star Street last night. Before I even got here."

His eyebrows up, Grey unfolded a pie and consumed it quickly and neatly. He brushed the crumbs from his fingers. "Who?"

"Lovax. He got ideas about breaking me to service."

"And you killed him."

She nodded and bent her head, feeling sick at the reminder. Hastily, to clean away the bad taste in her mouth, she gulped at the cha, draining the cup. She filled it again before speaking. "He panicked and came at me with a knife. I don't want to talk about it."

He looked at the omnicron on his wrist. "You'll be late for work."

"I'll go when I feel like it. Dryknolte gets impatient. He can chew on himself. What's Wolff like?"

"Cold. About twice as heavy as this world."

She stretched and yawned. "Sounds good. First time I set foot on this ball of mud I nearly bruised my nose. Hard to stand up straight. Kept tripping over my own feet." She sniffed at the cha, sighing with pleasure, then swallowed a sip. "What you say about Wolff reminds me of my homeworld. In winter, most times we had snow higher than the roof of a three-story building. And an honest pull on our muscles. Not like this, bounding through fluff."

He nodded briefly, his face sharpened with interest. "You'll like Wolff. I'll set my winters against yours anytime. The storms come sweeping down across the plains like a wall of killing ice, freezing everything they roll over. We dig in and let them roll. It's a good time." He smiled as he ate the last pie, remembering the warm closeness of the winter. "Then there's a time of peace when we break up through the crust, and make up a noisy, sometimes rowdy, crowd riding snowboats from house to house. Damn, that's a good time."

"What are your summers like?" Aleytys patted her mouth with a napkin and sipped at the last of the cha. "Mine were a standard year long and hot enough to singe the hair off your head." Her mouth tugged up in a rueful grin. "Though I've sampled a lot of worlds since I left, it still makes me uneasy to see an unpaired sun in the sky."

"A year of summer." He shook his head. "Excessive, Amber. Now we on Wolff take a connoisseur's approach to summertime." He grinned at her, wiping greasy hands on the napkins. "Keep 'em short. Keep 'em intense. You can see things grow, even watch fruit ripen. A lot of hard work. More hard playing. You don't go to bed in the summertime. Well, not much. You'll see." He stared past her shoulder at the wall. "A hard world and a poor world. We needed so much to make our lives more than barely supportable. But there was nothing to pay for what we needed. No heavy metals. No industry. Nothing but what we could make and grow. Some years there was enough for everyone. Some years whole families starved. The only real resource we had was our people." His eyes refocused on her, crinkling into narrow slits with amusement. "Stubborn bastards, all of us. With the trick of surviving, and an obsession with puzzles. Show me a puzzle . . ." His eyes ran over Aleytys, bright and curious. "And I'll bust my ass solving it."

Ignoring the hint, Aleytys dumped the throwaway cup into the bucket and stuffed the used napkins in after it. "You finished with those?" She pointed at the paper napkins beside his knee. At his nod, she said, "Throw them over here. I suppose Hunters Associates is your world's answer to famine."

Crumpling the napkins into a ball, he threw it to her. "Right. About three generations back we scraped through a cycle of years where crops failed and a lot of good people died. A young man called Elro Rohin scratched his way to University by methods he never talked much about later. After several years there, he came up with the idea of Hunters Associates, and eventually managed to use his contacts to get a small grant. Sent out a couple friends to hunt down a few rebels on a Company world. Was successful. Another time was one of a survey party on a new, wild world. Brought out a comprehensive report when everyone was killed. It went on like that for awhile, getting bigger and bigger as his reputation grew. He wasn't an admirable man, but we owe him a lot." He leaned forward, grinning. "End of lecture. Sorry you asked?"

She heard his pride through the imposed lightness. That it showed at all was evidence of the depth of his commitment to the Associates. She felt a warmth of her own since his invitation to join was quite a compliment. Then she came briskly to earth. "If I sit around here much longer, I'll get fired. I'm not ready for that yet. Damn. How do you tactfully refuse to sleep with your boss?"

Stretched out on the bed, hands linked behind his head, Grey grinned at her. "I never had that problem."

"I hope you do sometime, fool." She thrust the key in her pocket and went out.

Dryknolte was waiting for her, frowning in annoyance. "You're late."

"I was hungry. So I took lunch to my room."

"You could've eaten here."

"I didn't feel like it." She brushed past him and went through the door behind the bar.

The day went much as before, but there were more customers so she was soon awash with cold cha. Dryknolte's eyes kept following her and, somehow, he was close behind her whenever she turned around. It began to wear on her nerves, but she kept misunderstanding and not noticing, preserving, with difficulty, a bland ignorance of what he was up to, knowing he was going to set out his desires too explicitly for her to ignore before too long. All she could do was push away that crisis as long as possible.

About three hours before quitting, when she was just finishing a last song, the RMoahl came in. She laid the harp on the bar and slid off the stool.

Dryknolte loomed beside her, his huge hand landing heavily on her shoulder. "Let 'em sit. You don't have to go."

Aleytys fixed a smile on her face and moved casually from under his grip. Without looking back she threaded through the crowded tables, mouth curled in the meaningless professional smile, head shaking coolly at shouted words, body swaying expertly away from clutching hands, murmuring later . . . later . . . later . . .

She stopped by the RMoahl table. "Buy me a drink, despoites."

Sensayii clicked his nippers in consent and waited for the Actor to bring her glass. When the big blond man ambled off,

she sat down, picked up the glass, and sipped at the cha.
"Well, Hounds?"

"Have you decided to come with us, woman?"

"Certainly not."

"We will force you."

"We seem to have had this conversation before. Look.
There's no way I'm going to go with you. You can't get at
the diadem without killing me. Is that what you plan? Are
you going to kill me?"

Waves of shock swept out from the three. Sensayii's feelers
twisted frantically and the orange pompons fluttered as if a
storm wind prowled through the wiry fibers. "N . . . n . . .
no," he stammered. "No!" He sucked in a long long breath,
his black matte nostrils flaring wide. "We are NOT killers.
We would not even have killed the thief had we caught him."

She nodded, then set the glass down on the table. She
crossed her legs and rested her hands on her knees. "The only
option you have is to wait for my death from other causes. I
tell you frankly, Hounds, I'm not going to spend the rest of
what I hope will be a very long life on Roal. Can't we reach
some sort of compromise?"

Sensayii tapped his nippers on the table. "We are merely
Hounds, despina. If you would come back with us, we could
put that question to the Hoahlmoahl. Only The Nine have
the right to make such decisions."

Aleytys sighed. "No use going on with this." She pushed
the chair back and stood. "I suggest you go back and talk to
your . . . what did you call it . . . Hoahlmoahl." Leaving
them silent and looking a little doleful, the crisp black hair
on their rotund bodies drooping disconsolately, she headed
toward a collection of engine crew from several ships who
were grinning and beckoning to her.

She kept away from the bar the rest of the evening, staying
so involved with her patrons—laughing and fending off groping hands, listening to sad stories and ancient jokes and wild
exaggerations—that she managed to avoid Dryknolte's creeping encirclement.

A few minutes after midnight, she came out of the back
room, once more in her worn and comfortable tunic and
pants. The Actor escorted her across the room while the remaining drinkers yelled noisy farewells. Dryknolte stood
beside the door. The intense smothering possessiveness exud-

ing from his pores like sweat convinced her that she could put off facing this particular problem very little longer.

As she pushed through the door she saw the little gray man standing on the far side of the street, watching her. Behind her, she heard a rising commotion as Dryknolte stopped the RMoahl from following her. She couldn't distinguish the words but had no doubt the big man was establishing his claim on her and demanding from the RMoahl what their interest in her was. She hoped they wouldn't tell him.

She moved hastily across the street, almost running as she stepped off the sidewalk.

Tintin looked up as she came in. "No visitors." He sounded almost pleased.

Aleytys nodded. She hurried up the stairs and burst into her room. "Grey?"

"Here. What's wrong?" He stepped away from the wall, palming on the light as he moved. "You look terrible."

"Thanks." She stretched and groaned, then flattened her back against the wardrobe door. "I'm going for my bath. Go look out the window a minute."

"Suddenly modest?" He strolled to the window but didn't bother pulling the curtain aside to look out.

Aleytys unlocked the closet and rummaged through her pack. Immediately, she became aware that someone had touched her things. Everything was exactly as she had left it, but she knew in her bones that strange hands had been rummaging through her things. She opened the kerchief tied around the jewels she had liberated from the nayids. All there. Just curiosity then. She took the energy gun from the pack, then folded the flap down and tied the thongs. She shut the door behind her and locked it.

"All right, come on back."

He turned, raised eyebrows at the gun in her hand. "What's that for?"

"You've had a busy day."

He examined her face, then shrugged. "I got bored. How'd you know? I'm pretty good at making a clean search."

She nodded. "You are." She tossed the gun on the bed and sat down at the dressing table. "I felt your fingerprints."

He shook his head and sat down on the bed. "Still another talent." At her inquiring look, he said, "Psychometry. The ability to sense things about objects." He looked at the gun. "Like I said, what's that for?"

"You. While I'm gone for my bath. There are a bunch . . . no, several bunches of creeps who might think it's a good idea to break in here and wait for me. Tintin talks a good fight, but catch him right and he'd give out his master key without a second thought. He doesn't like me, anyway.'"

"You want me to tackle anyone coming in?"

"Right. Could be Dryknolte. I've been ignoring a lot of signals from him and he might be tired of that. He's an impatient man. The RMoahl have threatened to force me onto their ship. They're a bit wary of me. They haven't come out well on our previous encounters. Then there's Chu Manhanu. If the parasite decides he wants my body right now . . ." She picked up the soap dish and slung her towel over her shoulder. "Things are getting a bit tight."

Grey laughed and settled on the bed, back against the wall, the gun resting in his lap. "Have a nice bath, Amber. I'll keep the homestead free of lice."

She came back, her body softened by the warm water, her brain relaxed and gently tired. She didn't want to have to stay on alert any longer. So tired . . .

At her door, she sighed and straightened. There were no problems she could sense waiting for her behind the door. She slapped the key on the lock and stepped inside.

Grey moved away from the wall. "No visitors."

She let the air trickle from her lungs. "No." Draping the towel over the doorknob, she tossed the key onto the dressing table and crossed to the bed. "Madar, I'm tired."

"Lie down. I'll give you a back rub."

She lay on her face and let him slide the wrapper down off her shoulders. His long, narrow hands were warm and strong as they worked the ache out of her body. When he turned her over and lay beside her, she was ready for him. His hands moved over her, caressing, rousing, until she wanted him with an urgency that blanked out everything else.

"Starwitch!" The word boomed through the room like the note of a great bronze gong.

Grey leaped away from her, his hand closing around the gun. He landed crouched beside the bed, the gun held steady on the wavering apparition floating in the center of the room.

Anger and frustration exploded in Aleytys. She bounced onto her knees. "Get out!"

The image shredded under the impact of her anger. It lifted a protesting hand. "I am Synwedda." The words were growled and broken, hard to comprehend. "Come to the island, starwitch. We need you. No . . ." As Aleytys frowned and opened her mouth to protest, the wavery image waved a hand frantically. "Don't interrupt. Hear me. The cerdd Gwynnor waits in a boat at the landing where he left you. Bring the Hunter and come." Like steam sublimating into the air, the image dissolved.

"Your friend's timing is the worst." Grey stood, unworried by his nakedness, the gun held by his thigh. "What was she talking about?"

"Then you don't understand the cathl maes."

"I don't have an automatic translator in my head, like you."

"You better get dressed. We're going to that island I was telling you about." She slid off the bed. "It's the best chance of getting to Manhanu." Rubbing at her tender breasts, she stumped to the chair and slid the grey tunic over her head. When she was dressed, she unlocked the wardrobe and stuffed her few possessions into the pack, swept the things off the dressing table on top of everything else, then tied off the leather thongs that held the flap closed. When she straightened, Grey was beside her.

"I've got to make contact with the others."

"Just as well. We can't leave here together."

He nodded and held out the gun.

She shook her head. "I don't need that." She handed him the pack. "I'd better not walk out carrying this or Tintin'll have a fit. Think I'm walking out on my bill. That reminds me." She dipped into her pocket and pulled out a fistful of coins. She counted out a week's rent and left the coins in a heap on the table. "This should soothe his nerves."

Grey's eyebrows rose as he took the pack. "Those jewels are worth a lot. You trust me with them?"

She touched her head, smiling. "Remember? Money isn't your weakness, Grey. Tell you what. Let me distract Tintin. While he's busy with me, you can slide out."

She went downstairs with Grey a shadow close behind.

In the lobby, Dryknolte was arguing with Tintin. Aleytys hesitated, grimaced, then nodded to Grey. He walked quietly to the door as Aleytys went up to the quarreling pair.

"I'm going for a walk." She tossed the key on the desk.

Tintin sniffed. "More trouble. You should go for a long walk and forget to come back," he grumbled.

Aleytys chuckled, amused by the little man's complaining. Then she looked up at Dryknolte. He was devouring her with his eyes.

"You shouldn't go out alone. It's dangerous."

Aleytys turned her shoulder to him. Grey had disappeared through the door, unnoticed. "I don't want company."

Dryknolte followed her to the door in time to see the gray man emerge from the shadow and trail after her. Mouth set in an angry line, he went back inside.

Aleytys was briefly grateful for the presence of the spy. As she sauntered along, looking casually around, she thought, Dryknolte will be waiting for me in my room. She grinned at the picture. "Hope he enjoys the wait."

"H . . . honey, cummon wi' me." A drunk fumbled at her arm. She pulled away, disgusted. "C . . . cummon. G . . . g . . . got a room." Behind her, the spy came up a little closer, watching calmly as she struggled with the clinging, stinking humanoid. All I need, she thought. She kicked out at his crotch. Giggling, he avoided her foot, neat on his large feet as a mountain goat.

"Freyka," Swardheld's rugged face swam out of the darkness in her head with a suddenness that threw her off-balance and made her stumble against the drunk, who caught her in a stifling bear hug and started dragging her into a stinking alley that was little more than a filthy crack between two raucous bars. "Let him take you further," the rumble went on, "until the spy comes in after you."

"I hate this, Swardheld," she mumbled. "Do I have to?"

"We have to deal with the spy. Or are you planning to keep him as a pet?"

"I suppose you're right." She relaxed against the bulging muscles of the amorous drunk. "But you better take over before I get sick to my stomach. Madar, this creature stinks!"

As they moved farther into the sordid crack, Swardheld flowed into control. The little man came hesitantly and warily into the alley, projecting a growing unease as he patently wondered whether he should interfere or let her take care of herself. He wasn't there to keep her from being raped, only to keep track of the body his master was interested in.

The drunk hauled her into a doorway and fumbled for a key. Swardheld attacked at that moment, taking advantage of the big humanoid's concentration on unlocking the door. He burst free and drove a thumb against the big vein throbbing behind a hairy bat ear. Within seconds, the huge body slumped against the door, unconscious.

The little gray man crept closer, his eyes darting about, searching for Aleytys.

Swardheld was out of the doorway and attacking, his hands chopping against the sticklike neck. The spy tried for his gun, was too slow, fell into a limp heap in the slime. Swardheld lifted him by his collar and the seat of his pants and stuffed him into the doorway on top of the snoring drunk. Then he thrust the small weapon into a tunic pocket and walked rapidly back to the street. Hand on the wall, still in the shadow of the alley, he murmured, "Business finished, freyka. And I didn't kill your little friend, though no doubt he deserved it a dozen times over."

"Thanks." Aleytys fitted herself back into her body with a feeling of relief, finding it easier this time. She moved onto the street as casually as she could.

Grey was waiting for her at the gate. "What now?"

"Through there. I don't know any other way. You saw your friends?"

"Yes." He looked back along the street. "I see you ditched your shadow."

"I didn't think he'd make a nice pet." She rubbed her thumb vigorously alongside her nose. "Let me think for a minute." She turned away from him, crowding her shoulder against the wall so her face was hidden from him by her back and the other shoulder. "Shadith. How do we get out through the iris?"

"Easy, Lee. There has to be some kind of on-off switch in the guard tower. You can pull it open for a minute, get through. Close it again. Easy. And no sirens to draw attention."

"Good."

"Get your friend ready to move. We don't want the guards getting nosy."

Aleytys opened her eyes and turned. Meeting Grey's curious gaze, she shook her head. "Don't ask." She could feel his puzzle-obsession building. "Don't ask, Grey. It's none of your business. Look. The forcefield in the arch is going off for a few seconds. Be ready to move when I tell you."

"Telekinesis."

"Right."

"Handy."

Guided by Shadith, she found the switch and dragged the handle down. The two of them darted through the opened iris, then she turned the field back on.

As they walked down the dark, silent road, a few cold raindrops splatted down.

"Storm coming."

Grey glanced up. "Good cover. You?"

"No." She glanced around. "A lot happens I've got nothing to do with. You don't think it's natural?"

"A bit too convenient."

"The Synwedda's doing, then. A cerdd told me she has some power over natural forces."

Soaked to the skin by the pouring rain, they climbed cautiously down the steep zigzags of the rickety wooden stairs that clung to the precipitous stonc. The rain made the worn boards slippery and treacherous. By the time the two of them reached the bottom, she was trembling with exhaustion.

The small boat was hidden under the landing. Gwynnor silently helped them in. When they were settled, he pushed out into the main current as hastily as possible. The storm thundered above them, too loud for comfortable speech, so the four of them sat in uneasy discomfort without saying anything.

Gwynnor raised the sail as soon as they were clear of the land. With a strong wind driving them, the little boat cut across the bay with surprising speed.

Aleytys huddled beside Grey on the floor of the boat, growing angry as she felt intense, hostile jealousy radiating from Gwynnor and the glowering resentment of the cerdd girl.

When the boat slid beside the jetty, Aleytys was about ready to scream. Her movements jerky and unnecessarily forceful, she lunged awkwardly from the boat, nearly falling into the water as it slid away from under her. She pulled herself onto the ladder and stamped up to the landing. Grey came up next, saw her furious face in the pale, watery moonlight, and moved away to the steps where he stood waiting for the rest of the party to join him.

Sioned came next. She watched Aleytys from the moment her head cleared the top of the jetty. With wary animal caution she circled Aleytys, the fine fur on her pointed ears rippling nervously.

Gwynnor stepped onto the stone.

"What the hell do you think you're playing at!" Aleytys confronted him, eyes blazing. "What right have you to sit there glooming at me like a whipped baby!"

Startled, he backed away. "Aleytys . . ."

"Amber," Grey's calm voice cut through the clashing, "you've got more sense than this. Come on." He started up the steps, startled at first by the amplified booming of his feet.

Aleytys sighed, her anger draining away leaving her tired and depressed. She followed Grey, leaving Gwynnor and Sioned to trail behind.

Chapter XI

Sioned looked up as the acolyte brought Aleytys and Grey into the patio. Aleytys nodded coolly to the cerdd girl who looked chastened this morning, her pointed ears drooping at the tips, her exuberant black curls flattened. With Grey silent and wary behind her, Aleytys crossed to the benches and sat down.

"Native?" Grey dropped beside her, looking appreciatively at the pleasant sunlit garden.

"A cerdd." She tapped her fingers on her thighs. "How much longer do we have to wait?"

Grey ran cool, ironic eyes over the slumping figure. "Your friend over there looks sour." Then he caught her drumming hand. "Calm down, Amber."

"My name is Aleytys." She jerked the hand loose. "Don't patronize me. I'll jitter if I damn well want to."

He laughed, then sobered and frowned toward the blank archway. "You're right, I'm afraid. Time's getting short."

"How much longer before the thing spores?"

"You know as much as I do."

"How long till the bombs?"

"No."

"I don't see . . . Tipylexne!" She jumped up and ran across

the grass to greet the cludair. Behind him, Qilasc smiled at her.

Gwynnor came quietly from behind the cludair. Ignoring Aleytys' rapid chatter with the forest people, he crossed to Sioned and sat down on the grass beside her. She reached out, touching him with tentative fingers. He pulled away. "I'm sorry about last night," he muttered.

"You were tired."

"I was useless."

"No!"

He shook his head. "She still disturbs me. I'm sorry, Sioned, but that's the truth."

"You'll get over it." Her fingers closed forcefully on his. And this time she didn't let him pull away.

"I have to, don't I." He looked back at the man sitting relaxed, but wary, under the tree. "He's her kind," he muttered. A sick, dark pain burned under his heart.

Hunter Grey was a tall man, a half meter taller than Gwynnor. His skin was a coppery russet, like polished wood. His hair was black and straight, blowing in tufts about a strong face with high, wide cheekbones, a narrow beaky nose, and a wide thin-lipped mouth. He sat relaxed, but there was a feeling of alertness about the long wiry body in the worn black shipsuit. He looked tough and competent. Watching him, Gwynnor felt weak and unsure of himself, dominated to insignificance. He forced himself to remember the sense of maturity he had gained on his trek with Aleytys, and the respect his older brother had shown him. But when he opened his eyes, the casual force of the starman shriveled him back to nothing.

Sioned wriggled closer to him. "He makes me shiver," she whispered. "I don't like him. I wish the Synwedda hadn't asked him to come here. Or her." She scowled at Aleytys.

Gwynnor moved impatiently, turning his anger on her. "You don't know what you're talking about."

The Synwedda came quietly through the arch. She stopped and waited until all eyes were focused on her. "Aleytys."

Gwynnor jumped to his feet, watching the starwoman talk quietly to the Synwedda. After a short, inaudible conversation, she broke away and went across the grass to the Hunter. Gwynnor hesitated, then went across to the old woman. Dropping a hand on his arm, she drew him into the middle of the oval grassy plot. "Sit here, minstrel. In contact with the earth."

She brought Sioned to sit beside him and rapidly placed the others until they formed a rough circle on the grass. Synwedda. Qilasc. Tipylexne. Grey. Aleytys. Gwynnor. Sioned. Synwedda, again, to close the circle—a round of diverse beings who felt a little uncomfortable with each other. Gwynnor had a chill, uneasy shaking around his stomach.

Aleytys smiled at him, touched his knee. He pulled away and she shrugged and turned to the Synwedda, saying, "Do you know what changed the Company men's behavior to the cerdd?"

"I only know that it has changed."

"Hunter Grey knows the cause."

The Synwedda nodded but said nothing. Gwynnor turned to look with curiosity at the hunter. Hunter. It suited him. The others stared at him also, but the barrage of eyes brought no change to his cool composure. Since he could speak neither the cludair tongue nor the cathl maes, he sat quietly, watching them as a detached observer.

"Company Director Chu Manhanu, who has total control over the activities of the Company men, has been invaded by an intelligent and inimical parasite. This parasite will be sporing soon. If it is allowed to do so, it will eventually have the bodies of every man, woman, and child of Maeve and reach out from Maeve to other worlds. It is amoral and willing to do anything at all to assure its physical survival."

"And the maranhedd?"

"Maranhedd means power and wealth, both useful for survival."

"A number of young cerdd have been stolen from their homes."

Aleytys looked briefly at Grey, then spoke rapidly, translating this new information for him. He frowned, then nodded. She faced the Synwedda again. "I . . . we didn't know that. It's more evidence that the parasite is about to spore. The cerdd were stolen for their bodies. They are to furnish hosts for the spores."

Gwynnor shuddered, sickened to his depths by what he heard. He could feel a similar sickness in Sioned and reached for her hand, finding comfort himself in the cool, clean touch.

"There's more." The Synwedda's quiet voice brought his

attention back to Aleytys. Her bright hair shifted as she nodded.

"I'd stop it if I could." She paused, looked at the Hunter again, then stared down at her hands. "If the parasite sets its spores before we can destroy it, there is a ship . . ." She tilted her head and stared somberly at the brilliant blue sky. "Up there. A warship. Set to burn the life off this world if we fail."

Gwynnor sucked in his breath and stared up at the blue. Beside him, Sioned struggled to swallow her horror. Her fingers closed on his with painful strength. He could feel her tremble and wondered if she could feel the shaking in his bones. At the same time, the threat seemed strangely unreal.

The Synwedda nodded quietly. "I understand."

Gwynnor was shocked. He opened his mouth to protest, met the Synwedda's stern gaze and subsided. He turned back to Aleytys. She was staring at her hands again, silent and unhappy. The Hunter touched her shoulder and spoke to her softly. For the first time, Gwynnor was forced fully and finally to understand that no matter how gently and kindly she treated him, he had no place in her life. Somewhat to his surprise, now that he saw her as alien, he didn't want any part of her. Though he still felt pain around the heart whenever he looked at her, he knew he would be utterly miserable at her side. She was too strong for him. She would swallow him whole, leaving nothing behind. He felt Sioned's hand move in his and he smiled at her, settling back, content at last to be who he was and where he was. With quiet curiosity he scanned Grey, wondering if the Hunter was strong enough to avoid being absorbed. Because he no longer envied the starman, he could look at him without the distorting veil of jealousy.

The Synwedda cleared her throat and ran her eyes around the circle, demanding their attention. "The problem, then, is to bring Manhanu here. Get him here, then destroy man and spores both." She paused, then spoke slowly and forcefully. "With your support, with your strength which I shall borrow, I shall try to summon him."

Aleytys lifted a hand slightly and the Synwedda waited for her to speak. "Tell him who's waiting here."

"You think that will bring him?"

Her mouth twisting into a self-mocking smile, Aleytys

nodded. "Where else would he find a collection of such fine hosts? Of beings with such a concentration of power?"

The Synwedda pinched her lips together, distaste strong in her ascetic face. "I agree. Tell the Hunter what he's expected to do."

Gwynnor watched Aleytys lean toward the man until the bright and dark heads were nearly touching. The Hunter listened a minute, then he spoke. Aleytys shook her head. He protested.

She turned to the Synwedda. "Hunter Grey wishes to have his weapons here."

The Synwedda shook her head. "Not in the circle."

"I understand that. But . . ." She ran her hands through her hair, looking distracted. "I think he should be armed before Chu Manhanu gets here."

"Those things are disturbing."

"Manhanu will be armed." Aleytys spread out her hands. "If he comes willingly, then the Hunter can be excused from the circle. Can you be sure the parasite won't be stronger than all of us?"

"I cannot," the Synwedda said reluctantly.

"Then we'll need the backup. His gun might not be necessary, but we'd be fools to take the chance."

The Synwedda sat with her head down, staring at her hands. The two cludair moved closer together while Sioned and Gwynnor openly clung to each other for support. Grey sat frowning and annoyed. Finally the old woman jerked her head in a brief nod. "Agreed," she snapped.

Aleytys smiled, then explained the situation to Grey. He straightened and nodded grimly at the Synwedda. "He accepts the stipulation, recognizing that he is dealing with something he knows little about."

The Synwedda reached impatiently for Qilasc's hand on her left and Sioned's on her right. "Take hands all."

When the circle was complete, Aleytys lifted her head. "Before we begin, tell Chu Manhanu to bring another man with him. One called Han Lushan. Don't ask why right now. You'll see later."

The Synwedda's brown-gold eyes searched her face. "Very well." Then she moved her eyes around the circle. "Lend your wills to me. You will feel the power coming up through your bodies. This you will direct to me. Tell the Hunter, Aleytys."

As the Synwedda began a humming chant, Gwynnor felt the down on his body begin to crackle. Then, as the power flow increased, he smelled burning, the ends of the hair on his head and body crisping as the power flooded over and through him. He felt the flow build, passing from him to Sioned and from Aleytys into him. Around and around the circle. Around and around. Building. One to the other. Faster and faster. Faster and faster. Building . . .

Until . . .

Until . . .

. . . the seven-fold entity stood suddenly in Chu Manhanu's office, a glass-walled room high on the tallest turret of the Director's citadel.

Manhanu stared at the intrusion, then reached for an alarm. Then froze, unable to move, as the seven-part being moved at him, its fingers gently touching his arm.

"What do you want?"

"We wait for you on the island."

"Who?"

"Synwedda. Cerdd Gwynnor. Cerdd Sioned. Cludair Qilasc. Cludair Tipylexne. Hunter Grey. Starwitch Aleytys."

Chu Manhanu relaxed and leaned back in the chair, which hummed musically and adjusted to his altered center of gravity. "Interesting. Why should I walk into a trap?"

"Why not?" The seven-part entity drifted back from the man. "Aren't we what you want? Bring what weapons you choose. We can't stop you from arming yourself."

"You confess to a weakness?"

"You may count it a weakness."

"I do. I will come. Armed."

"When you come, bring another with you, Han Lushan, or you will not be permitted to land. The starwitch will see to that."

"What guarantee do I have that she won't blow the skimmer to pieces around me?"

"Our word. We will not."

"Why should I trust you?"

"You quibble. You trust us. And we don't have to trust you."

"What good are weapons against the witch?"

"That's for you to say. She's not omnipotent."

"What man did you say?"

"Han Lushan."

Chu Manhanu narrowed his dark almond eyes, then nodded.

"Come. Today."

He swung the floating chair around and touched a button. A holograph image of a young male face appeared over the desk. The head bowed obsequiously, then straightened.

"Find Han Lushan and bring him here."

Chapter XII

The acolyte stepped through the arch, still anonymous in the white robe with its overhanging cowl and too-long sleeves. She came in a silent glide across the grass and bowed before the regal figure of the old cerdd. The Synwedda acknowledged her with a small movement of her head while her old gold eyes watched the two starmen blinking in the sudden brightness of the garden.

Ignoring the acolyte as she slipped past him and disappeared into the building, leaving Han Lushan hesitating inside the archway, Manhanu strode across the grass toward them. He stopped in front of Aleytys and lifted a stunner, pointing it at her. "This worked on you before."

Her eyes narrowed. "Planning to use it?"

"Do I need to?"

"That's for you to decide."

The Synwedda lifted a hand, drawing his cold, dark eyes back to her. "We know what you are."

"I see." He looked past her at Grey, sitting in the shadow of the oak, the dull, heavy energy gun resting unobtrusively on his lap. One hand curled around the butt, a forefinger hovering above the firing sensor. "You're supposed to be dead."

Grey shifted slightly on the bench. "I'm not."

"I find it difficult to understand your present lively condition. Two purportedly fatal wounds, heart and stomach, my man said. I suppose he lied."

"No."

"Ah." His eyes moved back to Aleytys. "Healer?"

"You already know that. Psi-freak. Like the doctor said . . ."

Moving impatiently, the Synwedda snapped, "Form the circle. Aleytys, stand in place. Quickly. We waste time."

The corners of Chu Manhanu's mouth curled in a sardonic smile as he watched them drop onto the grass and reach out for hands to complete the circle around Aleytys, who stood alone in the center. He ran his eyes over the grim-faced figures. "The cerdd cub. My men went to the village for you. How'd they miss?" Gwynnor glared at him without answering. "No matter. This must be the female who got away. Mmmmm." He smiled at Sioned, visible relishing her nervous pallor. "A waste of effort." His eyes moved on to Qilasc. "I remember you." His smile stretched into an exultant grin. "Xalpsalp, of the cludair. I owe you some humiliation, hairy beast."

Qilasc kept her large, reddish-brown eyes fixed on his face, ignoring his verbal jabs.

"And the Speaker for Men. Men!" He sneered at Tipylexne. "Still, you beasts are healthy and have a measure of power among your kind. When the spores take you, you'll be taking a large step up the evolutionary ladder. But, of course, you won't be able to appreciate that."

Tipylexne was about to speak but Qilasc tugged on his hand. He settled back, watching the Director with a deep anger, hard and cold, behind the shallow red-brown of his eyes.

When Manhanu focused his reptilian gaze on her, Aleytys trembled with fear and excitement. She smoothed shaking hands down over her body. "Harskari," she whispered, "you promised."

Gwynnor saw Aleytys start shaking, then she swayed, almost falling. Before he could say anything, she straightened and seemed to grow taller, her face lengthening into a stern mask. As the Synwedda began a slow chant, he felt tentative touches of the energy come up through the earth into his body and flow through his arms into Sioned, a slow, calm trickle, nothing like the raw torrent of yesterday. Then the flow came through his hand from Tipylexne. The circuit was completed.

Manhanu watched with contempt and amusement.

Gwynnor saw him beckon to Lushan as Aleytys began a murmuring chant of her own that moved in and around the syllables issuing from the Synwedda. Lushan came reluctantly from the shadows. When he was an arm's length away from him, Manhanu leveled the stunner and shot him down.

With the engineer crumpled in a heap a meter from his feet, Manhanu turned the stunner on Aleytys.

Grey lifted his hand and blew the stunner into red-hot scrap. Manhanu dropped it instantly and jumped back. "You should have killed me," he said softly.

"I wanted to, but a promise was made." Grey sighted along the top of the gun, aiming it at Manhanu's middle. Then he dropped it back in his lap.

Shaking his tingling fingers, Manhanu lifted his uninjured hand, a tiny sleeve gun suddenly peeping from his fist. It snapped, blatted, flared, and Grey crumpled, the energy gun spilling onto the ground as his body folded in on itself and rolled off the bench. Before the snarling Director could turn the sleeve gun on Aleytys, Tipylexne jerked his hands free and surged onto his feet. With a cat-quick lunge at Manhanu he snatched the silvery tube and flung it at the side wall where it crashed against the stone with a tinkle of shattering elements.

The Synwedda cried out as the circle broke, jerking her hands free with violent haste. "Break," she said hoarsely. "Break!"

Gwynnor felt heat building with terrifying rapidity. Snatching his hand from Sioned, he imitated the Synwedda and held both hands up, letting the power which was running wild dissipate into the air above his head. He twisted around to look at Sioned, sighed with relief as he saw her hands up, also.

The Synwedda glared at Tipylexne. "Don't do that again, cludair! You could kill us all."

Tipylexne shrugged. Without bothering to reply, he stepped over Han Lushan's unconscious body, and walked quietly to the archway where he stationed himself before the single exit to the garden, crossing his arms over his chest and fixing his eyes on Manhanu.

The Synwedda sighed and stretched out her hands; the circle reformed. She glanced at the swaying, chanting figure in the center of the circle, then began the chant that would feed her own power into that gathered by the starwitch.

Manhanu sneered. "Useless melodrama." He stepped back. For a moment, his eyes met Gwynnor's, then he laughed. "Poor little cerdd. You think all this nonsense makes any difference?" Still laughing, he turned and took a step toward Grey's crumpled figure. Gwynnor stifled a shout as he realized the Director's goal, the Hunter's gun. But he didn't dare break the circle again.

Tipylexne blurred past the starman, plucked the gun from the Hunter's half-open hand, and was back in the archway before the startled Director could stop his futile rush. Settling back with angry satisfaction, Gwynnor concentrated on shifting the building power through his aching limbs, sneaking occasional glimpses of Aleytys.

She ignored the disturbance around her. Standing with hands lifted, she was chanting serenely. Then the chant changed and her hands began moving, catching the sunlight, rolling it into a fine, pale strand that fell in glowing coils at her feet as she spun golden light into shimmering thread.

He held his breath each time he looked at her. Beautiful. Terrible. The little flow of power moving through him paled before that fierce glow surrounding her. The nameless, numinous power caught him, trapped him, he couldn't bear to look at her, he couldn't tear his eyes from her. He sensed dimly the vortex he was part of stripping away from them all, adding itself to the building glow that extended half a meter from her body.

After a while, after an endless, timeless while, she stopped her spinning; the pale, fine thread lay in heaps about her feet. Once again the chant altered. Slowed. Deepened. She pulled at the thread trailing from her fingers, tossing a length into the air in front of her where it clung to the glow space. Again and again, she jerked the coiled thread and threw it upward until vertical lines burned red-gold in a nearly opaque curtain. Then she changed the chant once more and whipped a horizontal line across the verticals. Back and forth the lines flew, weaving a fine meshed net one meter wide and two long.

The Director cursed suddenly and broke free from the daze the chant induced in him. In them all. He took half a dozen swift strides. Unnoticed. Forgotten. He snatched the gun from Tipylexne and darted away, though there was no need for hurry. The cludair was woven into the spell and aware of little that went on around him.

Manhanu twisted the aperture wide and dropped a finger on the sensor. The killing light snapped out. Mingled with the golden glow. Brightened it. Fed it. Mutated into the force that built the aura. Did no harm at all to the woman standing with only hands moving inside the shimmer.

Manhanu screamed. His eyes turned back in his head and he collapsed a little distance from the stirring figure of Lushan, his mouth gaping wide, his body twitching like a puppet whose strings were plucked by a playful child.

A mass of orange-shot, dull gray jelly oozed from the open mouth, gradually obscuring the high-cheeked narrow face. Near the top of the mass, a number of small black specks stirred restlessly. Gradually, the shapeless jelly around those dots hardened into a transparent horny bubble that began swelling and thinning.

The net was finished, with so fine a mesh that it looked like a solid sheet of gold. The chant rose to a vibrant, demanding note. She caught the edge of the net as it began to fall and flung it over the Director's body, the flying edges just missing Lushan as he recovered enough to jerk himself farther away from the hideous thing at his feet.

As the net floated down to cling around the crumpled body, Gwynnor heard a woody pop as the horny bubble split. The spores were flung out and slammed against the mesh. He saw the net, spun from sunlight, surge and jerk and bump. Then it closed tightly around the dead man, pressing the spores back against his flesh.

A thread of pale gray smoke crept through the mesh. Then Chu Manhanu burned. With a soundless, heatless, flameless fire, the body burned until nothing was left but a fine dust.

The terrible pressure dissipated. Gwynnor felt drained. His hands fell away from Qilasc and Sioned, who slumped beside him, drained as he was, close to exhaustion, too tired to speak now that their minds and bodies had dropped free from the spell. After a minute, Gwynnor lifted his head and looked up at Aleytys.

The starwitch let her hands fall. The wildly swirling red hair dropped to hang lank and lifeless around a tired face, with several strands clinging to her skin, glued there by a slick of sweat. The brightness around her melted like smoke into the stirring air. She spoke one final word . . . "Finished" . . . stumbled, almost fell.

Then she straightened. Running shaking hands through her

hair, she stepped past Qilasc and kicked at the faint haze of dust on the withered grass. Then she walked heavily to the benches and sank down beside Grey.

The Hunter took her hands and held them between his. "You're right. You don't need a gun."

"You saw?"

"I came round somewhere in the middle, when the parasite took a shot at you."

"It did?" She let her head fall against his shoulder. "I ache all over. Even my hair hurts."

He laughed, more to encourage her than because he felt like laughing, and stroked a finger over her cheek, holding her close while she recovered a littel of her strength.

Watching them from his seat on the grass, Gwynnor felt all jealousy burnt out of him. He pulled Sioned against him, feeling her breath warm on his cheek. "You all right?"

"I'm too tired to know yet. Do I still have feet?"

"Stretch out your legs. Let me help you."

Groaning at the pain of moving legs gone to sleep, she straightened them with his help, then leaned back against his shoulder, fitting neatly into the space between the curve of his arm and the curve of his side. "Ah Mannh, Gwynnor. Holy Maeve grant I never get mixed up in something like this again."

"I know. Mind settling down with a landless minstrel and raising a pack of younglings?"

"Sounds . . . good. Good!" She took his hand and held it tightly. "I'm not made for high and noble deeds. Just small, comfortable, ordinary doings." She turned her head against his shoulder to look across at Aleytys. "I've stopped being jealous of her. In a way, I almost feel sorry for her."

"Think you can stand?"

"I'm comfortable here. Do we have to move?"

He dropped his head back and looked up, surprised to see the sun still in the morning half of the sky. "If we leave soon, we can be home before dark."

"I suppose so." She tucked her legs under and began struggling to her feet.

The Synwedda came through the arch, followed by an array of acolytes who carried in the paraphernalia for lunch. Table and chairs. Covered earthern pots that steamed copiously and sent out enticing odors.

Aleytys sniffed. She swung her legs around and stood. "I'm starved."

"You sound surprised." Grey rose beside her, stretching his body like a lazy cat. His hands came down on her shoulders and he gently massaged the taut muscles. "Relax. It's over."

The Synwedda beckoned them over.

The company, Han Lushan included, ate with intense concentration for several minutes. When the first edge of her hunger was blunted, Aleytys turned to Lushan. "Manhanu appointed you his successor?"

Lushan lifted the clear, crystal glass to his lips and sipped at the chilled water, his eyes moving over the varied faces of those sitting around the table. Mouth hidden behind the glass, he spoke softly. "You expected that?"

"I knew the parasite planned to spore here. And that the sporing would kill Manhanu's body. I suspected the original parasite would want another host available. Ready to take over. Naturally, he'd want that host confirmed into Manhanu's power."

"And you thought of me." He set the glass back on the table. "Thanks."

Aleytys pushed a piece of meat around with the tip of her spoon. "For me, Lushan," she said slowly, her eyes on the fragment of meat, "the best solution would be for the Company to pack up and leave Maeve. No," she looked up, smiling, "I know that won't happen. The Company is too big, with too many resources. Without the pressure of outside opinions, who knows what happens on Company worlds? Who cares?" She shrugged. "I fished around for what I thought might be an optimum solution. I thought of you. When we talked in the forest, I found you open to dealing with beings unlike yourself with a certain respect. I also found you amoral and ambitious, clever and flawed." She lifted her hands apologetically. "And, in a way, I owed you a favor."

"You don't temper your descriptions." He eyed her with dislike.

"But the house of Han can start back from exile, if you're clever enough. And if you remember you need the help of the people of Maeve."

"I see." His eyes glittered. "Something of a dubious favor. However," he rubbed his hands together, "favor it is. Han thanks you. Whatever we have is yours."

"Don't promise what you won't perform. Gratitude is a

shadow," She held up her hand so it made a shadow on the table. "Try to catch hold of it and it slides away."

"How profound." His mouth twisted in a mocking smile.

"Hunh. I'm serious, fool."

"Heavily so."

"Heavy or not, you should listen. You have a toehold here. Don't try to keep it by wringing Maeve dry."

He leaned back in the chair. "It shouldn't be hard to improve on Manhanu's record."

She sighed. "I don't know much about the maneuvering that goes on behind scenes. I suspect that your appointment will continue precarious no matter how strongly the parasite sealed you in position. So. Good luck in your balancing act."

"Will the cludair keep the bargain they made with Chu?"

Qilasc flattened her small, powerful hands on the table. "If the starmen keep out of the forest. The cludair wish to live their lives undisturbed by intruders. The wood will be provided as agreed to maintain our privacy."

Lushan chuckled. "Since that means we get a product without the expense of harvesting it, it is to our advantage to honor the agreement." He rubbed a long forefinger beside his mouth. "As long as we can make a reasonable profit on the amount of wood you provide."

Gwynnor leaned forward tensely. "The stolen maranhedd."

Han glanced at the Synwedda. "What happens if I keep it?"

"Do you enjoy thunderstorms?"

"Not particularly." Eyes narrowed, he glanced at the empty sky, then at her thin face. "It usually doesn't rain this time of year."

"And in the past few days there were two major storms."

"You?"

"I demonstrate." The Synwedda gestured and a miniature cloud, a small, black thunderhead the size of a double fist, formed over Lushan's head. A tiny lightning bolt sizzled past his nose, then the cloud opened up and poured rain on his undefended head.

Sputtering, he shoved his chair back and batted at the cloud, which followed as he moved his head. "All right." He used both hands to wipe rain from his face, a futile gesture since the tiny cloud continued to squeeze rain from its interior. "I get the message!"

The Synwedda lowered her hand and the cloud evaporated.

Brushing the water from his head and shoulders, Lushan pulled the chair back and sat. "The maranhedd that was stolen will be returned." He frowned. "Where?"

"Here," the Synwedda said briskly. "I'll see it is redistributed."

He leaned back in his chair. "Each month a supply of maranhedd was sent to the City. That is not negotiable."

The Synwedda pursed her lips. "Maranhedd partakes of the sacred for the cerdd."

Han Lushan shook his head slowly. "You know the alternative, Synwedda. You and your predecessors accepted the necessity long ago. No one man could negate that agreement. It is Company policy. If you try, I have no choice. I'm sure you don't want to force this issue. Put me in a box and I will get out of it, however I must."

The Synwedda looked across at Aleytys.

Aleytys nodded. "Unless you want to make it an all-out fight, you must keep the pact. However, I wouldn't presume to advise you. You know your strength and the needs of your world."

Quietly, the old woman touched her fingertips together. "The shipments will continue."

Sioned licked her lips, then slapped her hand on the table. "You're all forgetting. My father was killed! My mother was killed! Gwynnor, how can you even listen? Your father, too. They killed him! They stole the cerdd. Where are our people?"

Gwynnor looked at her in surprise, then nodded his agreement. Her hand came down on his arm. He could feel her trembling with pain and anger.

Lushan shook his head, his eyes hard. "You can't blame that on me or the Company. Manhanu took them when he was ridden by the parasite."

The Synwedda pressed her hand down hard on Sioned's arm. "The children of Maeve will be returned. The dead must lie in the earth. Let them lie." She flicked a finger at Gwynnor. "Your life should be unfolding, not twisting back on itself. Don't poison your children with your present anger." She turned back to Han Lushan. "You will find and return the stolen cerdd."

He was relaxed and smiling but his eyes were chill. "I see no profit in keeping them." He tapped his fingers on the table. "In return for my time and effort, I'd like to see the cerdd return to the market village and open the market again."

Synwedda nodded. "I will send word." She turned to Sioned and Gwynnor. "I will also expect your cooperation in this," she said firmly.

Gwynnor nodded, though he felt Sioned's fingers digging into his arm muscles. "There's something else. The drieu Dylaw." He fixed his dark-green eyes on Lushan's face. "We haven't got anything to say about what he does."

Lushan shrugged. "We'll deal with him. Every house has vermin in the walls."

The two cludair stood. Qilasc bowed her silver head. "There's no reason for us to stay longer. What we came to do has been done. The forest calls."

Tipylexne walked around the table and touched Aleytys' shoulder. "May your days be blessed, Lawilwit, wise onc. And may you find what you search for."

She touched the hand pressing down on her shoulder. "Sometimes I wonder if I really know what that is."

"You will."

He turned and moved with a quiet dignity out of the garden, one step behind Qilasc.

Gwynnor stood. "It's time we were leaving if we are to get home before dark." He bowed slightly to Lushan. "Not long ago, I would have fought you without compromise. You don't belong here. I haven't changed my mind about that. But I've learned to accept the reality of power. You have the power." He shrugged. "If cooperating with you will make life easier for the cerdd, you have my cooperation." He pulled Sioned up beside him, feeling her resentment and resistance to letting Lushan escape punishment. "I'm sure you realize it will take some time to get the cerdd to trust your intentions."

"Intentions, phah! It's a matter of business."

Gwynnor felt Sioned stiffen. "Shut up, love," he muttered. He pulled her away from the table and started moving out of the garden. At the arch, he turned. "Point taken, Lushan. A cerdd knows the value of his goods. We can deal." He gazed at Aleytys for a long minute then waved to her and pulled Sioned into the corridor with him.

Aleytys yawned and wriggled in her chair. Switching to interlingue, she reported lazily to Grey what had happened. "Another chapter closed. I think it's time for us to go, too."

Lushan strolled over to them. "Hunters Associates?"

"Yes. You got a skimmer out there?" He nodded toward the west where the exit of the building was situated.

"On the jetty. You want a lift?"

"Right."

"Her?"

"She belongs with me."

Lushan glanced at Aleytys. "I wish I'd known that before." He touched her hair where it fell over her shoulder. "Hunter. Fantastic. McNeis, after all?"

"My god, you don't give up. No, Lushan. I am not McNeis. Not. I hope you hear it this time." She stepped away from him. "Grey, I have to stop on Star Street for a few minutes to tie up some loose ends."

Grey chuckled. "Going to kiss Dryknolte goodby?"

"Hah!" She turned and bowed to the Synwedda. Switching to the cathl maes, she said, "Is there anything else you need from me?"

"No. May your days and ways be blessed, Aleytys."

Aleytys bowed again and glared at the two men until they did likewise. An acolyte waited in the corridor to guide them out. As they followed the gliding white figure, Aleytys turned to Lushan. "Has that gratitude you mentioned melted away yet?"

"No." She could feel a wary withdrawal.

She turned back to the hunter. "Grey?"

"What?"

"How many ships do you and your people have at the port?"

"None. Just a lander, later. If I can convince the University people that the parasite is really destroyed."

"You expect that to be hard?"

He shrugged. "Take time."

"Still got room for me?"

"There's room."

"Han Lushan."

"My will is yours."

"Lovely. I want you to ground all other ships until the Hunters are away."

"And you?"

"Me with them. I've got a little problem I'd prefer to leave behind. Far behind."

"I hate to see what would make you run scared."

"Nothing that would bother you. Will you do it?"

"How long do you want me to keep the lid on?"

"Seven hours standard. Beginning soon as we get back to Star Street."

"Done."

She chuckled. "And you'd rest more easily with us somewhere else."

At the front of the temple, the acolyte turned. In her hidden hands she held Aleytys' pack. Aleytys took it and slung it over her back, following the others out onto the redstone path. They walked down the neatly raked rock, feet crunching solidly, marring the smooth surface with their kick-toed prints. At the top of the stairs, they stopped a moment. The skimmer rested on the jetty below but it was a steep climb and all three were tired. Aleytys looked out across the bay.

Drawing close to the outflow of the river, a triangular sail was a fragment of brilliant white against the blue sparkle of the water. Gwynnor and Sioned. Halfway home again. Aleytys felt a sudden pang, close to jealousy. Home. A sane, ordered life. She pulled her gaze away and looked to the north. A second sail was on point of dipping behind the horizon. The cludair, going back to the forest. Going home.

Lushan's gaze was fixed on the dark blotch against the western horizon that marked the position of the city. He turned impatiently. "If you want to come with me, get a move on."

Aleytys jumped. She ran her hands over her face, then stretched with a long groan. "Funny, this is the first time I leave a world without having precipitated some kind of massacre. I like the feeling." She touched Grey's arm. "I just might like being a Hunter, after all."

Han looked at Grey accusingly. "You implied she was already a Hunter."

"She will be." He moved to the head of the booming stairs. "What's the difference?"

As Aleytys started to follow, Lushan caught hold of her arm. "Stay here. I'll top any offer he made you."

Aleytys glanced over her shoulder at him. "Changed your mind?"

"Now that I know you're not one of them."

"You'd use my talents cleverly, Han Lushan. I see that." He pulled at her arm but she jerked loose. "I suppose I could do well for myself here." Shaking her head, she moved down a step, then looked up into his frowning face. "Grey offers me freedom. You, a larger trap." Without waiting for an answer, she began running down the echoing steps.

Chapter XIII

Although it was only midafternoon, Star Street was empty, most shops and bars shuttered. Apparently the inhabitants of the enclave, along with visitors and crews, were keeping their heads low after the events of last night.

The cookshop was open. Aleytys pushed through the beads and crossed to the counter. Bran was briskly washing mugs and glasses, setting them to drain on the rack beside the sink. There was no one else in the shop.

Aleytys slid onto the stool and tapped on the counter with a half-drach piece. "Cup of cha."

Bran wheeled, almost dropping the soap-slippery glass in her hand. She grinned broadly, then sobered. "You stirred up something, hon. You want to be careful."

"I just came to say goodby. I couldn't leave Maeve without thanking you."

Bran shook her head. "You're a fool to come back. Them spiders were caterwaulin' about, threatenin' to level the place if they couldn't find you. Dryknolte looked fit to kill someone if he breathed funny. Tintin nearly had a heart attack when he thought you'd stiffed him. And the lid blew off the whole mess when they found your pet spy knocked cold in a doorway. You should have killed him. He's got one hell of a hate built up for you."

"Sounds like Star Street was jumping for awhile."

"Crawlin' with Company lice after that. The rest of us dived under cover. Deadest night and mornin' I seen in years."

"Mm. Mad at me?"

"Not me."

"Well, I finagled a ride offworld, so things will quiet down soon." She reached in her pocket and pulled out a small packet, a lumpy object wrapped in a paper napkin. "I wanted to give you these. Nobody's looking for them, so wear them in peace."

When Bran unfolded the napkin, a pair of earrings dropped onto the counter. Made for pierced ears, they were stylized flower shapes around firedrop centers, of a delicate filigree worked in pure gold. The filigree of one was a little bent and Bran smoothed it flat with her thumb. The two firestones were large and clear without any of the black stippling that marred so many of them. She touched the stones and saw them brighten, the fires beginning to glow in their crimson hearts. "They can't be real."

"I don't know." Aleytys hopped off the stool and stood beside the counter. "The being who owned them before wasn't the kind to fool with imitations." As Bran looked up, she continued hastily, "And is in no condition to worry about jewelry now."

Bran stroked the glowing stones. Reluctantly, she said, "They're too valuable to give away."

"Not to me. What you gave me means a hell of a lot more." She moved across to the curtain while Bran was still staring down at the earrings. "Think about me sometimes, will you?"

It was a hot, sunny day with a little breeze kicking at littered paper scraps and broken cups. But the street was still empty of people. She glanced at Dryknolte's tavern, wishing she could somehow get hold of the harp for Shadith, but there was no way she could think of to do that. At the side gate, she used her talent to switch off the iris and walk through without disturbing the guard.

Hunter Grey waited in a small, dusty groundcar. "Get your business done?"

"Yeah. What about you? Did you convince the University people to send the lander?"

He grimaced. "After a half-hour's wasted breath. They'll still test us one by one before they let us inside."

"Where are the others?"

"Waiting for us by the lander." He started the car moving. "By the way, we can make a stop on your world."

"Jaydugar?"

"Computer located it. Turned up a reference to the name with a physical description that matched what you told me.

Not too far out of the way. Tokeel has agreed to stop there
briefly." He slid the car through the gate onto the landing
field. "We transfer to the Huntership after the University
people check us out."

"Thanks." She leaned forward and watched intently as he
maneuvered the ground car to the landing dock where the
lander waited. "Grey."

"What is it?"

"I love this, this stepping off into anywhere. It's addictive."

He chuckled. "Hooked. I knew it. By the way, Han's done
it. The lid's clamped tight. Your spider friends are very unhappy."

"Good."

"Vindictive bitch." His voice was amiable and reeked of
satisfaction now that he had what he wanted.

"I don't like their plans for me."

He chuckled complacently, brought the car to a stop by
the lander, and escorted her inside. The man seated by the
silent pilot turned and grinned at her. She remembered seeing
him at Dryknolte's looking grave and dignified, with neat
gray hair, the image of the staid starship captain. The gray
was gone and his stern sobriety had disappeared somewhere.
His broad grin and twinkling eyes welcomed her as he identified himself. "Hunter Ticutt."

Across the chamber, in a wall seat, a girl watched her from
cool, assessing eyes. "Hunter Sybille," she said languorously.

Beside her, a man nodded at Aleytys. "Hunter Taggert."
He still had a stubbly beard and bags under his eyes, a hold-
over from his role of decrepit bum. But his hands were clean
and his slouching body had taken on a tigerish competence.
"You ready, Grey?"

"In a minute." Hunter Grey led Aleytys to an auxiliary
seat and strapped her in. Then he took his own seat. "All
set."

Taggert grunted. "Boot us out of here."

The pilot nodded briefly and began moving his hands over
the console.

Chapter XIV

Aleytys shivered. The air was chill on this autumn evening. The suns hung low in the sky, part of red Horli already gone behind the jagged horizon while all of blue Hesh was still visible, sitting like a boil on Horli's side. Autumn was only beginning. The horans and the other trees beside the river Kard still had most of their foliage, though the leaves had turned a dozen shades of red and gold. As the corner of one of the houses jutted beyond a clump of bushes, she stopped and looked uneasily ahead, unconsciously running her hands repeatedly over her dull-colored tunic.

The road was empty. This was the time when the women were preparing the eveing meal and the men were putting the animals to bed or in the fields bringing in the last loads of the day. Aleytys frowned, annoyed at having forgotten how much labor it took, how much time, to do the tasks common to life in the vadis. On the breeze drifting down the river she could smell the acid-sweet scent of the nearly ripe hullu fruit. Her frown melted as she remembered hullu festival, when the first fruit was pressed and the juice set aside to ferment. All the old wine was finished off in a wild, joyous revelry. Soon, she thought. Then sighed. She wouldn't be there.

Unwilling to endure the excitement and demanding curiosity her arrival would provoke, she left the main road and moved through the trees to the path she expected to find running along the edge of the river. Zardagul bushes hid her from the upper road and made music for her with their huge, amber bell-pods that tinkled in the breeze, ringing much louder when her arm happened to brush one of the branches. She walked slowly, savoring the familiar sounds and smells until she was almost dizzy. She knelt beside the river.

Mountain River. Clear. Cold. Singing to her. Laughing and crying at once, she splashed the water onto her face, then bent lower and drank. Cold leafy taste. It cut through the memory haze so she became aware once again of why she was here. She jumped up and walked on.

The sound of the lyrelike barbat brought her to a stop, heart beating in her throat. She even remembered the tune. Oh god, she thought, how many times did I hear him play that? How many times . . .

Loneliness was an aching, pulsating pain that poured through her body. Her bones shook with it. Shook with a marrow-deep sense of loss. The loss of roots. The loss of home. Of family. Of culture. Of lover. Of child. She stood, her feet in alien boots, her body encased in too-tight alien clothes. She looked down at herself. Even her flesh seemed changed. She had come back knowing too much, having experienced too much. And the loss was . . . incalculable.

The barbat sang. The music changed to a gentle ripple, a sound almost melting into the song of the river. Aleytys straightened her back and started on. Regret was futile. She couldn't make the things she'd seen and done unhappen. She couldn't force herself back into the mold of the ignorant native girl who fled from a witchburning.

She followed the sound and saw Vajd sitting beside the river on a bench built in a circle around the trunk of an ancient horan. As she watched him walk his fingers across the strings, hunting a song, she felt a dizzying surge of desire that muted after a little while to a deep affection. He's older, she thought, then laughed inwardly at her foolishness. His image hadn't changed in her mind, and somehow she had expected to find him unchanged, also. There was a lot more white in his soft, unruly hair, and his face was savagely scarred around the eyes. She felt again a terrible guilt. Blinded. Because of her. She sucked in an unsteady breath.

He heard her. "Who is it?" The blind face swung about trying to locate the source of the sound.

"Me," she said quietly. "How are you, Vajd?"

"Aleytys."

"I wondered if you'd remember me."

"I've been expecting you."

She dropped on the bench beside him, struggling to regain control of her tumbling emotions. "I forgot about your dreaming."

"You forgot a lot of things. I've been waiting for you the past three-year."

Reaching down on either side of her knees, she closed her

fingers hard around the edge of the bench. "Then Stavver brought him here."

"My son." A cold note in Vajd's voice jerked her head up and she stared into his face, feeling a suppressed anger in him and an implacable distaste. "You abandoned him."

"You don't understand." She scrubbed at her face, appalled. "Didn't Stavver tell you what happened?"

"He came late one night. I couldn't sleep; the stench of expectation kept me restless. He asked my name and when I told him, he put the boy down beside me and took my hand and put it on him. The boy flinched and started crying, not the full-throated roar of an angry boy but a flinching wail, like that of a hurt animal. He said, 'This is your son.' He said that a damn witch woman called Aleytys had forced him to track down the boy and bring him to me. He said that he was done with you and with me and the whole damn clan. And then he left." Vajd turned his scarred, accusing face on her. "He lied?"

"No. But there was . . . he left out everything. Vajd, I didn't abandon my baby. Madar! I couldn't do that. No. He was stolen from me by a crazy woman. And that woman sold me to slavers. I couldn't go after them, Vajd. There was no way I could go after them. So I set a geas on him and made him go. I . . . there . . . there was no telling where I'd end up. It depended on who bought me. So I told him to take Sharl to you. What else could I do?"

Vajd's hands moved restlessly over the wood of the barbat. When he spoke, the edge had gone off his voice. "He sounded tormented."

Aleytys sighed and leaned her head back against the horan, relishing the scent, although only at the edge of her awareness since the emotion-fogged atmosphere commanded most of her attention. "Miks Stavver was a thief, Vajd. A loner. A man used to moving at his own whims. Even when we were together, he was half-ready to dump me all the time. It must have been hell for him, being driven on a path with no turning. I suppose he fought the compulsion more than once." She touched his hand. Quietly, he moved it away. "I've changed, haven't I?"

"The girl I remember couldn't have done what you did."

"The girl you remember. I begin to suspect she never existed." She felt a wrenching ache. Her feeling for him hadn't changed. She wanted to touch the softly flyaway curls fluttering about his tired, lined face. She wanted to feel his body against her, wanted to know again the warm exploding rapture of those nights in the vadi Raqsidan. In that moment, she knew that Vajd had been the reason for her return. Her desire for him drowned her desire to find her son. And at the same moment, she knew the futility of it. With her bare-nerved sensitivity to what he was feeling she knew inescapably that the passion he'd felt for her once had eroded into strong aversion. Not only had he stopped loving her, he didn't even like her. That thing in her which reached out and trapped men into her service had betrayed her again. Vajd had only been the first of her victims; the love she remembered was illusion. She almost couldn't deal with the pain of that sudden realization.

For several minutes she didn't speak, not trusting her voice, not wanting him to hear her anguish. All she had left was her pride and she knew she couldn't afford to lose that—pride to stiffen her back and steady her voice. "How is Zavar?"

"Well. She's in tanha. We're expecting a second child by the end of the month."

"Oh." She stood. "I want to see my son."

"It's your right." Sliding his arm through the barbat's leather strap, he reached for the staff leaning against the tree and stood stiffly. He tapped down the path to the back of the Kardi Mari'fat where he and Zavar lived. He held the door open for her then brushed past to tap-tap up the stairs to the second floor. Aleytys shivered. It was like stepping back into a former lifetime. The night candles cast demon shadows on the walls of the dim-lit hallway.

He pushed open a childroom door and stepped aside.

Aleytys moved past him, tiptoeing, trembling, tense. She saw two small forms in the beds but it was too dark to see more. On the ledge formed by the deep window embrasure she found a stub of a candle in a plain pewter candlestick. She brought it out and lit it at the night candle, then moved back inside.

The boy in the bed on the left had Vajd's tumbled dark curls and Zavar's dreamy, vulnerable look. He murmured as she touched his shoulder, but didn't wake.

She turned to the other bed. In the candlelight, the sleeping boy's hair glowed like fire. "My son," she murmured. "Three standard years . . . A three-year since I saw you . . ." My god, she thought, I can't . . . if I saw him running around with a bunch of other boys I wouldn't even recognize him . . . except for the hair . . . She bent closer.

He was frowning, a small fist pressed tight against his mouth. He slept with dramatic intensity. She stretched out her hand but stopped it before she touched him. With a hair's width between her palm and his flesh she ran her hand caressingly over his small body. She began to tremble.

Close to a noisy loss of self-control she blew out the candle, fumbled it back onto the window ledge and ran from the room. Vajd pulled the door shut and waited for her to say something.

She leaned against the wall hugging her arms to her body, forcing her erratic breathing to steady, a discipline Vajd had taught her long before. Before . . . "We have to talk. Here or outside?" When he didn't answer, she pushed away from the wall and touched his arm. "Well?"

Quietly, he moved away from her. "The Records room. No one will be using that now."

As they moved down the corridor toward the stairs at the front of the house, she heard the gong sound for the start of the evening meal. "Won't they miss you?"

"I seldom eat in company." He sounded impatient.

"Oh."

Alone and unnoticed as the latecomers straggled into the dining hall, they went down the stairs and crossed the front hall.

"In here. There's a fire to keep the books dry."

On either side of the fireplace large high-backed seats of carved wood stood with massive dignity. Aleytys settled herself comfortably among the bright-colored cushions. Vajd sat down quietly on the one opposite. The heat from the fire and its soothing crackle damped down her agitation as the silence between them deepened.

"Why did you come back?" he said suddenly.

She turned her head to look at him, so tired suddenly it was difficult to keep her thoughts tracking. The harrowing of her emotions had tipped her into a lethargy more profound than any physical exhaustion. She blinked. "I came as soon as I could get transport. It's not easy." Her voice was dull and slow, the usually crisp syllables of her native tongue blurring one into the other. "To get my son. Why else should I be here?"

"My son."

She blinked. Her hands jerked repeatedly. "What?"

"Sharl is my son. I want him." He leaned forward tensely, his scarred face grim in the flickering firelight. "I won't let you take him."

"You can't stop me."

"Maybe not. What will you do when he wakes screaming for his mother?"

"I'm his mother."

"Zavar is his mother; Kadin is his brother. You're a terrifying stranger."

"He'll remember me. If he doesn't, he'll get to know me. He's my baby, Vajd."

"Your pet? Your small animal? That's what he was when that man brought him here, a beaten, broken animal. Someone had tortured him, Aleytys. Tortured a helpless baby." At Aleytys' exclamation, he nodded. "It's taken Zavar a full three-year to stop his nightmares. He used to scream at night. Over and over until he was exhausted. You dragged my son into danger, then lost him. Don't tell me you didn't know what that woman was. Oh yes, I accept your sad tale. Fooled. Sold. Baby stolen. You had no business taking a baby into such danger."

"I had no choice . . ." she began weakly.

He snorted. "There's always some kind of choice. Can you give him a better life than the one he has here?"

"I . . ." She licked her lips, then pressed the heels of her hands against her eyes. "I have a secure position now. I can support him, take care of him, give him a home."

"For Sharl, Zavar is his mother. He loves her."

"Ah!" Aleytys bent over under that blow, clutching at her middle. "That was low, Vajd," she whispered.

"It's the truth. If you disrupt his life now, how long will it take you to stop the screams? I'm not objective about this, Aleytys. He's my son and I've had a three-year to understand just how badly he's been hurt."

"You're asking me to abandon him."

"No, Aleytys."

"Calling it by another name wouldn't change it."

His wide, mobile mouth curled into a sad smile. "Settle here in the Kard. People have forgotten. There'd be no trouble." He shook his head. "You didn't even think of that."

Aleytys sucked in a breath. He was right. She could come

back. No! The negative was immediate and instinctive. "No," she said. "I can't stay."

"I didn't think so. You're too much like your mother."

Aleytys shivered. She jumped to her feet and began pacing back and forth in front of the fireplace. "I can't abandon my baby. What kind of person would I be to do that? I love him. I want him. I don't want to fight you. My god, I don't want that."

"You say you love him. If you do, if you aren't thinking only of appearances, then do what's best for him."

She collapsed back on the seat, her head dropping onto her hands. "I don't know what's best."

Vajd's voice was gentler as he spoke. "Sharl is surrounded by love here. He has the stability he needs and an assured place in life. When he's hurt in body or spirit he has someone immediately available to comfort him. Friends. Brother. A father. A mother. Will you be with him day and night as Zavar was? When he's hurt, would you be there? Or would you have to be off somewhere else doing the work you are paid for? Will you teach him what it is to be a man? Will you find a father for him to take my place?"

"I see." She sighed. "I don't need to ask you those questions, do I? Zavar has already taken my place." Closing her eyes, she leaned her head back. "What about Sharl? How will he feel if his mother just goes off and leaves him like mine did to me."

"The two cases are different, Aleytys." She could feel the beginning of triumph in him. She was beaten and he knew it. "The boy will feel nothing because he'll never know about you."

Aleytys winced and closed her lips over a protest. She knew her son would be better off here and that undermined all her resolution. She opened her eyes a slit and watched Vajd sitting quietly, his beautiful, skilled hands resting lightly on his knees. He still had a preference for broad stripes in his abbas, she thought, using trivial detail to avoid temporarily the wrenching decision she knew she had to make. The heavy avrishum with its dark blue and silver stripes glowed with a supple, silky sheen in the firelight.

"I shouldn't have come back," she said abruptly. Then she stood. "This is twice you've made me grow up, Vajd. I liked your first shot better. I was . . . I came here clinging to a dream of love and joy, like a child clinging to its mother's sleeve. You used the knife skillfully on that. You've cut me loose finally from my roots, stripped off my last illusions. You've won on all counts. I can't take Sharl away from you. And I won't be back to trouble you again." She stepped up close to him, reached out a hand to touch his face, then ran stumbling out of the room, through the still empty hall, and out the back.

On the river path she fell to her knees, arms hugged tight across her breasts, shaking so hard she lost balance and tumbled into the sand. She wanted tears to release some of the agony but her eyes were stubbornly dry. For several minutes she lay twitching spasmodically, then she pulled herself back onto her knees. She crawled to the river's edge and splashed the icy water over her face. Then she lay on her stomach and drank from the river until the clean, alive taste of the water brought her out of her fog into a painful but vigorous realization that she was still alive and intended to stay that way.

She stood, brushing leaves and dirt off herself. Then she moved hastily down the river path back to the crossroads at the mouth of the valley where Grey was waiting with a skimmer.

He opened the hatch for her and tactfully made no comment when he saw she was alone.

As the skimmer rose and darted off to join the orbiting mothership, she struggled to do something about the turbulent tides of emotion surging under her brittle calm. Her flashes of rage alternated with black fits of depression until her head threatened to burst. Once, she laughed when she had a sudden vision of her body as an expanding balloon about to go pop! Grey glanced at her, then returned to his silent handling of the controls.

When the skimmer was stowed, Grey hesitated. "You want to go straight to the cabin?"

She shivered, rubbing her hands up and down her arms. "I don't know. No. I don't know."

Shaking his head, Grey led her up several levels into the passenger lounge where the other Hunters were sitting about, talking desultorily. Leaving Aleytys standing uncertainly just inside the door, Grey crossed to the communicator and touched a sensor. "Captain Tokeel."

The captain's calm, chocolate face came into the small viewer. "I see you're back. Business finished?"

"Right."

The screen blanked out and Grey turned to find a situation developing. Sybille was lying in a graceful pose on one of the couches, every shining blond hair in place, every fold of her delicate white gown disciplined into perfection. Long, elegant hands stroking with intense sensuality over her torso and thighs, she ran milky blue eyes over Aleytys, her slight smile a deliberate provocation.

Aleytys looked drained and knew it. Her red hair hung in untidy tangles down her back. A fragment of leaf was caught in the dulled mass over one ear. Her tunic was worn and old with ugly, damp splotches and smudges of dirt. Without saying a word, Sybille made her feel clumsy and ludicrous. Her blue-green eyes began to glitter.

Sybille's smile widened microscopically. "Didn't we come out of our way to pick up your son, witch? Bring him in. Let us see your wunderkind."

Aleytys seemed to swell. The limp tangled hair stirred on her head and blew out as if in a strong wind. Even the air around her quivered visibly, stirred by the terrible rage building to a point of no control.

Grey strode hastily back across the room and caught her arm. "Aleytys!" he said sharply. At the sound of her name she tore her eyes off Sybille's mocking face and turned them on him. The fury in her struck at him like a physical blow. She was on the verge of exploding and the thought of what she might do made a chill hollow in his middle. He stepped between her and Sybille. "Aleytys," he said more softly, "we're your friends. Don't mind Sybille. She's a stainless steel bitch but a good Hunter in her way. You'll be able to laugh at her later when you're feeling better. Come on. A hot bath while I get you some food. A pot of cha. Then lots of rest. I want you rested and happy when you see Wolff."

She deflated suddenly and collapsed against him, tears gathering in her eyes and dripping silently down her smudged face. Grey patted her back and glared over her shoulder at Sybille, daring her to open her mouth.

Aleytys woke and stretched cautiously, unwilling to wake Grey who lay on his stomach, deeply asleep beside her. Somehow the pain of losing Sharl and the realization that she'd never really had Vajd was diminished by time and distance. She began to feel a rising excitement at the thought of seeing a new world. She was still somewhat dubious about whether she'd like being a Hunter, but there was an excitement in that also. "Wolff," she whispered into the darkness, savoring the crisp, tough feel of the word. "I wonder what it's going to be like."

DAW=sf BOOKS

10th Year as the SF Leader!
Outstanding science fiction

By John Brunner
THE WRONG END OF TIME   (#UE1598—$1.75)
THE AVENGERS OF CARRIG   (#UE1509—$1.75)
TO CONQUER CHAOS   (#UJ1596—$1.95)
THE REPAIRMEN OF
  CYCLOPS   (#UE1638—$2.25)
INTERSTELLAR EMPIRE   (#UE1668—$2.25)

By Arthur H. Landis
A WORLD CALLED CAMELOT (#UE1418—$1.75)
CAMELOT IN ORBIT   (#UE1417—$1.75)
THE MAGICK OF CAMELOT   (#UE1623—$2.25)

By M. A. Foster
THE WARRIORS OF DAWN   (#UE1751—$2.50)
THE GAMEPLAYERS OF ZAN (#UE1497—$2.25)
THE DAY OF THE KLESH   (#UE1514—$2.25)
WAVES   (#UE1569—$2.25)
THE MORPHODITE   (#UE1669—$2.75)

By Gordon R. Dickson
ANCIENT, MY ENEMY   (#UE1552—$1.75)
NONE BUT MAN   (#UE1621—$2.25)
HOUR OF THE HORDE   (#UJ1689—$1.95)
THE STAR ROAD   (#UE1711—$2.25)

By Ansen Dibell
PURSUIT OF THE SCREAMER (#UE1580—$2.25)
CIRCLE, CRESCENT, STAR   (#UE1603—$2.25)

THE NEW AMERICAN LIBRARY, INC.,
P.O. Box 999, Bergenfield, New Jersey 07621

Please send me the DAW BOOKS I have checked above. I am enclosing
$_____ (check or money order—no currency or C.O.D.'s).
Please include the list price plus $1.00 per order to cover handling
costs.

Name _____

Address _____

City _____ State _____ Zip Code _____
Please allow at least 4 weeks for delivery

Presenting C. J. CHERRYH

☐ **DOWNBELOW STATION.** A blockbuster of a novel! Interstellar warfare as humanity's colonies rise in cosmic rebellion. (#UE1594—$2.75)

☐ **SERPENT'S REACH.** Two races lived in harmony in a quarantined constellation—until one person broke the truce! (#UE1682—$2.50)

☐ **FIRES OF AZEROTH.** Armageddon at the last gate of three worlds. (#UJ1466—$1.95)

☐ **HUNTER OF WORLDS.** Triple fetters of the mind served to keep their human prey in bondage to this city-sized starship. (#UE1559—$2.25)

☐ **BROTHERS OF EARTH:** This in-depth novel of an alien world and a human who had to adjust or die was a Science Fiction Book Club Selection. (#UJ1470—$1.95)

☐ **THE FADED SUN: KESRITH.** Universal praise for this novel of the last members of humanity's warrior-enemies . . . and the Earthman who was fated to save them. (#UE1692—$2.50)

☐ **THE FADED SUN: SHON'JIR.** Across the untracked stars to the forgotten world of the Mri go the last of that warrior race and the man who had betrayed humanity. (#UE1753—$2.50)

☐ **THE FADED SUN: KUTATH.** The final and dramatic conclusion of this bestselling trilogy—with three worlds in militant confrontation. (#UE1743—$2.50)

☐ **HESTIA.** A single engineer faces the terrors and problems of an endangered colony planet. (#UE1680—$2.25)

DAW BOOKS are represented by the publisher of Signet and Mentor Books, **THE NEW AMERICAN LIBRARY, INC.**

THE NEW AMERICAN LIBRARY, INC.,
P.O. Box 999, Bergenfield, New Jersey 07621

Please send me the DAW BOOKS I have checked above. I am enclosing
$_____ (check or money order—no currency or C.O.D.'s).
Please include the list price plus $1.00 per order to cover handling
costs.

Name _____

Address _____

City _____ State _____ Zip Code _____
Please allow at least 4 weeks for delivery

PRESENTS AMAZONS AND WOMEN OF POWER

☐ **THE CRYSTALS OF MIDA** by Sharon Green
Jalav the Amazon leads her legions in the War between the
Sexes. (#UE1735—$2.95)

☐ **THE WARRIOR WITHIN** by Sharon Green
Secret agent on a barbaric world. (#UE1707—$2.50)

☐ **THE SHATTERED CHAIN** by Marion Zimmer Bradley
Challenge to the Free Amazons of Darkover!
(#UE1683—$2.50)

☐ **GATE OF IVREL** by C. J. Cherryh
Morgaine fights to close the door between worlds.
(#UE1615—$1.75)

☐ **REBEL OF ANTARES** by Dray Prescot (Akers)
Jaezila, princess of Vallia, versus the Empress of Evil.
(#UJ1582—$1.95)

☐ **THE NOWHERE HUNT** by Jo Clayton
Aleytys the Star Hunter seeks the fallen starship.
(#UE1665—$2.25)

☐ **HECATE'S CAULDRON** Edited by Susan M. Shwartz
An original anothology of witches and women of magic.
(#UE1705—$2.95)

☐ **THE SILVER METAL LOVER** by Tanith Lee
She purchased a robot—and defended him against all!
(#UE1721—$2.75)

☐ **THE DIMENSIONEERS** by Doris Piserchia
Battle between the worlds with this orphan of power.
(#UE1738—$2.25)

THE NEW AMERICAN LIBRARY, INC.,
P.O. Box 999, Bergenfield, New Jersey 07621

Please send me the DAW BOOKS I have checked above. I am enclosing
$_____ (check or money order—no currency or C.O.D.'s).
Please include the list price plus $1.00 per order to cover handling
costs.

Name _____

Address _____

City _____ State _____ Zip Code _____
Please allow at least 4 weeks for delivery